I0714997

RIGHT THIS WAY

Miriam N. Kotzin

SPUYTEN DUYVIL

New York   Paris

© 2023 Miriam Kotzin
ISBN 978-1-956005-47-9

Cover art by Joseph Danciger

Library of Congress Cataloging-in-Publication Data

Names: Kotzin, Miriam N., 1943- author.
Title: Right this way / Miriam N. Kotzin.
Description: New York City : Spuyten Duyvil, [2022]
Identifiers: LCCN 2022012957 | ISBN 9781956005479 (paperback)
Subjects: LCGFT: Novels.
Classification: LCC PS3611.O74939 R54 2022 | DDC 813/.6--dc23
LC record available at https://lccn.loc.gov/2022012957

to Joseph Danciger

Chapter 1

When he was in his suburban garden weeding the pole beans, Ely Cutter saw God's face in the sky. He'd been paying attention to the ground, careful not to cut through the beans, and the world darkened. He looked up to see if a cloud had covered the sun, and, in the cloudless sky, he saw the face the sun would have if it had a face. Or God. He wanted to believe he hadn't seen the face, but he'd seen it, all right, and he was ashamed that the face looked like their neighbor's terracotta garden ornament.

When he told his wife what had happened, Lynne narrowed her eyes, warned him not to tell anyone else, and then left him standing in their kitchen still holding his soiled white canvass garden gloves. Maybe she'd have been impressed if he'd seen the hand of God as painted in the Sistine Chapel instead of his cut-rate vision. She might have stayed to talk with him about what happened instead of keeping her appointment to get a perm.

Cutter knew that she'd tell everyone at the salon. Women will look up from their glossy magazines and lean out from under their dryers to hear what she says. Lynne's manicurist will have a new story. In a week or two, most of Cherry Hill will know all about him. He'll become as infamous as any philandering husband, though without the pleasure—or the guilt. He reconsidered: perhaps a real womanizer feels no guilt, but a man who has only one woman besides his wife, such a man is another story. He pays for the transitory thrill, available to long-married men, of looking, once more, at the face of a woman who wants to see him.

Eleanor would have listened to his story. Raptly. She wouldn't have dismissed him after a few sentences. She would have asked him for details. How he felt just before he saw the face in the sky. How he felt while he was looking at the face. What he did afterwards and whether he'd spoken to it. Or heard it speak to him. All the questions he asked himself and more. Many, many more.

After years with Lynne, he'd found Eleanor's insistent questions, her extraordinary concentration on him, exhausting and un-nerving. That, as much as the guilt, was his reason for having broken it off. Since then, imagining the conversation that would ensue had kept him from phoning her. Curious, these words with their common root: raptly, rapture, raptor. No, he would not call Eleanor.

Their yearbook, with the photo of Ely and Lynne, who were voted Cutest Couple, was taken from its place on the top shelf of the bookcase on some, but not all, wedding anniversaries. Always by Lynne. And once, while he was embroiled with Eleanor, he walked into the den and found Lynne looking at the photo of the two of them. When she looked up at him with tears in her eyes, Ely felt her accusation, but she said nothing other than, "We were cute, weren't we?"

"We still are," he said, but did not stay for an answer.

Later he was abashed by his cowardice and his failure to feel sufficient shame. Sufficient, that is, to cause him to stop seeing Eleanor. Instead, his shame increased his eagerness to see Eleanor. He wanted to unburden himself, and she was the only one he could tell. The next time he was with Eleanor, he told her about the incident.

"Manipulative," she said. She ripped open the tan packets of sugar two at a time and emptied them into her espresso. "Lynne was being manipulative."

"But how? She couldn't have known I was coming in. Those were real tears."

Eleanor tore open two more packets—four in one cup of espresso—then made rapid circles with the wooden stirrer. "She knows you like she knows herself."

Cutter was fascinated. The thick sweet coffee swirled, finally slowing to a tremble. He had never said his wife didn't understand him, just that she sometimes discounted him. Eleanor's mouth would taste like coffee candy.

Eleanor twisted the lemon rind. In the sunlight a fragrant mist rose and vanished. She rubbed the rim of her cup with the rind then dropped it in, splashing coffee onto the saucer. She wiped it clean with the corner of her napkin, then sipped and smiled at Cutter. "What are you going to do about it?"

The first word that came to Cutter's mind was "confess" though he would not. He had nothing to tell his wife that she didn't already know. To tell her again would be worse than an insult.

"Do you want to quit me—us?" Eleanor asked.

Cutter admired her bluntness, her risk taking. Perhaps just as Lynne knew him, he knew Eleanor—at least well enough to have anticipated her response. He told her about the incident with the yearbook knowing that she would ask this question. He told her so he could say "no."

He knew enough about women to understand that he shouldn't give a quick answer. He had to put up a show of struggle. No sacrifice for him, no gain for her. The dramatic pause, the furrowed brow, the crumpled napkin—all these preceded his response. "I'm not quitting, as you put it."

Here Cutter put his hand, palm up, on the table. Eleanor was not such a fool as to take it. For his part, with his hand on the table he had the advantage of appearing to be the supplicant. He would get his later.

"I'm not abandoning you. I'm just letting you know what's happening." He paused, then added in his most serious tone. "We're going to have to be more careful."

Eleanor laughed. Cutter recognized the familiar, bitter tone, he had to appear empathic. He didn't want to—couldn't afford to—make an enemy of Eleanor. "I just mean 'careful,' that's all. I want to see you more," he said. "I'd be with you every night if I could. There's nothing I'd like more than to wake up in the morning and see you next to me."

"Nothing, that is, besides your marriage. Besides Lynne."

Lynne wasn't a name that lent itself to spitting out—all the wrong consonants and vowels. It couldn't even be hissed. Even so, Eleanor had done a fine job of expelling it from her mouth like something rotten.

"You're right, of course. I'm not ready to leave Lynne. It would be too hard on us," he said, with a nod of his head so Eleanor would understand. Then, to make sure, he added, "way too hard for you and me."

"What?" Eleanor said, lifting one eyebrow.

"We'd have to break off first. Not see each other for a long time," Cutter said, dropping his voice even lower so that he was almost mouthing the words. "I can't drag you through the scandal. It would have to look like all Lynne's idea, you see. You'd have to be well out of it." He hoped that would do.

"You're full of shit, Ely. You just want us both."

Cutter kept quiet. He thought for a while, then said, "Yes, I suppose you're right."

Eleanor smirked, and Cutter was relieved. He'd rather have her pleased at being right than angry with him. Besides, he could fix it. "I'd rather have you both than not be able to be with you. I know, I know," he said. He held up his hands, placating. "You think it's just an excuse. It's not. I'm old-fashioned enough to not want to drag you through a scandal."

"I said it was bullshit, Ely, not an excuse."

In fact, Ely silently noted that she hadn't said it was bullshit, she'd said that he was full of shit. The two were different, quite so. Nonetheless, he forged on. "But not old-fashioned enough not to want you."

Cutter checked Eleanor's face. She no longer looked cynical. A simple compliment had done it. And it was true, besides: Cutter thought of himself as old-fashioned, and he did want Eleanor. He even, he was afraid, needed her. Or needed the way she looked at him as though he might vanish at any moment, dissolve into the air like an apparition.

And, he assumed, that was the way he looked at her. It was in the nature of an affair. He was not an expert in affairs, nor did he aspire to be. As for Lynne's tears, if she could cry, be worried, would she start to see him again? And if she did, maybe Eleanor would be superfluous.

He dipped his chocolate-covered biscotti in his coffee, careful not to leave it in so long that it would fall to mush.

He examined Eleanor's face for a hint of disapproval. Nothing of the sort. Another reason he wanted to be with her. "Lynne hates me to dip," he said.

"You sleep with that woman every night. Can't you at least leave her at home when you're with me?"

So, Eleanor was peeved. Or hurt. He wasn't sure which. He knew it mattered, which. But either would be fixed, he hoped, by a sincere apology and then, with effort, for today at least, by banishing Lynne from his conversation. He couldn't banish her from his thoughts, even if he'd wanted to.

He apologized to Eleanor, then added, "I hate it that I said something wrong." He didn't say, "hurt you." Eleanor didn't like to be seen as weak. And he didn't want to remind her of her anger. He put his hand on the table again. Eleanor looked him in the eye, gave a quick squeeze of his fingers and let go.

"How long do we stay here?" she asked.

He recognized her invitation, and Cutter was all set to go.

He tried to draw a picture of what he had seen before he forgot what it looked like. It wasn't so much a face as an image of a face. He got a piece of paper from the computer printer and traced a saucer to make a circle, but he was afraid of making a child's drawing of the sun. It wasn't a child's drawing of the sun that he'd seen, though it had been as bright and as flat.

He used pencils and colored markers, newspaper under the sheet of typing paper, which he still called typing paper though no working typewriter was in the house. He tried several drawings, each inadequate. He stopped, fearful that his crude drawings would replace his memory of what he'd seen. He said that to himself with some satisfaction. He had seen something. It wasn't his fault that "garden ornament" were the best words to describe it. Sam and Ruth, on whose wall such a plaque hung, would be amused to hear about his vision.

He crumpled the papers and threw them in the trash. Then he tied up the bag and took it out to the garbage. He didn't want Lynne to find his drawings and cross-examine him, or, worse, laugh at him. When he came back in, he folded the newspapers and put them on the stack waiting to be tied and recycled. He opened a new trash bag and lined the can. Lynne hated to have to line the can when she wanted to throw something away. For that matter, so did he; no sense in pretending to be hen-pecked. Lynne wouldn't be home until two o'clock at the earliest. He was on his own for lunch. He made himself a sandwich laying the corned beef on the bread just the way he liked it, with both Russian dressing and mustard. He always felt cheated by a deli sandwich heaped high in the middle and almost nothing at the edges. Life is like that, and he's he still in the fat part, but the thin comes next.

He ate at the kitchen table, drank his beer from the bottle, considered just for a moment about having a second one, and listened to the radio. He tuned the radio to the all-news station, in part because he was happy to have everything he needed to know about the world in 22 minutes, and today because he wanted to find out if he was the only person to have seen the face in the sky. Nothing.

Cutter was unperturbed. He hadn't reported his sighting to anyone official. He supposed that no one else had reported one either. If anyone else had seen it.

A little nap before Lynne came home, a little nap on the

sofa would be just the ticket, he thought, slipping out of his shoes. Lynne would wake him when she returned. He might even wake when he heard the car door slam in the driveway. He switched the radio to National Public Radio. Nothing alarming ever happened on NPR, not on weekends, that is. And so he slept, with the soothing voices floating over his head like busy, politically savvy angels.

Cutter dreamed he was in high school on his way to pick up Lynne for the senior prom when his car got a flat. Instead of the tuxedo that he'd, in fact, worn, he was dressed in a white dinner jacket that made him look like a waiter in the Catskills. He'd seen photographs in his parents' album, and his father had been such a waiter.

He fixed the flat, but his jacket, which he hadn't removed, was smudged. He was afraid Lynne would be angry at him for being so late, even though it wasn't his fault. When he arrived to pick her up, she didn't complain about his lateness, but she asked him whose lipstick was on his jacket.

"I don't have lipstick," he said, "this is grease from when I changed the tire." But when he looked at the jacket, it was lipstick.

"Here," Lynne said. She handed him a tissue.

The jacket was immaculate again. The tissue turned into a violet silk handkerchief, which he tucked into the front pocket of his dinner jacket. It drooped over the edge of the pocket, and as he was reaching to adjust it, Lynne said, "I'll fix it." She came up to him and tried to stuff the handkerchief into the pocket with just the right amount of poof.

"Don't," he said, "I'll do it." She kept on fussing with the hanky until she ripped his pocket from the jacket. "Don't." he said, "Don't."

He was awakened by Lynne who stood on the other side of the coffee table frowning, asking, "Don't what, Ely? I was only going into the kitchen."

"I must have been dreaming," Cutter said. "I don't remember what," he added, though he did. He didn't understand his dream any more than he had understood the face in the sky.

Cutter stretched and padded into the kitchen, following Lynne. "Your hair looks nice," he said. He said this every time she went to the beauty parlor. It wasn't a lie, though "nice" was an execrable word, and he knew it.

Lynne leaned against the counter and held her hands out, fingers spread. "A new color," she said, "I'm not sure. What do you think?"

That was a trick question. He stared at his wife's fingers, then took one of her hands in his, her cool fingers resting on his palm. Her nails were an opalescent pink, a comic book version of radioactive cotton candy. "You have such beautiful hands," he said. "I've always thought..."

"Ely, darling, I'm glad you think my hands are beautiful. Really I am, but the polish?"

"It's different from the coral."

"Of course it's different. That's why I'm asking. It's a summer color."

Cutter responded to the exasperation that was in her voice again. She's out of patience so soon these days. "I have to get used to it," he said.

"That means you don't like it."

"Why can't I mean what I say—just what I say?" Cutter said. After a brief pause, he added, "I have trouble with change, I guess."

"See," Lynne said. She sounded almost triumphant. "That's what I said. You don't like it. If you did, you wouldn't have trouble with it. You have trouble with bad change, not good change."

"Just change, Lynne. I know what I have trouble with."

"I think it makes my hands look sallow." She examined her hands, then said, "It looked pretty in the bottle." She sighed. "My toes are that color, too."

Cutter put his arms around his wife. "Your fingernails look just fine. You have beautiful hands, and your toes..." he paused, "I'm sure they look fine pink, too."

His wife's head rested against his chest. He closed his eyes. It's nail polish, not a terminal illness, he thought and said, "Let me look again."

She stepped back and held her hands out like a small child having her fingernails checked for dirt. "They twinkle," he said.

"Frosted, they call it frosted cotton candy."

He'd got that right. "I thought so," he said, leaving out the radioactive part. "I dreamt I took you to the prom again," he said.

"I thought you didn't remember..."

"I didn't," he said, "but I remember it now. Every bit of it." He bent to kiss her. "I wore a dinner jacket," he said, editing, "and you arranged a silk hanky in my pocket."

"It sounds romantic."

"Yes," he said, "It does sound romantic, doesn't it?"

After all, in spite of the rough patches, they were still married, while in the forty years since their graduation many of their classmates had divorced. Sometimes he wasn't sure if it was envy or pity in his classmates' eyes.

At the last reunion. Barnett, who was holding a half-empty glass of Scotch, had asked him "What's your secret?"

That was soon after Cutter had begun to see Eleanor. He tried not to look like he was hiding something, but he must have seemed startled because Barnett had laughed and said, "Your happy marriage. Never could do it myself. Tried three times."

Cutter had felt a surge of pride, but a wave of sorrow and anxiety followed. With all his problems, he was grateful he wasn't single.

"The secret of my happy marriage? No secret at all. It's Lynne." He smiled, aiming at joviality, careful to keep his expression free of condescension and irony.

"You're a lucky man," Barnett said. He looked down into his glass. "I'll buy you a drink," he said.

"No, no. I'm fine," Cutter said, holding up his full glass of Chardonnay.

When the lights were out and Cutter closed his eyes, he saw the image of the face in the sky. The face vanished, however, when he tried to concentrate on it. Lynne lay with her back to him. "I did see it, you know," he said.

"It's late, Ely," she said. "It's not good to get all stirred up at bedtime."

He laid his hand on the curve of her hip. "I'm not 'stirred up,' Lynne. It's just," he paused and searched for the right way to say it, "I wanted you to understand. I wasn't making it up."

"Of course, you weren't making it up." Lynne reached over and switched on the light next to the bed, then turned over to face him. "Why would you make it up? Nobody would invent such a thing."

This was not a good direction for the conversation. So, she believed that seeing something the way he had was crazy, to claim it, stupid... still, they ought to talk about it. "You sound upset, Lynne. Does this upset you?"

She shook her head, no.

"Then say it." Cutter guessed that she didn't trust her voice. She wouldn't be able to hide her deception. Too bad, he thought, I know about it anyway. "Come on, Lynne. I wouldn't blame you..."

"Suppose I said something like that, Ely. Suppose I started saying that I saw statues weeping, or images of the Virgin Mary in cut potatoes..."

"Lynne, we're not Catholic. Make it a burning bush," he said with a chuckle.

"This isn't funny," she said. "I'm worried about you. What if you start hearing voices? Bad ones?"

Cutter sighed. Lynne was sitting straight up and looking down at him. He ought to sit up, too, make it official, but wasn't pillow talk all lying down? Too bad he hadn't softened her up a bit before he had this conversation Too late for that now. "I promise that if I start hearing voices, I'll tell you."

"But suppose the voices tell you not to? What if they say to smother me in my sleep? What then?"

Cutter closed his eyes. Over the years Lynne had ignored him, discounted him, been angry with him and been impatient. She had never said she was afraid of him. This was worse than her thinking that he was stupid. Far worse. "Lynne, how many times have you told me to do something, and I haven't? Why would I do something some strange voice says to do? I love you."

He hoped he didn't sound insincere. He did love her, whatever love means these days.

Lynne frowned. "I'm sorry if I told you to do things. I meant to ask."

"It's okay, Lynne, you're okay." Cutter scratched his chest. "I'm just trying to reassure you that I won't do anything I shouldn't, anything I'll be sorry for. I'd never hurt you." Saying that was a mistake. Now she'll be thinking about Eleanor. She's never forgotten about her, and why should she? I haven't.

"Let's go to sleep," she said. "We can talk about this again tomorrow. Or not at all. It's up to you." She switched off the light and lay down again, once more with her back to him.

Cutter was sure she'd meant to settle it, then, for tonight. Maybe she could sleep. He was wide awake, and hearing voices. But they weren't the voices Lynne had feared.

"You can't be serious," Cutter was saying.

"But I am, entirely. Why shouldn't I be? We've known each other, well, forever."

"I know. But after all, you're her friend, too," he said. They were leaning against the kitchen counter in Cutter's house. Cutter turned and examined the array of wine bottles on the counter. He chose one and poured a little into his wine glass, swirled it around and tasted it. He wrinkled his nose, shrugged and downed the rest, rinsed his glass, dried it with a paper towel, and poured from another bottle. "Better." He held up the bottle and waggled it as an offer to pour.

"You're such a wine snob," she said. "By the way, that first bottle you had was one I brought."

"Sorry, I didn't mean to offend." He grinned, "But what should I expect from a bourbon drinker."

"Bourbon never gives me a headache. Wine is...unreliable. I like reliable."

Cutter laughed. "If you wanted reliable, I'd think you'd want something...someone...no, something else."

"I know what I'd be getting," Eleanor said. "You've been a good husband. If you were in the habit of screwing around, I would have heard, either from your wife, or more likely from someone else. Nothing stays secret forever."

"Right. So why risk everything?"

"You or me?" Eleanor asked.

"Both."

"I have nothing to lose, everything to gain. You have something to lose. But you won't lose Lynne. She won't leave you for that."

"No?" He stared into his wineglass as though it held the answer. "What then?"

"You kissed me," Eleanor said, "You must have had something in mind."

"Nothing," he said with a wry smile." If I'd had my brain engaged, I wouldn't have kissed you."

"A gentleman," Eleanor said, drinking from her glass of bourbon, "wouldn't say that. It's insulting."

"You know what I mean. But how can you be sure about Lynne?"

"What you mean, Ely, is how can you be sure about Lynne? I only need to be sure about you. And I am."

"I have to think about it," Cutter said. He sounded somber, even to himself. "I'll think about it."

Eleanor chucked him under his chin and ran her hand down his shirtfront stopping at his belt. She rested her fingers on his belt buckle. "I'm sure you will, Ely. You do that. Think about it all you like." And then she turned, brushing against him with her hip, and walked from the room.

Cutter turned to the counter and busied himself with the wine bottles, waiting for his erection to subside. It took longer than he expected. That night he thought again about sex with Eleanor, and he made love to Lynne. When they'd finished, she leaned over and kissed him on the cheek. "We should give parties more often," she said.

"Anything you say, Darling," Cutter replied, trying to keep his voice light, not even trying to brush away the memory of Eleanor's hand and what it had promised.

Even now, thinking about it, Cutter was aroused. He supposed he was lucky considering his age. The advertising wouldn't be so heavy for the pills if more men could get it up as easily as he did. Still, it all was slower, less urgent. Someday he'd be talking to Harvey asking for a script—that is, if

Harvey hadn't retired. Maybe by then they'd be available over the counter. Would he be as self-conscious taking them to the register as he had been when he'd first bought condoms? No pride in it. That would be a difference. Or Lynne could pick them up along with the shampoo and deodorant. Everything in the same category. And if she forgot? A message, there, he decided. Borrowing trouble.

He'd done that before. Lynne too. They were alike in that way, borrowing trouble. If one of them had been more sanguine, perhaps they might have been happier. Probably not. As it happened, neither of them had been prepared for the worst.

Strange that he wasn't upset now in the same way she was about his vision. Vision—that's how he thought about it. Not a glitch in his perception, or some bizarre fluke of light, or disturbance in his sight, or even an imbalance in electrolytes. But what could it have meant? It hadn't been on the news at all. Not like a UFO. Maybe he could be subtle and still ask around without asking, "Anybody else see a face in the sky Saturday morning?" No, that wouldn't do.

If this got around, would it affect his ability to sell houses? He liked being in on people's dreams. And the percentage was good, too, though he could have made more in commercial deals and had fewer hassles, too. He'd been talking about it for years, and now he was too old to make the switch.

The ghost of desire floated over the bed, hovered so close to Cutter that he thought about Eleanor. He tried to remember her hands and her mouth. Nothing. She'd become as elusive as his memory of the face.

CHAPTER 2

Cutter woke with the sun in his eyes, feeling as though he were on the last day of a vacation at a fancy resort and about to miss the last moments of the lavish buffet breakfast, and he'd been anticipating the huevos rancheros, tangerine juice, and the pastries whose names he hadn't yet learned.

"I was up early," Lynne said when he got down to the kitchen. "I went out in the garden before it gets too hot."

He listened for a tone he might be missing, a message saying so hot that, like you, I'd be seeing things that aren't there. No. He was being too sensitive.

"I'll finish the beans," he said. "I'll wear a hat. I'll be fine." It wouldn't take long to change into gardening clothes.

"Oh," she said, "the beans. Right." She handed him a big glass of something pink and opaque. "Potassium, calcium, vitamin D, vitamin C, low fat."

He'd rather hear something like, "Banana, strawberries, yogurt, orange juice." The days when they ate things that they liked seemed to be gone. Back then from time to time something was tagged "good for you," and they'd eaten it feeling rather smug. Now food was presented as a list of nutritional qualities. Dinner plates had turned into hospital trays.

The local radio expert on physical fitness and nutrition had keeled at about the age he was now. Cutter said none of this. Instead, he thanked Lynne for making such a good breakfast.

The garden shimmered in the sun.

Cutter stepped out of his cool kitchen into the garden. The shimmer had changed to a glare. The ground needed watering, but to do it now risked scorching the plants. Still, he needed to finish looking after the beans. The weeds were doing just fine. Too bad more weeds weren't edible, though he'd heard somewhere that purslane made a passing salad. He imagined it tasted a bit like okra, mucilaginous, cooked. The strands of dusty purslane hung limp in his gloved hand. He considered purslane's possible nutritional value as a selling point, and, with a modicum of guilt. tossed it on the pile for compost.

He took off his gloves, reached down and pinched off one of the purslane leaves, then rinsed it in water from the hose. He found himself trying to remember the words for the blessing for vegetables before he popped the purslane in his mouth. He could call up only the first part, *"Baruch atah...*Blessed art Thou, Lord" He looked at the sky. Nothing watching that he could see. The purslane was fine. Maybe he'd bring in the rest of it as a surprise for Lynne. He wouldn't tell her he'd tried to say a blessing. One thing at a time.

Cutter got a bowl, put in a tray of ice cubes and water, and took it with him back out to the garden. He picked up a rosette of purslane and put it in the bowl. He swooshed it around, and the earth sank to the bottom of the bowl. A few bunches would do. He'd serve them at dinner. He wouldn't spring the whole range of found vegetables at once. Maybe it would be better to pick them at the last moment, like corn, and, after more consideration than he thought that the problem merited, he decided it wouldn't make much difference.

After he'd rinsed a good handful of the purslane, he tipped

the water onto the ground near a tomato, careful not to splash the leaves, hoping the water wouldn't be too cold.

He carried the purslane back to the house in the bowl he'd just used. The mucilaginous quality he'd worried about wasn't bad uncooked. Besides, both of them liked okra. He couldn't wrap it in a paper towel and put in the refrigerator without telling Lynne even though he would have liked this to be a surprise. Looked at from another point of view, the surprise might be an ambush.

"What's that?" She pointed to the bowl with the strands of purslane in it.

"Purslane," he said. He pulled two sheets of paper towel from the roll and lay them flat on the table. He set the purslane on the towels.

"I know it's purslane. I meant why is it in the kitchen instead of on the compost heap."

"I'm going to make a salad for dinner." He wrapped the purslane in the paper towels.

"With a weed?"

"It's good. You'll like it." Cutter opened the cabinet and took out the box of plastic bags. He pulled one bag from the box and returned the rest, feeling pleased at his efficiency.

"How do you know it's good?"

Cutter put the purslane in the bag before answering.

"I ate some. Well," he said, being strict with himself, "I ate a leaf." He put the bag with the purslane in the vegetable bin as he was talking to Lynne.

"OK. Let's see if I follow this. You go out to weed the beans?"

"Right."

"And you do?"

"Right."

"And then you decide to sample the weeds."

"Only the purslane." He kept his voice almost level, with a tilt towards cheerful. "It's fine. I'll make a salad at dinner. If you don't like it, you don't have to eat it." This sounded so familiar. He'd heard it dozens of times.

Lynne doesn't like change any more than I do, he thought. Maybe even less.

The number of recipes Cutter found by Googling purslane astonished him. He found it gratifying to learn that it was high in vitamins A and C, potassium, and calcium. He could present it to Lynne in the same way she handed him his smoothies. He printed two recipes for salads, thinking that the recipe with onions might mask the taste of the purslane more than the other. For a moment he considered asking Lynne which she would prefer. No. This was his baby. Cucumbers, fresh cilantro and mint—he'd do that. They had some cold salmon. It would be perfect.

Cutter stood at the counter chopping the cilantro and the mint, the purslane in the baggie next to the maple cutting board that had been his mother's. He'd asked his mother if they could eat the wild onions that grew in the lawn. They looked so much like scallions to him when he was a boy. Her answer had been unequivocal: no.

Now he wondered if she'd been right, and what she'd say if she knew about the purslane. She'd probably give him what for.

He felt Lynne's presence though she hadn't said anything. Sure enough, she was standing behind him, leaning against the doorjamb. Her hair was up in a towel. "They're coming for dinner, remember?"

He hadn't, but now he did. Sam and Ruth "I'd forgotten. Thanks for reminding me." He kept on chopping.

"We're not going to serve them weeds."

"No indeed. No indeed. We surely wouldn't serve a weed," Cutter turned to smile at his wife. "We mustn't swerve. We couldn't serve, we wouldn't serve, unless we've grown it from a seed. As Dr. Seuss would have said it if he'd had to," Cutter said, wanting to shift the topic.

"How did you do that?' Lynne asked, "You don't talk in verse."

He shrugged. "Inspiration. I'm feeling inspired."

"Ely, really, Sam and Ruth..." she paused, said in an affected tone, "Do have some weed salad. We made it because you were coming."

"What is a weed, Lynne? Just a plant that's growing where you don't want it. As soon as you want it, it's not a weed anymore."

"Nonsense."

"Crocus. It grows in the lawn. We plant the bulbs, they grow. They're in the lawn, but they're not weeds. Dandelions are weeds—unless you want to eat them."

Cutter peeled the cucumber as he spoke. "I wish they didn't wax these."

"I wish you wouldn't go on like this."

"I'm not going on. I just said that I don't like wax on my cucumbers once. Today."

"Not the cucumber, Ely. The weed."

"Weed, Lynne? Be careful. The feds will think you're talking about a controlled substance." He laughed and gestured with the vegetable peeler. "The walls have ears."

"You know what I mean. You're being difficult."

"It's my turn, Lynne. I haven't been difficult in three months, two weeks and four days. You, on the other hand..." Cutter was feeling pleased with himself.

"Oh, never mind. We can serve tomatoes if no one will eat the salad."

"Right. Fall-back for picky eaters. Are you getting picky, Lynne? Off your feed?"

"What is the matter with you, Ely? I'm just saying, ...oh, never mind. It'll be fine."

"Just don't make a big deal of it, Lynne. It really will be fine. I promise." Cutter wished the rest of it were as easy.

Had Lynne said anything to Ruth about the vision? If she had, Ruth would have told Sam, even if Lynne had made her promise not to. Don't tell your husband translated to "Don't tell anyone except your husband. And I mean anyone. Not even your other best friend."

"Where do you want to eat?" Cutter asked.

"It's hot," Lynne said.

"If you say so," Cutter said.

"Don't you think it's too hot to eat outside?"

Cutter heard the peevish note, repented, and covered, "I just wanted to make sure," he said. "In case."

"In case?"

"Oh, I don't know. In case you wanted to fire up the tiki

torches and get out the tiny paper umbrellas and serve Mai Tais or Margaritas. Something summer."

"Gin and tonic is all Sam drinks," Lynne said. "Besides, we don't have tequila or rum. Or paper umbrellas for that matter."

"I guess that takes care of that. We'll have to eat inside if we don't have paper umbrellas." He paused and shook his head. "It's a shame."

"What?"

"The tiki torches. We never use them."

Lynne sighed. "For God's sake, Ely. Are you saying you want to eat outside in ninety-degree heat so you can light tiki torches?"

"It might be nice."

Cutter calibrated Lynne's glare. She looks flushed. "I'll set the table. You can go take a shower."

"My hair is barely dry. I'll set the table," she said, "If you want to eat on the patio, I suppose it's not unbearable."

Cutter laughed. "Sounds inviting, the way you put it. 'Not unbearable.' We'll wait for a cooler evening. It's bound to come. Sometime."

"Have some salad," Cutter said, passing the bowl to Ruth. Would Lynne say anything about his ingredients? Maybe she'd done so already talking about his vision, "My husband saw a garden ornament—one quite like yours—in the sky, something he thought was God's face—and now he's serving us all weeds for dinner." No, he couldn't believe she'd have done that.

Ruth looked at the salad, "Such pretty colors, Lynne!"

Lynne said, "Say that to Ely. It's his salad. He gets all the credit for this one."

Good, Cutter thought, by the tone in her voice she hasn't told them. He was almost sorry she hadn't. He'd rather they helped themselves knowing what they were eating. He wasn't, after all, intending to hide anything from them. The market was filled with unrecognizable imported fruits and vegetables. He was finding vegetables he'd read about in fourth grade social studies, and what the hell was star fruit, anyway? He wasn't sure what to do with them, maybe it was time to learn.

Ruth turned to Ely, "What is it, Ely? I see cucumber and, what, mint? Something else flat that I don't recognize? "Yogurt," Sam said.

"I know yogurt," she said. "It's the other green?"

"Coriander and purslane," Cutter said.

"Parsley?" Sam asked. "I've never seen parsley like that. But it looks familiar."

"It does," Ruth said, "but I can't place it."

"*Purs*-lane," Lynne said, enunciating. "It should look familiar."

Cutter sighed. "She's trying to say it's a weed. It's a vegetable now. It was a weed yesterday."

"A weed?" Ruth asked.

Cutter forked some salad into his mouth. "Some would say." He chewed and swallowed, took another bite. "Wine?" He offered the bottle of chilled Chablis.

Sam poured wine for himself and Ruth

"It's from the garden. Very high in antioxidants. Calcium. Iron. Trace minerals. Tasty, too," Cutter added, thinking of the smoothie he'd had for breakfast. Sam and Ruth gave one another "the look," the one he and Lynne exchanged when they sensed something odd going on with another couple and they wanted to stay out of it. "We have tomatoes, too," he said.

"What's the verdict?" Cutter asked as Lynne, Ruth, and Sam poked at the salad, trying to pick out the purslane, like kids avoiding raisins. Tomatoes. We have plenty of tomatoes, he thought, reassuring himself that he can eat the salad if they don't want it. But then they stopped examining the salad and were eating it, good friends, good guests. Lynne, smiled at him as though he'd brought her a birthday gift on the wrong day.

He said a silent thanks, his eyes closed, trying to remember the expression on the face he'd seen in the sky. Was it, perhaps, amusement? If not, it should have been. Or would be now.

"So, Ely, how'd you think of the salad?" Sam asked.

Sam didn't look at him while he asked the question. What was on his mind? Cutter didn't think it was the salad.

"I got the recipe online," Cutter said. He applied the sales method of interpreting a question to give the sort of answer that was to his advantage. He'd learned it forty years earlier in high school debating with less practical applications. Now it was coming in handy again. Or might have, had Sam been less persistent.

"C'mon you know that's not what I mean. The purslane." Sam leaned towards Cutter even though the women were in the other room. "Who'd you hear it from? You seeing Eleanor again?"

"What?" Cutter was puzzled. But that explained why Sam seemed embarrassed. Less the weed, more the woman.

"She has odd ideas," Sam said, "though I admit I never heard she ate weeds."

"Look," Cutter said, "I don't get it. I try something a little different and you're accusing me of taking up with her again."

"I owe you an apology?"

"Forget it," Cutter said, "I think about her now and then—that's all, I swear—but…"

Sam waved his hand, like clearing smoke, dismissing the subject. "Sorry I mentioned it."

Purslane was a safer topic. "I must have read it somewhere, and I don't know what, why, I tried a bit. It was good, and, all kidding aside, I Googled it and found all sorts of stuff about it on the web," Cutter said.

"Ruth… well, actually Ruth told me Lynne said you'd been acting odd, and she asked me if I thought you'd been seeing Eleanor again. I told her it was none of our business."

Cutter raised an eyebrow.

"And that I wouldn't say anything to you about it, but then when the purslane came out, even though I wouldn't let anything slip, I wondered. We've been friends…"

"So," Cutter said, pushing forward, "I Googled." He stopped and waited until Sam spoke again. Cutter hated that Sam had asked him. He'd been dragged into the mess with Eleanor years before. You'd think he'd have kept his mouth shut, but Ruth must have been on him. Cutter kept quiet. Another sales technique. In time, Sam would say something.

Sam shifted in his chair, then said, "Amazing, this technology."

"I'm sorry I pulled so much of it out before I realized..."

"The weed eater. Remember?" Sam asked.

"Isn't that some garden gadget?"

"No, no, a guy, hunting the wild something." Sam smiled, shook his head. "He was, you remember, maybe thirty, forty years ago?"

He called out, "Ruth, remember a book, some fellow in plaid, hunting something. He ate wild things."

"Gibson," Ruth called. "Something Gibson."

"Even before Earth Day, I think," Sam said.

Ruth said, "Definitely before Earth Day. After Earth Day you wouldn't dare eat a wild plant. They were all protected."

Cutter was sure she'd got it wrong. That wasn't what Earth Day was about, but he didn't want to start a fight, not tonight when Ruth had a bee in her bonnet. If she says something to Lynne about her suspicions, he'll be in for it later.

Lynne came up behind him, put her hands on his shoulders, and kissed the thinning spot on the top of his head, before sitting beside him on the couch.

He hoped the women heard their conversation about Eleanor. He wouldn't have wanted Lynne to be hurt—or suspicious. A crumb. A trail of crumbs leading not out of, but into the woods. Cutter wasn't lost now, but for a time he'd come close.

Although the affair with Eleanor had been over for years, Cutter still wasn't free of her. He wouldn't be free until he'd stopped thinking that he wanted to tell her about something, and, in that sense, Ruth's suspicious were correct. Still, since the affair had ended, he hadn't called Eleanor. He liked to think of himself as having been caught up in the affair like a mouse in the talons of a hawk on a wild ride high above verdant fields and trees. His world was far below, and, in spite of the wonderful new view, he was in danger—falling from a height he could not calculate or, worse, remaining in the grip and meeting a different, even less pleasant, fate.

Eleanor had insisted that he'd started it. And, if he counted the kiss in the kitchen as the start, well, she was right. He didn't know when it had started, whether he had begun, or she had. The kiss had seemed at the time natural, or at least inevitable. They had been circling one another for weeks. Only later had he felt as though he wanted to be out of Eleanor's reach, out of her sight.

Getting into it was easy. His job had given him ample time for which he could not be held accountable. Clients. Driving around looking at houses. Good reason to be unreachable. He had been, in practice, available to Eleanor far too often.

It gave him pleasure even now to tell himself that it had not been all about sex. As often as they had gone to bed, they'd spent their hour or two driving around or having coffee or walking around the small parks, his hands jammed in his pockets.

They behaved like teenagers just once. The sky had darkened with clouds. Wind tugged at the branches, sent dust devils whirling, and Cutter's car was alone on the narrow road that wound through the park. Eleanor had leaned against a tree, and he'd kissed her, sucking her lip into his mouth and biting until she moaned. He'd taken her wrist and put her hand on his erection, looked her full in the eyes and then let go. She had kept her hand on him and squeezed. And then the rain swept in, spattering on the maple leaves above them, soaking their shoulders as they ran to the car. The smell of rain rose from the earth.

He'd entertained a theory that not being able to touch Eleanor freely made him want to touch her all the more. At parties they were careful, so intent on being careful, that he was certain everyone could see how careful they were being. Being careful would be their undoing. If not that, then surely something else. From the start he'd known it would not last, though sometimes it was almost fun to pretend otherwise.

CHAPTER 3

Lynne leaned against the closed front door. She'd drunk more than usual, especially after dinner when she and Ruth had come into the den where he'd been sitting with Sam. If she'd overheard Sam asking about Eleanor, she might have heard his answer. He'd have some explaining to do.

"Ruth said she thinks you've been seeing Eleanor," Lynne said. "I told her that was nonsense."

Cutter didn't want to be drawn into talking about his discussion with Sam, just as much as he didn't want to appear to be hiding anything, so he said, "I know. Sam told me Ruth had instructed him to ferret out the truth." Cutter made a wiggling gesture with his hand to accompany the word ferret.

"Do you mind?" Lynne asked.

Cutter nodded. He said that of course he minded, but he realized he'd opened the door to discussions like this when he made his mistake. He knew he'd been stupid and cruel, that what he'd done was wrong, but it was over, and he hopes that as long as he and Lynne were all right again—and they are, aren't they? —that everyone else could go on and at least pretend it had never happened. Even good friends. Good friends, in particular. And then he was quiet.

"Ruth said you've been acting preoccupied. She said she's run into you a few times and you barely said hello, that she practically had to put her hand on your arm to get your attention."

"Oh?" he said. "I don't remember. But that would make sense that I don't—after all, she said I was preoccupied."

"I told her," Lynne said.

"What?" Cutter was puzzled.

"What you'd seen. That you'd seen it. You know, the face."

She'd told him not to tell anyone, and then she had. It figures. Ruth, at least, was a friend. Besides, he didn't have anything to hide. "And?"

"She asked if you'd showed it to me!" Lynne laughed. "And if I'd seen it too."

"I could have kept it to myself, but that would have been..."

"Crazy for you to hide it from me. What if you'd seen it again?" She took a deep breath, "You haven't, have you?"

"No," he said. "But I've looked."

"You sound sorry," she said.

"Not sorry, exactly. Disappointed isn't the right word either. It's just, you see something like that once, you keep looking. If you see it again, you know you weren't imagining."

"You're not seeing her, are you?"

Eleanor again. "No. I told you no."

"Never? Not even in public?"

"Lynne, I promise you, it's over."

"You didn't answer my question."

"Lynne, I answered. I promised you. It's over. I'm sorry it ever happened—that I let it happen. I'd do anything if I could make it different. I've told you that before, and that hasn't changed. Nothing's changed."

Cutter waited for her to say something.

"You made promises before," she said. "You broke a promise every time you were with her. Every time was like new lie, another broken promise."

"Lynne," Cutter said, "please...don't."

"Why not, Ely?" she asked, "does it hurt your feelings?"

"Yes," he said, "but that's not why you should stop."

"You want to protect yourself," she said.

"Okay, I do, but I want to protect you, too," he said. "It hurts you, Lynne. And us."

"You should have thought about that before."

"It's too late for that," Cutter couldn't tell her that he had thought about it, hurting her, losing her. That he'd taken the gamble. Except for times like this, he'd won.

After all, he'd had his time with Eleanor. Eleanor had been right: Lynne hadn't left him when she found out. From time to time, however, he endured her bitter remonstrances and accommodated her grief. He couldn't begin to measure her misery, which she had seasoned with rage.

After the third miscarriage Lynne had said she wanted to stop trying. Nothing can be worse than this, he'd concluded, the hope, a tender shoot gone. And then, like a miracle, she'd carried to term. They named their son Isaac after her grandfather and Isaac whose name meant laughter, had, in his third month, died in his sleep.

Their mourning had gone in cycles, through the traditional rituals, not only the birthday, but the anniversary of his death, marked twice each year, once on the Gregorian calendar, then again, the lunar. Each year the notice came, the fifteenth of Kislev, a small glass filled with a candle flickered on the sideboard. They stood together to light it, but no matter how many times they passed by, neither was there when the flame went out. Ely hated throwing out the glass, and Lynne would not. The first year, the glass, darkened by smoke from the guttering flame, sat on the sideboard for a week. Then Ely looked and it was gone. Neither said anything.

The year their son would have started school, Lynne sat, stricken, her lap covered by bright advertisements for notebooks, pencils, and back-to-school clothing. Together they noted what would have been landmarks: the date of his Bar Mitzvah, his high school graduation, his college graduation all passed. And the questions of marriage, children, these were phantom anniversaries.

Several months into his affair with Eleanor, Lynne confronted Cutter. She asked him if he would have "done this thing," a phrase in which he heard her contempt as well as her sorrow, if his son, his only son, Isaac had been alive. Eli told her the truth. He said, "I don't know." As soon as he spoke, he regretted it, but her question had stung like a scourge.

Now he waited for Lynne to mention Isaac, but she did not. Nonetheless Ely imagined Isaac, who would have been older now than Cutter had been when he was born, standing behind Lynne, looking like pictures he'd seen of Lynne's father as a young man. Life gets so complicated.

"I hate fighting at bedtime," Cutter said.

"I hate fighting, too," she said, "I hate not trusting you. I hate knowing people are still..."

"Not people. Ruth," Cutter said, "She's family."

"You know what I mean."

"I wish she hadn't worried you," Cutter said. He got up and paced.

"Don't be mad at her. It's not fair."

"I'm not mad—I'm disappointed. She doesn't trust me, and she's spreading it to you."

"You can't blame her, Ely."

"I can. I do." He stood in front of his wife and looked down at her. He held out his hand. "Come upstairs, Lynne. It's been a long day. We can fight again tomorrow if we feel like it," he said only half-kidding. 'But let's put it aside now."

He looked over at where he'd imagined Isaac standing. Gone, nothing.

"You know what your mother said about going to bed angry." Cutter's shrewdest last resort had always been Lynne's mother's bits of wisdom, which had won many arguments for him. Or, if not won, at least ended.

In bed, Lynne lay with her head on Cutter's shoulder. "I wish..." she began.

"What, Lynne?" Her voice had been wistful, and his voice was soft, matching hers. He wasn't afraid of how she'd finish her sentence. He could think of lots of things that he wished, too. In spite of everything he'd said to Lynne, he didn't wish he'd never had the affair with Eleanor. He did wish the affair had dissolved without pain—his, Eleanor's, Lynne's. He wished no one had found out about it. He wished it could vanish from everyone's memory—with two exceptions.

He didn't want to forget the good times with Eleanor. Even now he thought about them with pleasure. He had felt alive, brimming with anticipation. He wanted to remember how that felt, to re-create the feeling. But he didn't want to start up again. He'd rather immolate himself; it would be quicker and less painful than the consequences of sleeping with Eleanor again. He was satisfied with wanting to sleep with her. Even that held its dangers.

Lynne nuzzled in closer, kissed Cutter's shoulder, then pulled away. "You know what I wish," she said. "Let's not talk about it anymore tonight. It won't do us any good anyway." Then she turned, her back to Cutter.

He considered curling up with her, his arm over her body, and if she responded, he would make love to her. She was stiff, as though she wouldn't welcome his sexual touch. And yet, with her head on his shoulder, for a moment it had seemed to him as though they could move on. If Lynne had intuited his thinking about Eleanor, they'd move on, but in a bad direction. That was unlikely. He let his mind drift.

"Ely! Ely!"

His name carried on the wind down the sidewalk through a crowd of students leaving the school. Lynne was standing on the high school steps waving. She wore her cheerleader outfit, and waved with her free hand, not with the pompoms, which she held by her side.

In the spotlight of gold afternoon sun, Lynne was luminous.

He stopped and waved back. Then he turned and started walking away again. He figured she didn't want to talk to him much anyway. A guy from their geometry class tapped him on the shoulder and pointed, "She's trying to talk to you, Ely. Don't be a jerk."

Feeling stupid, Ely headed back to school, walking

against the stream of students. What did Lynne want from him? Homework? There was a game this weekend, and he had a ticket. He'd be happy to give her one of those big curly chrysanthemums with blue and gold ribbons, the school colors, but she wasn't his date.

Cutter had stood at the bottom of the steps; he could see up Lynne's skirt almost to the electric blue panties that were a part of the cheerleader's outfit. He looked away. And then Lynne ran down the steps, as breathless as if she'd been running around the track.

To his amazement she asked him if he'd go with her to the post-game party.

His father was still driving him on dates, and Ely sat in the back seat with Lynne, holding her hand while she chattered with his father. When they got to her house Ely walked her to her door. She leaned forward and held her face up without saying anything until he knew that he should kiss her. He hoped her parents wouldn't open the door—it was bad enough that his father was in the car, watching.

From then on, Ely didn't miss a home game. He went to cheer for the cheerleaders, for Lynne, more than for the teams. In college, when he had exams, Lynne had adapted some of the cheers to change them to his name. She had waved invisible pompoms, jumped, spelled out his name—and he had aced exams. If he asked her, would Lynne cheer for him now or had she grown too old for such antics, or too jaded and bitter? She slept beside him as he fretted. If she refused, he couldn't blame her.

Sleepless, next to his sleeping wife, Ely looked at the clock.

One a.m. It was late, but not that late. Taking care to be quiet, he left their bed.

His fingers would remember Eleanor's phone number, the places on the keypad that made such a perfect pattern. One nine three seven. He'd liked the symmetry. It was something to talk about when he was getting started with her. At first, he told her that he memorized her number, and later he said that he tapped it in by instinct. Making the call tonight would be easy; extricating himself—again—would be difficult. He would have to lie.

He hadn't lied before, he told himself, not a real lie. Lynne hadn't asked him if Eleanor had phoned him. He'd just said he hadn't called her. No point in telling Lynne the rest of it. If he were going to risk everything, it should be for something big. Not for what had happened then.

Cutter was showing a house when his cell phone rang. Whether he answered or not, the phone was an intrusion. The first few houses were important, that was when the couple— and it was usually a couple, though not today—decided whether or not they wanted to work with him. They had to feel he was looking after their interests, pretending that it didn't matter, after all, that he was being paid by the seller.

It was a tricky business to set up what he called win-win situations. Time is money, he'd say. He'd show the sellers how much they were losing in interest, while they were still paying maintenance and taxes. And when interest rates were low, he'd opine that they might go up, an argument that worked with both seller—who knew that the price of a house was determined by what the buyer could afford in monthly payments—and the buyer who could get more house for the money. Win win.

Cutter, however, won only when a sale was made. No sale, no commission. The ringing cell phone was bad for business. If he didn't answer the current client would be thinking, "what if I need to call him?"

Cutter checked his phone. Eleanor. "Good morning," he said, trying to sound pleasant and professional. "I'm showing a house now..."

"Ely, I have to talk to you."

"Fine," he said, cutting her off, hoping the volume was low enough so that his client wouldn't hear Eleanor's tone. She could be unpredictable. "I'll be in touch later."

This sales business was as tricky as any courtship. He had to be attentive but know when to disappear. Women often wanted the house. This one wanted out, a new place, or thought she did. She wanted, she said, "A fresh start."

"Grace," he said, turning to his client, "I apologize for the interruption."

She shook her head, waved her hand, as though to say, "it's nothing." How had Grace deployed that little hand-wave in her marriage? He thanked her and pointed out the construction of the kitchen cabinets. He tried to push the phone call from his mind. He'd learn soon enough what Eleanor had wanted.

Grace sighed. Cutter had heard that sigh before. He kept quiet. Silence is a salesman's friend.

"I could paint," Grace said, looking around. "A coat of paint would brighten things up in here."

"That it would," Cutter said. As always, he offered no suggestion about color.

"A butter yellow," Grace said, "Don't you think?"

"Butter yellow's a fine color for a kitchen, pulls the morning sunshine into a room."

"What would it look like with this tile floor?"

"You can always bring over some paint chips," Cutter said.

"Do you mind if we look at the closet in the bedroom again?" Grace asked.

Cutter didn't mind. He had other houses he could show Grace if she didn't want this one. And as soon as he was through with Grace, he'd be free to return Eleanor's call.

"I always wanted a butter-yellow kitchen," Grace said.

"Well," Cutter replied, "we'll see to it."

"Yes," Grace said.

Cutter felt her gaze of appraisal on him, not much different than that she'd given the closets and cabinets. He didn't flinch when she finished by saying, "We will."

When he and Lynne were first married, she'd asked him, teasing, about his showing houses to all the widows and divorcées, and she'd just pretended to be jealous.

"I've been in more bedrooms with women in the last week," he'd said. "And the only things the women noticed were the closets and placement of the windows." And, for the most part, that was the truth.

Now with Grace, driving to the next house, he was careful to keep both hands on the wheel.

"I don't want to look at split levels," Grace said. "And cathedral ceilings make me nervous. Picture windows facing the street... I could never see the point. You have to cover them up with curtains, or you're the picture."

"OK," Cutter said. "We'll keep that in mind." Grace knows what she doesn't want, he thought, and what she does. "This next house has a yellow kitchen, but not the yellow you want."

"I'm not expecting to find a perfect house," she said.

"You're flexible."

"Yoga," Grace said, laughing.

"But no cathedral ceilings," Cutter said, picturing Grace in a leotard or less, which, he assumed was her point.

Cutter would have preferred to feign ignorance when Eleanor asked, "What does she look like?" Eleanor always knew if, when she called, Cutter was showing a house to a couple or to a single woman.

He wouldn't get away with a lie, and so he told the truth. Even as he spoke, he knew he was making a mistake. "Dark hair, hazel eyes, about five one. Lots of gold."

"What kind of shoes?"

"I don't know," Cutter said.

"You noticed her jewelry and not her shoes?"

"The jewelry made noise," Cutter said. "Bangles. You could get a headache from the clanging."

"I don't believe you, Ely. You're hiding something."

"You called me," he said, "I'm calling back."

"You're calling back—and you're hiding something."

"Eleanor. Please. Lynne is expecting me. Let's not..."

"Fight? Or let's not talk about what's-her-name?"

"I'm not responsible for what a client wears."

Eleanor's jealousy was one of her least attractive qualities. Still, he could understand why she would have been possessive. She knew he could stray. But why now, after so much time apart?

"Ely. Don't bullshit me. I hear you saw God?"

It hadn't taken long, then, for word to spread. "You heard," he said. "Everything we hear, we shouldn't believe."

"It's not true? First you lie about the shoes and now this? Why didn't you call me?"

"You want me to say black backless heels and an ankle bracelet?"

"I want you to talk to me, Ely. Like before. You see an ankle bracelet, you don't see an ankle bracelet—who cares? But God's face?"

"It's not a long story," Ely said, "And apparently you already heard it."

"I hate pretending."

She's shifting topics, turning it to her, Ely observed. We're back to that again. "I hated it too."

"Hated? Pretending's over?"

"We're friends. What was, it was. I'm not saying it wasn't."

"I don't believe you."

"Today's theme?" Ely asked. "About seeing God, that you believe?"

"Is it true?"

"The shoes?" He'd pay for giving her a hard time.

"I'll be at Barnes & Noble tonight, 8:30," she said. "I'm still here, for you Ely."

He didn't say anything.

"Good, I'll see you then," she said and left him wondering what lie he'd tell Lynne.

CHAPTER 4

The Starbucks in Barnes & Noble was always crowded, perfect for clandestine meetings: you might be sharing a table for convenience. Cutter picked up a Fodor's Caribbean 2009 as a prop. He considered getting a café Grande as a second flourish to make Eleanor's presence at his table seem coincidental, but when he saw one open table for two along the wall, he took it. As usual almost no tables were available. The tables for two were prime real estate, desirable to couples and single readers.

He had no interest in going to the Caribbean. He chose the guidebook only because it was the sort of book anyone might be seen browsing without arousing suspicion. He opened it at random and stared at a page: Jamaica. A smudge of something, perhaps chocolate, was a clue that someone had been reading and eating. Maybe the previous reader had been indulging in a fantasy vacation or had been waiting for someone as he was now waiting for Eleanor, who had, more often, waited for him.

He'd never been late on purpose. Eleanor had always glanced at her watch before she smiled at him—not that she'd actually complained about his arrival time. Nonetheless, her tic of checking the time had been an unmistakable wordless reproach. Tonight, Cutter made sure he'd be first. He was determined that tonight he'd be blameless.

He'd just stopped staring blankly at a page and had begun to read about a Sandals Resort, when he became aware that someone was standing just behind his right shoulder.

"Ely," she said, walking around to stand next to him,

"What a coincidence!" She glanced at the empty seat and set her full cup of cappuccino on his table. "May I?"

Before Ely could answer, Grace slid into the empty chair.

Cutter assessed his options while Grace chattered about the potential of the last house they'd seen. He curbed his instinct to check his watch, nodding and smiling, in his best pleasant but non-committal manner.

Grace was still wearing her bangles, but she'd changed from the modest blouse and slacks she'd had on earlier to a short white skirt and black tank top, a style he'd never seen on a woman her age. He checked her upper arm for slackness; maybe her yoga kept her body looking young.

"Planning a winter vacation?"

He'd forgotten the Fodor's. He'd missed Eleanor, but not the intrigue, the excuses, the lies. And now, because Eleanor had heard the gossip, here he was. Again. "Oh," he said, "This..." He patted the book. "Dreaming."

"Do you hate the winters, Ely?" Grace said. "We go...we used to go...I used.... Shit!"

"It's all right," Ely said. "You went where?" he changed the emphasis from her husband to her destination. Separated, he decided.

"We went to Mexico," Grace said, confident now, "Robert was interested in the Aztecs. Chechen Itza, Tulum, Teotihuacán...."

"And you?" Ely asked.

"Oh," Grace said, her voice trailing off, "whether or not I was interested didn't matter."

Was she passing herself off as a self-sacrificing wife? He

looked at his watch and realized too late that his gesture was ill-timed.

"I'm sorry, to have bored you," Grace said, her voice icy. "Am I keeping you from something?"

"No," said Cutter, "nothing. A bad habit, this checking the time. It comes from wanting to be on time for appointments. Can't shake it." I'm babbling, he thought, and added, "You're not keeping me from anything. I've all the time in the world."

"Good," she said, lowering her voice in volume and pitch to a level of intimacy, "I'm so glad we met tonight. I was feeling lonely."

Cutter looked over her shoulder. Eleanor was standing a few feet away, holding a cup. His back had been towards the counter, and he hadn't seen her there. Now, having caught his eye, she headed towards their table.

Eleanor put her cup on the table, smiled and held her right hand out to Grace, "Eleanor Levy," she said.

"Grace Cooper," Grace said, reaching up to shake her hand. The gold bangles slid down her arm.

Noisy, Ely thought.

Eleanor looked around, "Oh dear! All the tables are taken."

Cutter glanced at the tables nearby. All the four tops had one or two people sitting at them. Just as well.

"...It gets so crowded in here..." Eleanor continued.

"Yes," Grace murmured, and took a sip of her cappuccino.

"I hate sitting with strangers," Eleanor said, "It's not that I'm shy, I just feel it's such an imposition."

Ely listened and watched: cobra and mongoose. Eleanor was speaking with italics. That's not like her. Well, this must be awkward for her, too. Eleanor had put her cup in the middle of the table. She's not leaving.

"What can you do?" Grace said. She shrugged, then beamed at Ely. "I was so lucky to run into Ely. He's such good company." He'd made a mistake telling Grace he had plenty of time. If Eleanor left him with Grace, he'd get home so late that he'd a fancy excuse.

"I'd ask to pull over a chair and join you two" Eleanor said, "but I don't want to intrude."

Her cup on the table said something else.

She's good, Cutter told himself. There's no possible response to that but to say something like, oh not at all, you're not intruding. He could say it, but it would be better coming from Grace. He had to speak up soon; his silence would be a tacit agreement to her assessment of the intrusion.

Grace was silent. Smiling, but silent. So Cutter rose, "Please do," he said, embarrassed that he'd unintentionally acknowledged Eleanor's arrival as an intrusion.

"I'll pull a chair over and sit here," he said, gesturing at the third side of the tiny table. "There's plenty of room."

"Don't you want some coffee, Ely? As long as we'll all be here?" Grace said.

Cutter shook his head.

"Oh, do, Ely," Eleanor said. "I hate drinking alone." She laughed, having just annihilated Grace.

Cutter looked at the two women, appalled at the way they were colluding to get him to go for coffee. Crap, he thought, the second I leave this table, they start talking. If they were cobra and mongoose, what was he?

The counter was crowded. Getting anything at all would take a while. He was glum with the knowledge that he'd be gone far too long. At the counter, Cutter calculated what would take least time. No matter what he chose for himself, he'd have to wait through two cappuccinos and one skinny latté. What catastrophe could they bring about in his absence? Survival of the fittest, nature tooth and claw.

He turned to look at the women; they were engrossed in conversation. Grace was laughing. So far so good. Or maybe not. He focused his attention on the barista. He didn't want to lose his place in line.

When he returned with his iced coffee, Eleanor was alone.

"Grace left," Eleanor said.

Yes, of course. Eleanor's statement only seemed to be superfluous. She had vanquished Grace. He'd learn what they'd talked about, if not now, later—assuredly not at the time of his choosing. Each woman would make the report in the way most advantageous to herself. The loser? Ely.

"Charming woman. She thinks you're wonderful." Eleanor had a wicked smile.

"I'm sure you set her straight."

"Now, Ely. You know how I feel." Her voice was so soft that she was in no danger of being overheard; the expression on her face was far more neutral than the one Grace had been sporting. But then Eleanor may be more practiced than Grace at this sort of deception.

"Don't," he said.

"Don't? Or don't here?"

"This is your meeting, Eleanor. I don't have all night."

"Don't be mean."

Cutter looked at his coffee. No staring into one another's eyes. He hadn't been enjoying his time with Grace, but it was preferable to this. He didn't answer her.

"All right," she said. "You win. I'll drop it—for now." She took a deep breath and frowned. "So, Ely, is it true?"

"Is what true?"

"Don't play games with me. You've already said you don't have all night. What happened?"

"I'll tell you, but first tell me what you heard—and how."

"I don't see what difference that makes."

"It makes a difference to me. And maybe you already know what happened, so why hear it from me all over again?"

"Janet Korn told me that you were gardening, and you heard a deep voice coming from the sky. When you looked up, you saw God's face. He was angry."

Cutter sighed. Janet Korn wasn't in their circle of friends. "Do you know how Janet heard? And why did she tell you? Does she..."

"No. Of course not. She doesn't have a clue. She'd never have said a word if she'd even suspected..."

"Can't tell. She might have been trying to see how you'd react."

"Don't worry," she said, dismissing his concern. She paused not at all before asking, "Is it true?"

"Partly."

Eleanor was frowning and picking at the cuticle on her thumb. "I guess she heard from someone who goes to Marguerite," he said.

"She goes to Marguerite."

"Bingo."

"Bingo?"

"Lynne had an appointment the same day it happened. She must have told Marguerite. Figures."

"I don't want to say anything nice about Lynne…"

Cutter was skeptical.

"…but who wouldn't have said something?"

"He didn't say anything."

"What?"

"I didn't hear Him say anything. And He didn't look angry. I don't know where they got that." Cutter was sorry he'd stopped smoking. He wanted an excuse to go outside, get out of here. He felt as though he'd been sitting in the coffee shop for hours.

"Are you all right?"

"I'm fine, perfect. This has been a lovely evening. It's getting better every minute."

"I'm on your side, Ely."

"People are taking sides?" Cutter meant this, if not as a joke, as a rhetorical ploy to keep from giving more details. But when Eleanor didn't answer, Cutter saw that he'd hit the mark. He could sell clever tee shirts and mugs with a picture of…what, the face? In essence, an image of a garden ornament.

"What's wrong?"

He told her, even about his imaginary merchandise.

"You could give them away as a bonus when people buy a house from you, Ely. On the back it could say, "Ely Cutter, Heavenly Homes.""

"You can still write copy, Eleanor," he said though Heavenly Homes was more garden cemetery than suburban housing.

"But Ely, if He didn't call you, what then?"

"I'd never thought of it as His calling me...," Cutter said. "I just looked up, you know how you do when you're weeding and it's hot out. You stand up from time to time, look around."

"You were weeding, and it was hot. You stood up too fast in all that heat." Eleanor leaned forward over the table. "Dehydration. Were you blacking out?"

Cutter tried to remember if he'd heard a ringing in his ears or seen spots. He hadn't. "I was fine, Eleanor. Just fine. Awake as I am now."

"Don't get defensive."

"Sorry. This isn't easy, you know."

"I understand. That's why I was surprised when you didn't call me. I thought being able to talk to me was a comfort."

"I didn't have a right to call you, Eleanor." Cutter said, "Not under these circumstances."

"'These circumstances' as you call them, can change. We can go back." Eleanor drained her cup of cappuccino. "I'd like that, wouldn't you?"

Cutter was ready for this question. "That's not why we're here, is it? If so, we should just say goodnight now." His smile contradicted his words.

"You win, Ely. I'll let it drop—for now. But I see the way you look at me, still." She leaned forward, "And it's not discreet, especially..."

"Especially what?"

"When you're such a, how shall I say, local celebrity."

"Celebrity! You have a way of putting the best spin on things. Why don't you just say, subject of gossip?"

"Speculation?" she said, "Is that better?"

"It'll do. This whole thing is odd for me. But you know that." He smiled again, one of the boyish smiles she used to dote on. "You called me because you knew."

Cutter patted Eleanor's hand, which she had left on the table, in what he recognized as the "touch me" position. It can't do too much damage. Anyone looking would have seen the gesture of an old friend. Or that's what he hoped.

"Looking at it one way, it's simple. It was morning, and I was weeding, and I looked up and saw a face in the sky. No clouds, just a face."

"'Just a face!'"

"Well, yes. Like a garden ornament. They used to be everywhere. A sun with rays. Terracotta painted in blues and yellow, or sometimes unpainted." Cutter paused, elbows on the table, wiggling his fingers in the air to simulate the rays. He felt melancholy. "Now they're mostly painted metal, pierced metal. *Hecho en* China."

"So, you saw?"

"This face. You've seen dozens of them in gardens, no?"

"I know what you mean, but..."

"But why God? Or—why me?" Cutter sighed and then met her gaze. "I ask that too."

"You're certain it was God?"

"Certain? I know what I saw. If not God, then who?"

"Or what?"

"No—not what," he said.

"Well, what if it wasn't God, but...you know, the Other."

"I thought of that." If Satan were going to come for him, Eleanor would have something to do with it, "You think I can't tell the difference?"

Eleanor didn't answer.

"Well, I can. I said He looked like a garden ornament. Whoever heard of Satan in a garden?"

"Oh? Once upon a time there was a tree with forbidden fruit, remember. A Garden?"

"OK. But I'm sure, pretty sure, anyway. Otherwise, I wouldn't have..." Cutter caught himself before he told Eleanor about the purslane. And why would seeing God make him want to eat the weeds anyway. None of it made sense, which was one of the reasons Lynne had been so upset with him.

"Are you all right? You look unhappy," she said, her face set against him.

"I am. This isn't fun." Cutter shook his head. "Talking about this isn't fun, I mean. The whole experience I could have done without."

"Apparently not. Or it wouldn't have happened."

"I don't get it."

"Ely, think. You must have needed it," Eleanor said.

She sounded smug, but he didn't interrupt. Useless to interrupt when she had something on her mind. She'd just go back to it.

She went on, "If you did see God, and I believe you think you did—and not something or someone else up there—then it was destiny. Or God's will, however you want to say it."

"Purslane," Cutter said. He might as well tell her. She

hadn't heard about it yet or she would have said something. But she was sure to hear, especially since he had some ideas about other plants he'd seen. She might as well hear it from him.

And so Cutter gave Eleanor a short version of his having tried the purslane and found it good. He told her how he'd rinsed one of the plump leaves in cold hose water, how he'd tried to say the blessing for plants growing in the earth, and how he hadn't remembered anything past the first few words. He was ashamed. He wasn't sure if he felt ashamed of having forgotten the blessing, such a simple sentence after all, or his having attempted it.

"The blessing? The whole *Baruch-atah*, Blessed-art-Thou bit?" Eleanor asked.

Eleanor's use of "bit" to describe a blessing nettled him: he was ashamed of having forgotten the words, not at having tried to say the prayer thanking God for causing something to grow from the earth. At the time it had seemed natural to him to say the blessing. Why hasn't he continued to say them?

Eleanor had been chattering and he hadn't been listening. And now she was silent, staring, tapping the soft pads of her fingers next to her empty cup. But she was smiling as though she'd heard an old joke that she still found funny.

"And?" He heard her say.

"And I looked up recipes and made a salad." he said. "With yogurt," adding, "I found recipes on the net. Apparently, I'm not the only one." He decided against telling her about how he and Lynne had dinner with Ruth and Sam, that Ruth had decided he'd taken up with her again. And how he'd assured them it was over. No, he couldn't tell her that.

Cutter had been half-alive for some time. Or half-asleep. He could ask Eleanor if he'd been that way before his vision, and, if so, for how long. She'd know.

"Dreaming again, Ely?"

"I didn't realize," Cutter said. He looked at Eleanor, and wished he were at home with Lynne, emptying the dishwasher, or busying himself with whatever domestic task would let him feel ordinary again.

"What?"

"How often was I what you call 'dreaming'? Do I owe you an apology?"

Eleanor laughed. "Damn straight you do. But not for that."

She had a point. He'd allowed things with her to get out of hand. Had she been even slightly less demanding, he'd be with her yet.

He looked at his watch, this time with intention. He took longer than he needed.

"There's a clock on the wall over the menu," Eleanor said. "In your line of sight. You've been checking it since you came back to the table. Late date?"

Comments like these had kept him from calling her, and Cutter was grateful to be reminded of that, especially now, when he needed someone eager to listen to him think aloud. Grace. She thought he had a date with Grace. Or she was pretending to think so to bait him.

He shook his head. "I have to be going...," he said.

"So, you don't want to keep Lynne waiting?" she said.

Better let that pass. "I'll walk you to your car," Cutter said, pushing his chair back from the table. She used to park towards the back of the lot in back, away from traffic. They'd sat there together in the days he'd come to think of as "before." He'd felt like a teenager in the car with the windows steamed from their breath and body heat.

"No need," she said, "I'm just out front."

Cutter walked with her to the front of the store, but he hung back as she moved into the vestibule lined with posters and brochures. She pushed open the door, then turned and stopped. She lifted her hand as if to wave, a gesture left incomplete. Instead, she pivoted and walked away.

When he turned, he understood. It was Grace.

Chapter 5

The light in his living room was still on when Cutter pulled into his driveway. If he hurried, he could get in before the timer switched off at midnight. He disliked coming into the dark empty living room, which made him feel in varying ratios, both apprehensive and melancholy. Best of all options, he preferred coming in with the light on and Lynne already upstairs, half-awake or reading.

Cutter didn't call to Lynne; he didn't want to wake her up. She deserved a good night's sleep, and he needed a few more minutes alone. All the caffeine and Grace's chatter had left his head buzzing like a failing ballast in a fluorescent kitchen light. Between Eleanor and Grace, he'd had someone plucking at his sleeve—clucking at him—for hours.

He'd stop and pour himself a nightcap before he went upstairs. When he was seeing Eleanor, if they'd been drinking, he'd carry a drink upstairs to explain any alcohol on his breath. Tonight, he wouldn't take even a sip until he'd greeted Lynne. He could kiss her, and that would be a good start to "their little talk." It would be fine. After all, what had he done but have coffee in the bookstore with a client? And it had happened by chance. That part of it was true, anyway.

He carried his glass into the bedroom. Lynne looked up from her book and smiled. She took off her reading glasses and set them on the nightstand. He checked the smile for irony, none. This would be easier than he'd expected. He bent and kissed her, happy he had nothing much to hide.

Cutter held his glass out to her, and she shook her head.

He sat on the edge of the bed near her feet and took a sip, wondering why he drank when he didn't much like the taste. Nonetheless, this gin, would be good with cucumber. Maybe he could find a recipe for a cold cucumber soup spiked with gin.

"You're getting inventive, Ely," Lynne said when he told her his idea.

She sounded wistful, and perhaps he did, too. It was easier to play it straight. "You mean the purslane? I can't explain that."

"I think it had something to do with your vision."

"It seems so pretentious, 'vision.' It makes me sound like some sort of saint or prophet."

"What would you want me to call it, a psychotic episode?"

"Make it vision, then." He kept his voice flat. "What would you say about trying a few more things? I bought a book."

"Fine, Ely," Lynne put her glasses on and opened her book, the new best seller, stacks of it at B&N.

"We can read it together."

She didn't ask what book he'd bought, which might have rankled under other circumstances. Tonight, he simply was grateful that she hadn't asked any other questions about the evening except innocuous questions about the likelihood of making the sale.

Cutter hadn't brought the book into the house. He'd bought it because it was about finding and eating weeds, which he deemed oxymoronic. Eating wild plants, yes—but once something became edible, it was no longer a weed. You pull out weeds and throw them away; you harvest edible wild plants.

He'd keep the book in the car to read while waiting for clients, and then if he spotted a plant, he could—if he were alone—pull over and check it out. The difficulty would lie in finding plants he could eat safely, as roadside plants may have absorbed pollution and poisonous metals. He'd have to stay close to home in his search, or the yards of friends who didn't use herbicides or pesticides. It wouldn't be a spontaneous picnic. He said none of this to Lynne.

As he was about to get into bed after a long, cool shower, his cell phone began to ring. He'd left his phone in the pocket of his jacket that he'd thrown over the back of a chair. He made no move to dig the phone free until it stopped ringing.

"Sorry," he said to Lynne. He held his hands palms up. "I can't imagine..."

"I can," Lynne said.

Cutter was unsurprised by the suspicion in her voice.

"I'll take care of it," he said, as he retrieved his phone, turned it off, and plugged it into the charger, sorry that he couldn't take care of her imagination. She'd overheard too many calls from Eleanor.

"Aren't you going to see who phoned?"

"It's probably a wrong number. Or a client who assumes my phone's turned off and just wants to leave a message," he said. "Nothing that won't wait until morning."

He looked at Lynne to see how this was playing. "Who do we know who'd call my cell phone at this time of night?"

"Who indeed?" Lynne said, her tone its own answer.

Cutter shrugged, feigning calm ignorance. He didn't blame

Lynne for her reaction; he should have known better than to ask that question. It was a matter of damage control now. "I'll deal with it tomorrow."

"Aren't you even curious?"

"Frankly, my dear, I don't give a damn." Cutter smiled at Lynne. "I think this is where I carry you up the stairs to bed—except, how convenient...."

"Really, Ely. If I'd been in the mood before, I'm certainly not in the mood now."

That was just as well. He wasn't sure what he could manage beyond his murmured, "Sorry, Darling. Another time."

"Will the light bother you?" Lynne asked, her book still open.

The question was *pro forma*. The light never bothered him. He slid into bed and gave her a peck on the cheek, murmuring a good night. When he fell asleep Lynne was still reading.

Cutter woke. He'd heard someone call his name. Startled, he sat up and looked around—Lynne was sleeping, her back to him. He was certain he hadn't been dreaming. He got out of bed, taking care not to wake his wife, and pushed aside the curtain. In the moon light Lynne's white flowers seemed to float, untethered.

He felt as though he had slept through the night, and though he wasn't often a victim of insomnia, he was sure he wouldn't sleep again. The clock said 3:30. He'd go downstairs and sit a while in the garden. Nothing wrong with that.

He picked up the glass he'd left by the bed, just melted ice. He'd drunk more than he'd realized. He carried the glass down with him, poured the liquid down the drain. He refilled the glass with ice and orange juice and carried it out with him to the patio.

Cutter sat on the chaise. He'd never been in the garden at this hour, and having the place to himself at this hour felt strange, a bit lonely. But even if Lynne were awake, they wouldn't sit here in the middle of the night. He drank the juice all at once. He hadn't realized he was so thirsty.

He stretched out on the chaise, and he tried to push away his thoughts of Grace. He'll have to be careful with her. He was almost certain she'd been the one to phone. Already out of control. He didn't want to get into all that again.

He still had so much to be grateful for—he didn't want to lose it. He'd just lie here for a while and then go back in the house before Lynne awoke. The night was humid, but blessedly cool. He closed his eyes to concentrate on the fragrance that surrounded him, the Nicotiana and other white flowers Lynne had planted for her moon garden. And he slept.

When he woke, the sun had risen just high enough over the roof to light a corner of the garden. He'd never awakened outside before; even in the scouts he'd slept in a pup tent. He'd crawled out and been astonished by the dew, by how wet the world could be even without rain. Now he was amazed by the beauty of the garden, the shades of green, and, where the sun served as spotlight, the gaudy marigolds and zinnias, pink, yellow, orange, and red. He was content here, fortunate to breathe the morning air and to be, as he so often said, on the right side of the grass.

He peered at the glass he'd left by his side on the patio.

Empty. He'd fill a large glass with lots of ice cubes and in orange juice. He ought to get busy in the garden and weed, perhaps water, before it's too hot, but he wanted to just sit idle for a while.

But when he went into the kitchen, he found a fresh pot of coffee still running down into the carafe. Lynne must have gone back up to shower. He thought he'd take a cup of coffee to her but changed his mind. It would be more fun for both of them if he surprised her with a fancy breakfast on the terrace.

Cutter went out into the garden, harvested a tomato for an omelet and took it back to the house. Humming a tune that he made up as he went along, he set the table on the terrace and, on a whim, took out the hot-pink cloth napkins. He cut three pink roses, some green and purple basil, and sprigs of mint with their lavender blossoms, some lambs ear, and a few nasturtiums. He could use mint, basil, and nasturtium in a salad at dinner, too. That wouldn't be controversial.

He was chopping the tomato when Lynne came into the kitchen. She wasn't quite frowning, but something about the set of her mouth told him she was still bothered by last night's call. He was alone in his delight, enjoying the beauty of a splendid morning. Maybe the breakfast would cheer her up. Instead, it was his mood that changed. The ominous feeling that the late-night phone call would require damage control returned and intensified because it was possible that by now Lynne had checked the caller ID. Too bad he couldn't ask. He'd find out soon enough.

"Flowers?" Lynne asked, after she'd looked at the window.

"Sure," Cutter said.

"Why the basil and mint?"

"Looks good, smells good."

"Are you planning to eat these right out of the vase or wait until later?"

Cutter was embarrassed. He was almost afraid to tell her about his plans for the salad. The roses had never been sprayed. He could, in fact, eat the roses right out of the vase. He could eat all the arrangement, except the thorns.

"Don't worry. I'm not going to ruin this pretty arrangement," he said, silently modifying his assurance, "Not yet, anyhow."

"Don't you have a call to return?"

Cutter tried to read Lynne's expression. She'd have recognized Eleanor's phone number if she'd checked his phone, and he thought he'd broken Eleanor of phoning him so late. "No rush," he said, "I guess." He paused and added, "I don't know who called."

"Oh?"

"I came down here last night to sit awhile in the garden. I didn't mean to fall asleep."

"Do you want to make your call now?"

"I'm sure it's not important." Cutter said, hoping he was right. "And, besides, it's still too early to make a call. Work can wait."

"A call after midnight..." she began to say.

"Is most likely a wrong number." It would be a wrong number, he hoped. At any rate this was the best way to complete Lynne's sentence although that probably wasn't what she had in mind.

"A wonderful invention, caller ID."

For whom was it wonderful, was Cutter's silent question, but, aloud, he asked, "Do you want me to make the call now?"

"I thought you said it was a wrong number," she said.

"Lynne, I'm sorry I came down here last night. I didn't mean to fall asleep here."

"You said that before, Ely."

He wanted to compliment her on her moon garden, and he wanted to tell her everything that had happened the evening before at the bookstore. Maybe he could turn it into a funny story. "It was beautiful out here last night. And this morning. It was like waking up to a whole new world. You..."

"I what?" she said.

It was impossible to ignore her mood, but he was determined not to contribute to ruining the day. He'll find a way. He'll tell her another time. After breakfast. After he sees who called. He turned his attention again to chopping the tomato.

"Why the tomato?"

"Omelet. Maybe some cheddar. Live a little. Life is short."

"I'm not hungry, Ely. It's too early."

"Never too early for breakfast. I thought that's what you..."

"Right. Of course. But not now."

With the bright sunlight behind her, Lynne's face was inscrutable, but her voice was clear. She was distancing herself. That call last night had upset her far more than he'd realized. And, he reminded himself, he'd been late getting in.

"I'm going back upstairs," she said. She poured herself a cup of coffee and headed out to the hall. She called back to him, "The omelet sounds great. Enjoy."

"I'll wait for you," Ely said. "This'll keep." He wasn't sure about the vitamins, but the chopped tomatoes would be fine in the fridge with some cling wrap over the bowl. He'd drain the juice into a glass. The omelet would be almost as good if he made it in a few hours.

The table was festive with the bright napkins and the flowers. They'll keep too. Maybe he'd better go upstairs himself and check the cell. The call, whoever it had come from, had become too important for him to ignore. The longer he waited, the more significant it became. Lynne had made it important. And he couldn't blame her.

When he walked into the bedroom, Lynne was back in bed, the mug of coffee by her side. She was reading again and didn't look up even though he was certain she'd heard him.

"Hi," he said. How absurd he felt saying that. He felt as awkward as a freshman boy at his first college mixer. And this was his wife, in their bed.

"Hi," she said in the same blameless tone that she'd used telling him to enjoy. She kept her eyes fixed on her book, but she wasn't turning any pages.

He fumbled a bit with his cell phone, flinched at the characteristic sound of the phone turning on—it seemed far too loud in this silent room. He was surprised that his hands were cold, that he was so nervous. He didn't know if Lynne had looked earlier, but if she'd been snooping, she should be the one to be nervous.

Maybe that's why she was remote. "I had two missed calls,"

he said, hoping to redeem himself from whatever blame might settle on him. He'd learn soon enough how much trouble he was in.

The same number was on both calls. One had come in at 12:30, the other a half an hour later while the phone was turned off. Grace. Both times.

He tossed the phone on the bed next to Lynne. She turned a page of her book and looked up at him. She picked up the phone and held it out to him, as though she wanted to hand it over. "You dropped something."

"That's not the word I'd use."

"You'd prefer I say you threw it at me?"

This was far worse than he'd expected. And, for once, he was innocent. Well, that was true under some strict construction of the word. And under others, he was guilty. He hadn't sent Grace away. He'd used his business relationship with her as an excuse. "I'd prefer you look to see who called. That's why I gave it to you." He hadn't taken the phone.

"Gave?" She set the phone down.

"It's what I meant to do." Like the breakfast she wouldn't eat, the flowers and the napkins she'd dismissed; Cutter reassured himself that his intentions were good. Everything was going wrong, he told himself, then caught himself whining. He scooped up the phone and put it in his pocket.

"I'm sorry," Cutter said. "I didn't intend to do anything that would upset you."

Lynne raised her eyebrows as her only response.

"The calls upset me too, Lynne. Calls come in that late, even though nobody's sick now, I get frightened. We're at that age..."

"I thought you said it was a wrong number."

"I said—I thought I said—it was either a wrong number or a client who expected that my phone would be off. It was a client. I'm not responsible for..."

"What your clients do? Not entirely off the hook either. Unless you can explain why she called twice and so late."

"What makes you so sure it was she?" Even as he spoke, Cutter knew he was making a mistake.

"Tell me I'm wrong, Ely. I'd love to be wrong about this."

"I can't."

"Then why did you ask why I thought it was a woman? You're not playing Texas Hold'em with the boys."

Cutter was quiet. He'd never played Texas Hold'em. He had no "boys" with whom he played cards. Maybe if he kept silent, he'd learn why she was so suspicious now. He'd been an exemplary husband for the last several weeks. Until today.

Of course, it was yesterday, not today, that he'd met Eleanor. But that hadn't been his idea, and he'd wanted Eleanor to be on his side in the next months. He was going to need all the allies he could find as the word spread that he'd had a vision. He couldn't afford to alienate Eleanor. And besides, he did owe her something. Anyway, he was pretty sure he could count on her in a pinch.

As for Grace, well, she was something else. When she sat down with him before he could take a breath to invite her, he had an indication that she could be trouble, but he hadn't a clue about how much trouble she'd be. Even when he bumped into her after having seen Eleanor to the door at the bookstore, he wasn't sure that it hadn't been an accident. And she had retreated when Eleanor had come to the table, hadn't she?

But today, he'd tried a bluff, and Lynne hadn't fallen for it. He'd tried to fool her into thinking that Grace was just a client, one that was, perhaps, a bit clingy. He'd had clients like that before, and Lynne and he had laughed about them together. He might have gotten away with his deception. He might have, but he hadn't. "I was wrong, Lynne. Blame me for not wanting to worry you."

"How about for being defensive?"

"Okay, then, for being defensive." He took a deep breath. "I think Grace is a little off."

Cutter watched for clues as his wife set her book on the nightstand and placed her folded reading glasses on top of the closed book. He knew that he'd chanced on the right thing to say when Lynne looked at him and said, "So, Ely, tell me."

This was the opportunity he needed. He took a deep breath and sat on the bed at Lynne's feet where he could see her face. "I'm not sure where to begin," he said. That wasn't a figure of speech. He couldn't decide if he should begin with the butter-yellow kitchen or with Eleanor's unexpected call during the house showing. "I tell you what," he said, placing his hand on her leg with what he hoped would seem to be a comradely affection that grew out of their decades together. "Why don't we go down to the kitchen, together, and we can talk while I put together those omelets?"

One sigh from Lynne, and he'd have to get into it here. This wasn't pillow talk, and he'd rather be where Lynne had access to knives than to pollute their bedroom with this story.

If he did everything right, they could be sitting on the patio together eating a tomato omelet. To keep Lynne happy he'd skip the cheddar. It was a small price to pay for domestic tranquility.

Chapter 6

In the kitchen, Cutter began with Grace's gold bangles. "They made a racket," he said, "I'd have thought she was doing it on purpose, but why would she?" He hoped he was making her sound unattractive.

"Rings on her fingers, bells on her toes," Lynne said.

"No bells," Cutter said, "but rings. Rings and bracelets. Unless her money is all in jewelry, she should be able to buy a decent place. No wedding ring. Divorce."

"Divorce...." Lynne paused, and when Cutter didn't fill in the silence, continued, "She didn't get the house?"

"She doesn't want the house. Fresh start. All that. You've heard it before." And she had. Cutter's relationships with his freshly-divorced female clients were a frequent topic of conversation with Lynne. Doctors, lawyers, and spies who couldn't use work for small talk with their wives—what did they talk about?

"So you're going to help her with that fresh start?"

"Just with the house." He didn't tell Lynne that Grace expected him to help paint her kitchen. He'd meant his offer to be rhetorical, just a moment in his showing the house, and he'd spoken without imagining how Grace might misinterpret his casual rhetorical comment. He wouldn't compound his error by telling Lynne, who would be hurt and angry. This wasn't the time for that tidbit, and the right time for that might never come. He'd made too many mistakes already.

Leaving Grace alone with Eleanor had been another error. He'd found out just how much of a mistake after Grace ambushed him at the bookstore.

"You have a minute, Ely?" Grace asked.

She was standing close, too close. As the first part of his answer Cutter checked his watch but said nothing. It was after ten. Lynne had expected him to be home at nine. He should have phoned. Too late now. It would be awkward to break away from Grace, and, besides, he knew from experience that his cell phone wouldn't work in the bathroom of Barnes & Noble, so he couldn't call from there. "A minute? Of course," he said, with what he hoped would appear to be a sincere smile.

"Eleanor—do I have that right? or was it Evelyn?"

"Yes," Cutter said, enjoying the knowledge that his answer was perfectly ambiguous.

"Evelyn, sorry. I was distracted when you introduced us."

"No, no," Cutter said. "It happens." He ought to correct her, but he wished she'd get on with it. He wanted to go home. This had been a trying evening.

"She told me she was an old friend."

He nodded.

"She said she knew you very well."

This didn't sound like Eleanor. She'd always been discreet, even at the end when it was too late, and discretion was merely a matter of form. He nodded to see what would come next, what nasty revelation, what half-worm in a bitten fruit.

"She said you were someone who deserved..." her voice dropped, "everything he had."

So, Cutter mused, she's fishing. Well, let her. What harm can there be in that?

"Eleanor's always been generous of spirit."

"Eleanor? I thought you said her name was Evelyn?"

Grace sounded piqued. Cutter was amused at how little effort he had expended to tweak her so. "Did I? We must have had a misunderstanding. It's Eleanor. Definitely. I'm sure of it." Now he was fishing.

"Well, I guess you are sure. As I said, she told me you were awfully good friends."

"Oh?"

"She said you understood her better than anyone ever had," Grace said, "that you had a knack with women."

Cutter laughed. He couldn't help it. He was certain now. Grace was making this up. Eleanor would never have said those things about him even in an attempt to piss on the tree to mark her territory. If women could piss on trees—for damn sure they did something.

"Well, I think you do, Ely. You've been a big help to me already," she said, her hand on his arm.

Her hand was cold. No wonder, he thought. She's half-naked in that tank top—and those bracelets do nothing for warmth. "You're too kind," he said, emptying his voice of irony.

But what had Eleanor said? He'd better find out. Whatever it was, it'd been enough to get Grace to scram and leave them alone, but not enough to keep her away altogether. Or maybe that would have required more than even Eleanor was capable of accomplishing.

Tears were welling up in Grace's eyes, and she hadn't taken her hand off his arm.

"There, there," he said, patting her hand and stepping back, thus freeing himself while trying to appear sympathetic. Would it appear to an onlooker as though he was a source of consolation—or the cause of her misery? That would never do.

Grace wiped away her tears, smudging her mascara. Her eyes were red-rimmed. How, after only a mini moment of emotion, could she have red eyes? Didn't you have to cry to get those? He'd seen Lynne like that all too often, and, rarely, Eleanor, too.

Grace looked a mess. He'd have to say something. He couldn't be seen talking to her with her looking like that, and if she caught sight of herself in a mirror she'd be mortified and blame him. Women were always blaming men for things like that, he thought, pleased with his observation, and not in the least irritated by its content.

"Would you like me to get you a drink?" Cutter asked, trying to be solicitous. He hoped she'd suggest the freshening up.

"Lovely," Grace said. "I could use one. Where shall we go?"

"What?" He was taken off guard. All evening he'd been kept off balance both by Eleanor and Grace. Now this. It was one thing to be seen having coffee in the bookstore. Another in a venue so much less coincidental in appearance.

"For a drink?"

"I'm married, Grace," Cutter said, trying to sound gentle. That wasn't difficult.

"I know. Eve—Eleanor told me." She paused. "Besides, I'd assumed you were."

Cutter was at a loss. "I thought maybe a glass of spring water? Iced herbal tea?"

Grace laughed and made a sudden gesture that set her bangles to clanging. Did she always wear them? What did she do with them at Yoga? Surely, they'd get in the way.

"I thought maybe a gin and tonic? Or gin and lime on the rocks, or vodka," she countered. "Something cold and clear and soothing."

"It's awkward," Cutter said, looking at his watch, then a shrug, holding his hands palms up, as if helpless, asking what can I do?

"Well," Grace said, "You are the sly dog she said you were. All right then. My place it is."

"I hope that's all you're going to do," Lynne said.

"Right," Cutter said, trying to remember what it is he'd said.

"Would you mind if I go cut some herbs for this omelet?" He looked down at the tomatoes he'd cubed. "I should have thought of it before."

"You want me to go along?"

"I'll be right back," he said. "I'm not doing the grand tour."

"Those flowers do look sweet," Lynne said, with a nod to the terrace.

Was she trying, by being nice, to build a fortification against an invasion by Grace?

"I don't know, Grace," Cutter said. "It's getting kind of late."

"Just for a night cap, Ely." She took a deep breath. "You don't have to stay all night."

"Even if I wanted to, that's one thing I could never do," he said, conscious that he was in the middle of the bookstore aisle negotiating parameters of a relationship with a tank-top wearing, apparently braless, bangle-jangling, right-out-of-the-box, divorcée.

"We'll worry about that when we have to," Grace said. "You said you had all the time in the world."

Cutter struggled. What had he said? Had he used exactly those words? He'd have to be more careful. If he'd said that, she'd pounced on the phrase, and if he'd said something else, she'd twisted what he said to suit her.

Considering her red-rimmed eyes, smeared make up, and the fluorescent lights, she didn't look half-bad. For a woman her age. And a woman much younger wouldn't look at him twice, barely once. For a long time, he'd been feeling invisible, which had its advantages. Being invisible meant he didn't have to suck in his gut.

"I don't want to worry about it at all," he said.

"Let's not worry then. We can play it by ear—or anything else that comes up."

Cutter cringed. He hoped Grace hadn't noticed his reaction. "By ear then."

"So, you'll follow me? Or do you remember where I live?"

"You'd better lead the way," Cutter said, feeling as though this wasn't going to be his last capitulation.

Although Cutter had promised not to do what he and Lynne called the grand tour—his walking through the garden and making note of his day's chores—nonetheless he inspected the herb garden while he was pinching some green goddess basil. He was hoping he'd find some purslane or lambs quarters. None. He'd phone Sam later, wander by and check his garden for edibles that Sam wouldn't want.

He rinsed, stripped, and chiffonaded the basil to mix in with the tomatoes. He found a bowl of shredded cheddar. Lynne had worked quickly. "Got the cheese done! Nice work," he said.

A lambent grimace on Lynne's face became a weak smile, "Thanks, Sweetie," she said.

He'd have to be careful of using that hearty tone. Too much false cheer. They were both on good behavior, and he wasn't sure whether he preferred that to the sniping or clenched jaw. Cutter didn't like being careful, and his life had changed so that he had to be careful far more than before. He'd simplified his life when he'd broken off with Eleanor, or so he thought, but here she was back again. And Grace? Good grief! How had he let that happen?

Following Grace to her house, watching the taillights of her car as it picked up speed, Cutter considered his option of getting lost and then phoning her to say he couldn't make it tonight—now that he'd have to find his way from wherever— and he'd have to take a rain check. Grace had said what a good idea it was that he come by and see her home; he'd have a much better idea of what she liked and didn't like if he saw how she'd been living for thirty-two years.

Cutter hadn't wanted her to tear up again, so he'd agreed. Nonetheless, he knew that was a rationalization. Besides, she wanted to make a change, or so she'd said. She wouldn't want a duplicate of her present house. Or would she? After seeing how she lived, he could compare her home with what she'd said about features of the houses she'd seen so far. If he were a betting man, he'd wager that she just wanted a change of address. He might be able to figure out an angle once he'd seen her place.

Cutter knew the houses in this area: stone on the outside, apparently traditional center hall colonial—but then a surprise. Inside, instead of the two-story house one would expect from looking at the exterior, you found yourself in a split-level.

"The SOB took every Oriental rug we had in the house," were Grace's words to Cutter as she turned the key in the lock. She was standing under the porch light waiting for him. Cutter was certain that every word she said could be heard in the neighbors' homes, and he hoped they wouldn't look to determine the identity of her audience.

Cutter nodded. Voices carry at night. He didn't know who lived nearby.

"Home sweet home," Grace said, pushing open the door. "What's your professional opinion, Ely?"

Grace—or her husband—had poured a lot of money into upgrades. The floor, for example, granite in the entryway and exotic hardwood beyond. Acres of it, wholly without rugs. The granite wasn't in the least practical, not in this climate. Step on it in wet galoshes and you'll land on your keister.

"Gracious," Cutter said, careful not to make it an exclamation instead of a compliment. "Lovely."

"You should have seen it with the rugs," Grace said.

Cutter was afraid she was going to cry again, but instead she laughed. He was alarmed by the note of hysteria.

"What's your poison?" she asked.

"Heavy on the ice," Cutter said, "Light on water."

"My kind of man," Grace said. "Gin or Vodka?"

Cutter grinned. "Neither. Just water on the rocks. Light on water."

"You must be kidding."

"No. I'm making a little joke, but not kidding."

"Okay," Grace said, "Rain check on the booze. You don't mind, if I?"

"Not at all," Cutter said. "Rain check it is." He followed her to the kitchen and looked around: black granite counter, tile floor, nice backsplash, but the Italian tiles didn't go with the ultra-modern kitchen.

"The tiles were his idea," Grace said, her back to him.

Cutter was surprised; he hadn't said a word about the tiles. Grace held two glasses in the refrigerator icemaker, filling them with cloudy half-moons.

"Heavy on the ice it is," she said. She handed him a glass and said, smiling, "Here you go. You better add the water. I don't want to ruin our first drink together."

She opened the freezer and took out a green bottle. She poured until the ice in her glass was covered. Cutter held his glass and figured she must have poured herself at least four ounces of gin. She held her glass out, "Cheers!"

Bangles again! Does she know how much noise they make? Cutter lifted his ice water, *"L'chaim!"* He didn't touch his glass to hers but took a sip.

"You can change your mind, you know."

"I'm fine," Cutter said, shaking his head for emphasis.

"Ready for a house tour?"

Cutter was ready for the tour, but not for the extras. "Rain check," he said.

"You're taking a lot of those rain checks," Grace said, frowning.

"That I am," he said.

"I'm counting on your cashing them in, Ely," Grace said. "Evelyn...sorry, Eleanor, was right. You're a charming man. I feel like I've known you forever." She drank, then turned and opened the freezer. "Might as well freshen this up now."

"Ah, Grace, don't make any hasty judgments. I'm sure I'm not as nice as you've heard."

"I'm counting on that," she said, laughing. What was it you said, 'L'chaim?'" She held up her glass. "Anyway, I'll drink to that."

"You've become quite the chef, Ely," Lynne said. "And look at this table."

It did look beautiful. Cutter hoped that eating breakfast on the terrace, having flowers on the table might distract Lynne. He watched her fork the omelet into her mouth. "It's the tomatoes," Ely said. "Right out of the garden, they'll make anyone seem like a good cook."

"So, what did you promise her?"

Lynne's question startled him. He believed he'd answered that before, and he said so. He explained again that this was "a house sale, pure and simple."

"Pure and simple?" Lynne asked. "From what you've told me, Grace's intentions aren't all that pure. And she doesn't sound simple, either."

From what he'd told her? Cutter had made certain that he'd given Lynne a severely edited version of the evening. What had he said? More likely, what had he omitted that put her on the trail?

"You're right, Lynne. She's not simple." Cutter paused, looked her in the eye, and said, "But I'm not simple either. Give me some credit."

"For what?"

"For knowing better."

Lynne had sounded bitter, and she had a right to be. He'd put her through a lot with Eleanor. But he'd assured her that was over and done with. Even though he'd met Eleanor last night, it really was over. If Lynne chose not to believe him, well then, he might as well have the game if he had the name.

"For knowing better," he repeated.

He didn't like the smirk on Lynne's face. Not long ago he'd thought they were both on their best behavior and that she was trying to keep him close by being sweet.

"So, you were with Grace last night? The whole time?"

Cutter recognized a trick question when he heard it. He'd been out for close to five hours. If he'd spent the whole time with Grace, he had to come up with some fancy explanations. On the other hand, the truth wouldn't serve him well, either. Lynne would hate hearing about Eleanor.

"Cat got your tongue?" Lynne asked, "Or was it just some pussy?"

It wasn't like Lynne to be vulgar. Cutter scraped his chair back from the table, the wrought iron legs rasping on the patio. He leaned back and sat quiet. He'd wait this one out to see what else she had to say.

Usually, the salesman's trick worked the other way around. Ask the question and then shut up and wait for the answer. The silence was so uncomfortable for most people that you found out a lot of information. Now he'd use it on Lynne. He was happy in silence, could wait out nearly anyone. He wanted to know what she knew, but he'd be damned if he'd ask her. He couldn't think of a question she could ask that wouldn't spell out the worst of what he'd done, which, when he considered it, wasn't much at all.

"Do you want to sit in the garden, or stay in the living room?" Grace asked.

If they went outside, his voice might carry—worse, Grace's voice might carry; depending on how long he stayed, the liquor she was drinking would have time to kick in. Even sober, she might say something he wouldn't want people to hear. He was fairly certain that he'd sold the house next to hers. Give the neighbors the wrong impression, that's for sure. He wished she had a visible volume knob to turn down.

She's probably a screamer, and she most likely leaves the windows open to boot. He imagined her riding him, calling out his name. He shook his head at the image. Grace had been watching him.

"What's your pleasure?" she said.

Was she some sort of witch? She'd talked about the tiles

when he was looking at them and her back was to him, but that could have been a coincidence. Now this. No, she was talking about the indoors or garden question. He'd calculated the dangers of being outside. Inside he'd have more control. He could sit in the big armchair.

His choice of where to sit would be a message. And, besides, that big leather one looked comfortable, though he didn't want to seem too much at home. Why was that chair still here? The brown leather didn't go with the elegant white sofa. If her husband had taken the rugs, he might have taken that along with him, too. From what he knew of divorces, he surmised that a story lurked in that armchair.

No table beside the chair, he'd have to hold his glass. He couldn't put a sweating glass on the leather arm. Glass tables flanked the sofa, and the glass coffee table would be handy if he sat over there, but the sofa was out. He'd be safe on the chair.

"That big chair looks so comfortable," Cutter said.

"*Mi casa es su casa*," Grace said, raising her glass to him again.

Cutter sank into the chair. He was comfortable until Grace sat on the arm. This wasn't what he had in mind. She was far too close. "Comfy?" Grace asked.

Cutter turned to look at her. She leaned on the back of the chair, her arm inches from his head, her left breast inches from his face.

"You like the chair, Ely?" Grace asked. "It has a story. You want to hear?"

"Everything has a story, Grace. Every stick of furniture, every vase in every house. They've each got a story."

"That's profound, Ely. Let's trade stories."

"Sure, Grace, sure. But not tonight." He had to leverage himself out of the chair without bumping into her breast. He'd have to stand up without balancing on the arm of the chair, and one hand held the glass of ice water.

"Another rain check," Grace said. "We're going to be so busy we won't have time to look at houses."

"Let's find a house first," Cutter said. "And then we can catch up on the rain checks."

"Ely, if I hadn't seen the way you look at me," Grace said, "I'd think you were more interested in making a sale than in anything else."

"Let's make that the first order of business," he said.

"Will that make you happy?"

"We should find the house that you want to live in," Cutter said, "And then we can get the kitchen painted butter yellow. I can't look past that."

"I'm not sure about that color," she said. Her own kitchen was a pale blue. It went with the tiles and nothing else. The butter yellow was the complementary color of that blue.

"You can always paint when you've made up your mind," he said.

"'You?' You promised you'd help me," Grace said.

She sounded petulant. And the alcohol was already beginning to kick in. She'd be drunk soon. He'd have to get out of here while she was at least semi-sober.

"One step at a time. One baby step."

"Do you like children, Ely?"

"As much as anyone," he said.

"You have kids?"

Ely shook his head. He didn't want to tell Grace about his son, not now, maybe not at all.

"What about you?"

"Not to speak of. Now. None that will get in the way."

Cutter didn't even try to unpack her meaning; he sensed more there than he cared to deal with. More, he feared, than he would be able to handle.

"Rain check," Cutter said. It was the only thing he could think of saying. Then he thought of another. "Hold this, will you, please?" he said, raising his glass.

When she took it from him, Cutter realized that a secondary benefit was that Grace had both hands busy. He slid to the edge of the chair and leaned forward. The chair was comfortable, but the devil to get out of. He felt awkward and out of shape. Once he was standing, Grace looked tiny and cute, no longer predatory, as she sat on the arm of the chair. Her legs didn't reach the floor, and she was barefoot. When had she shed her shoes?

"So," Grace said, "Now what?"

"Now I go home," Cutter said.

"And then?"

"Then I ..." Cutter stopped realizing that he didn't know what to say. He wanted to say, "Then I can go to bed," but that was the wrong answer.

"You what?"

"I phone you in the morning, and we figure out what else might be available for you—for us to look at."

"You know what I'm looking for, right?"

"More or less," Cutter said. "I'm counting on you to tell me what you want—and what you don't."

Grace laughed. She set Cutter's drink on the coffee table, but she held onto hers. "I can tell you that now," she said, "but you keep saying you'll take a rain check."

She made a moue that Cutter found distasteful. He edged towards the door.

"Nothing happened with Grace," Cutter said to Lynne. "You could watch a video of the entire time we spent together, and you wouldn't flinch." This was a deliberate lie. Even though he hadn't done anything about it, his face had been so close to Grace's breast that he'd wanted to lean forward, mouth open. He hadn't had a clothed breast in his mouth since he was a teenager, and last night he'd been seconds away from it. Grace hadn't been wearing a bra under that black tank top.

No, Lynne, wouldn't have liked watching that. Still, he thought, a good video from the right angle would have emphasized his restraint.

Lynne said. "I know you're selling that woman a house. "That wasn't the question I asked you, Ely."

"Right. So, what's the big deal?" Cutter caught the flash of anger in his wife's face, and he hurried to appease her with an apology. He told Lynne how Grace had trapped him at the bookstore, how she'd been upset about, well, her marriage ending, about not being used to saying "I" rather than "we." He told her how Grace cried on a hair trigger, how she'd asked him to see her home. Cutter knew that this wasn't strictly the truth, either. And, from the expression on her face, Lynne wasn't buying it. "And I ought to have called, Lynne. To say I was running late. But she seemed so," he hesitated, looking for the word, rejected both fragile and scared, and settled on "needy. And unpredictable. She was talking far too loudly. I just wanted out."

"That's noble, Ely. So, you 'see her home' because you 'wanted out'? Really!"

"I was afraid she'd make a scene. Coming so soon after you-know-what," Ely said, confident Lynne would recognize his reference to his vision. "I didn't want people to have more to talk about."

"So that explains your cozy tête à tête with Eleanor?" Lynne stood up. "Honestly, Ely. Starbucks in Barnes & Noble! I don't know how you thought you'd get away with it."

Cutter looked at his wife as she stood across the table. I ought to stand up, too. I ought to apologize again. Someone had seen him talking with Eleanor and rushed to phone Lynne.

"You're not denying it, are you? At least there's that to be grateful for. But my God, Ely! My God! What were you thinking?"

And with that she turned and went back into the house, leaving the half-eaten omelet on the table. She slid the glass door closed behind her. All Ely could see was the reflection of their garden, but he imagined Lynne pouring herself a cup of coffee and retreating to their bedroom. He could do with another cup of coffee himself, but he didn't want to follow her into the house like a puppy.

Troublemakers. Why couldn't people mind their own

business? Or was the book she'd been reading brand new? Had she seen them at the bookstore herself? He'd been distracted by the cell-phone incident last night. Grace shouldn't have called so late. But she had. Alone in the garden, he closed his eyes. Grace moved from her perch on the arm of the chair to his lap. There they were together, their mouths too busy for words.

CHAPTER 7

Lynne ought to have told him straightaway that she'd seen him with Eleanor. He could have explained. She probably brooded all night long, he thought, forgetting that he'd been the one who'd had insomnia, not Lynne.

"Cat got your tongue? Or was it pussy?" No wonder she'd said that! How much had she heard or seen? With his luck Lynne would have caught him patting Eleanor's hand.

Now he'd have to call Eleanor and tell her what happened. Could she have noticed Lynne and not said anything? He didn't think so. Better prepare her for any fallout. He stopped at the top of the stairs and leaned against the wall, indulging himself with conscious self-pity, before calling, in as cheerful a tone as he could muster, "Lynne?"

No answer. So, it was the silent treatment. Worse. The bed was made, the book she'd been reading on the bedside table. Such a bright jacket! He ought to have known. And using the receipt as a bookmark! It was her way of telling him she'd been at Barnes & Noble, and he'd missed it. She was too subtle for him.

He looked at the clock. He'd been out there on the patio far longer than he'd realized. Grace had gotten him in trouble after all.

He went back down the stairs, calling Lynne's name. No answer. Lynne was gone. She'd left without a word to him, and Cutter smarted with the slight.

He tried phoning Lynne on her cell phone, and when he

got the message box, left none. She'd see that he called. That was enough. He didn't want to leave a conciliatory message that she was sure to listen to repeatedly, searching for signs of insincerity.

And besides, if he didn't hurry, he'd be late for his appointment with Grace.

Strictly speaking, he didn't have an appointment. But he was certain that if he called her, she'd set one up. Knowing her, she might even pretend that they did have one already. He was counting on it.

"I've been waiting for your call," she said. "I thought you'd be here a half hour ago. I was getting worried."

So, he'd been right. Too bad he couldn't take any pleasure in it. Not with Lynne being so upset with him. "I'm fine," he'd said, "Ready to find that house?"

"When you didn't call back, I thought something awful had happened to you." She paused, then added, "I phoned you last night." And another pause, and in lowered voice, "Twice."

And so it was that Cutter found himself sitting in Grace's driveway, debating whether to ring her bell or phone her to let her know he'd arrived.

Before he'd made up his mind, his cell vibrated in his pocket. Lynne would pick now to phone back. But better now than in a few minutes when he'd be with Grace. He took the call without looking at the ID, certain that it was his wife. "Hello," he said, his voice curling his greeting to a question.

"I'm sorry."

Grace! "No, no," Cutter said, while wondering why she was apologizing.

"I can't remember," Grace said, "And I feel awful about it."

"I'm sure you shouldn't," Cutter said, feeling now as though he'd been locked in a tilt-a-whirl. He'd better turn on the air conditioning or get out of the car. What can't she remember that would call for her being so upset?

"Iced coffee," Grace said, "Whether you take cream and sugar? So it's black."

Cutter turned the air conditioning on high. He held his cell with one hand, clutched the steering wheel with the other. "We'll have plenty of time for that later."

"But the ice will melt. It'll be watery."

She sounded as distressed as if all the ladies had come for lunch and her soufflé had fallen. Was she actually sobbing? Good Lord. "All right, Grace," he said, "I suppose there's time enough now."

At her worst, Eleanor hadn't been this bad. He shook his head and prepared to manage a smile; when he looked towards the house, Grace, dressed all in white, phone in her hand, was striding towards his car.

Cutter perched on a chair at the breakfast bar in Grace's kitchen. The glass of iced coffee was covered with beads of condensation. Grace was right about the ice melting, too. He had to give her that.

"It's espresso," she said. "A double. Is that right?" Her face twisted. "I used to know it all. What he put in coffee. What brand of underwear. His collar size and sleeve length. How long to steam his broccoli. What news program..."

Oh, Cutter thought. That. He knew without asking: she was talking about her husband. One woman had told him that for a year after her divorce she'd kept index cards for each of the men she dated. She said she'd never have done that before she was married.

He knew almost as much about women as a manicurist. They'd tell him things while they were in houses. The confidences came in the kitchens, mostly.

"It's all right, Grace."

"But I should remember," she said. "It's important."

Was she going to cry again? He hoped not.

"It's important," she said again.

Important? If he weren't married, he probably wouldn't care if a woman he'd dated once or twice remembered what he put in his coffee. Grace actually hadn't seen him drink coffee; she'd been gone when he got back to the table with his. Gone—vanquished by Eleanor, or so he had thought. But Eleanor's victory had been only temporary.

"Grace," he said, "You couldn't know what I put in my coffee." He went on to explain to her why, underplaying the Eleanor-Evelyn aspect. He expected that he'd make it all right with his explanation. Instead, she burst into tears, which she wiped from her face with the back of her hands. She snuffled and stood so close to Cutter that he felt cruel, unnatural, not reaching out to comfort her.

"I've made a fool of myself," she said.

"Look here, Grace," he said, "it's just me."

"That's what I mean," she said. "It's you!"

Cutter was confused. His pulse was beating quicker than

he would have liked. Should he blame it on the double espresso following his morning coffee and a poor night's sleep—or on Grace standing far too close.

A gold chain disappeared into her sheer white linen blouse. Whatever pendant was on the end must be nestling between her breasts.

"I'm ruining everything," she blurted.

"Ruining everything? Of course, you're not." Tears and divorce went together, he'd seen them before, but Grace was different, less restrained. She needed medication. Or therapy. Or friends. Didn't she have any lady friends? What did she mean, anyway, ruining everything?

"Now you'll..." she stopped short.

Cutter knew that he was supposed to ask her to finish her sentence. She wouldn't, and then the script called for him to urge her to confide in him, to feel safe. With him. But he wasn't following that script. He'd wait her out. With luck, in a few minutes she'll have calmed herself down, and they'll be on their way to see the first house on today's list.

"Oh, Ely!" she cried and flung herself against him.

The front legs of Cutter's chair left the floor. He threw his hands into the air, which further shifted his weight back as he tilted. His chair went over backwards, carrying him to the floor and Grace with him. As his body arced towards the ceramic tile, he had time only to think, "please, God," without completing the bargain in exchange for his safety. The rest was wordless. He closed his eyes as he went backwards, flashed on the image of the face he'd seen in the sky, heard the splintering wood, and Grace's wail. And then there he was on the floor, Grace on top of him. He'd never liked these tall chairs.

He'd been holding the glass of ice cubes and murky brown water that the espresso had become after the ice melted. When his hands had gone up the coffee had splashed out onto his shirt. When he'd fallen, he'd lost his grip on the glass, which flew up, landed on the tile floor, and shattered. Now he—and Grace—lay on the floor and on what was left of the chair. Shards of glass and melting ice cubes were scattered on the white tile floor.

Cutter became aware that his arms were around Grace, whose head was on his chest, her hands on his shoulders, as if she'd collapsed on him after making love. He turned his head to one side, relieved that he could move without excruciating pain. The shards and the splinters and slivers of glass sparkled with innumerable rainbows in the sun.

He'd barely had time to get his bearings when a series of unmistakable chimes gave notice: someone at the front door. Ely left his arms where they were, his hands on Grace's back. Grace spoke into his chest. She lifted and turned her head, still muttering, "Fuck. Fuck. Fuck."

The doorbell rang again. Then a familiar woman's voice called out from the living room, "Hello? Anyone home? Hello?" and then, softer, talking to someone with her, "I like to make sure that if the owner's home, I don't startle them."

And then laughter, a man and a woman. And then again, a musical "Hello?"

Cutter lay still. Grace started to giggle, putting her head

back down. Her laughter grew louder, as the voices came closer. Someone had used the key from the lockbox to let herself in to show the house.

"Hello?" she called again.

Cutter lifted his hands from Grace's back, and he held his hands up in the air, as though he were being robbed or surrendering to the law. Nothing to do for it now. Grace should say something, and when she laughed instead—of course they'd heard, how could they not?—he answered himself, "We're in the kitchen!" Which was literally true.

"Ely Cutter!"

Even from this bizarre angle, he recognized Joanne, who was married to Ruth's cousin. She was one of the part-time saleswomen who did this for what they called pin money. Twenty thousand here, twenty thousand there. Pin money, they called it.

"Good grief!" she said.

"Hello, Joanne." Cutter felt acute embarrassment. Grace, whose laughter had subsided, was now laughing again, moving towards hysteria. Perhaps hysteria was a normal state for her. "We've had a little accident," he said, chiding himself for saying something so obvious. He shouldn't be so hard on himself; after all, he wasn't at his best right now.

"Are you all right?" The man, whoever he was, walked over and stooped down next to Cutter. Glass crunched under his feet as he moved.

"You're walking through broken glass, Chet," a woman said. Cutter couldn't see her from where he was lying. "You'll track it all over the house."

"Oh. Right," Chet said, an absently. He looked at Cutter, and the two men exchanged sympathetic looks.

"We'd better get that glass up so that you can move," Joanne said, and added a perfunctory introduction of the couple she had in tow.

Cutter had never liked Joanne or her big hair. Now he thought she was enjoying this scene too much, especially his discomfort, and embarrassment; her voice fairly oozed assumed professionalism and phony concern.

"I see that I don't have to make introductions," Grace said. She put her palms on his chest and rested her chin on them. Joanne stood directly behind Cutter's head, so Grace would be staring at her shins. Or ankles.

A young woman handed Chet a wad of wet paper towels, and he dabbed at the floor around them. "This will pick up the glass and not scatter it around, so you can get up without cutting yourself. It won't take long." Then the young man asked, "You can get up, can't you? You are all right, aren't you?"

"Oh, yes," Cutter said, "Never been better—under the circumstances."

They all laughed. Cutter counted on his sense of humor to pull him through bad times. It was his love of the absurd. Still, he'd rather have been elsewhere.

"You want a hand?" Chet asked, still squatting next to Cutter and Grace.

Now that the glass was gone, Grace should be scrambling up, Cutter thought, not lying on him as though this were an old, comfortable position.

"I'm okay," Grace said as though she meant it, as though she were enjoying herself. Maybe she is on meds, Ely thought.

"Well, we'll leave you then," Joanne said, "To sort yourselves out."

Cutter managed a weak salute. Joanne led her clients off towards the bedrooms. As they walked, she pointed out features like a museum docent, well-trained and new enough at the job not to have become blasé.

Grace put her hands on either side of Cutter's torso. She was taking her time as she crawled on all fours towards his feet. Under slightly different circumstances he could have relished this, Cutter thought, then chided himself for not being grateful simply to have survived the fall.

His head could have smashed on the floor when he went over backwards. Good for a concussion, or worse. He'd gotten away with a bit of a damp shirt, which would probably wash clean. That and humiliation. Rotten luck that it was Joanne with her connection to Ruth who walked in on them.

They'd be back in the kitchen in minutes. "Are you all right?" he asked Grace. "Maybe you'd like to reschedule?"

"No, no, no, no, no," she said.

"Are you sure?" Cutter asked, trying to keep the irony from his voice. He would have liked to reschedule. Go home. Shower. Take a couple of aspirin. Tylenol maybe, just in case there was internal bleeding he didn't know about. He wished she'd cancel or at least ask him if he wanted to. But her series of emphatic no's left him little hope.

"You probably want to go home," Grace said, "You probably never want to see me again. ... I wouldn't blame you if you told me to find another agent."

"Please, Grace..."

"And now you'll never help me with my kitchen colors."

What was she talking about? Oh yes, the butter yellow. "It'll be fine, Grace," Cutter said. He looked around the room, his sales instinct kicking in. "Let's pick things up in here so the kitchen's back in shape. It won't take a minute." He tossed the crumpled paper towel into the trash. Under the sink, that's where she'd keep the trash, he thought, seeing no sign of it elsewhere. He knew from having shown her clients' houses that Joanne had them do that. This was Joanne's job, but she was in the bedroom. And if she made the sale, Grace would be motivated to find another place. And have the money to do it.

"What should I do with that chair?"

"Out," he said, "Next trash day." He shook his head. The wood had splintered. "You don't want to bother trying to fix this, do you? You can get some nice new chairs when you move. Besides, your new place might not have a breakfast bar...or is that a feature you really want?"

"What do you think of breakfast bars, Ely?"

What he thought shouldn't matter, and he didn't want her to be fawning over him when Joanne came back in. Grace shouldn't even be here while Joanne was showing the house. So he made a joke about how right now breakfast bars and tall chairs didn't rank high on his list of favorite furniture, and then he suggested they say a quick goodbye to Joanne and her clients and let them look at the kitchen.

"I thought I'd change clothes," Grace said, "These are all mussed, don't you think?" She made a sweeping gesture down over her clothes.

That would mean sitting around and waiting, staying out of Joanne's way, trying to look as though he didn't belong here more than he did, which was not at all. Except Grace kept trying to make him. "I think you look just fine," he said, "And it'd be best for us to leave so Joanne can show the house. She did explain all that didn't she?"

"Oh, yes," Grace sounded wistful. "I guess I'm all right."

"You're not hurt?"

"You broke my fall, you poor thing," she said. "Such a hero!"

"Is this a good time to show the kitchen?" Joanne asked.

Joanne would walk in just then! Well, it can't be helped. After a moment's silence, Cutter prompted, "Grace?"

"Oh, yes..." she said. The fall had provided an excuse for her to be vague.

"All right, then!" Cutter said, in his heartiest take-charge voice, and added his polite good-byes. "Let's be on our way, Grace, so these good folk can see your kitchen." That was a smirk followed by a quizzical look on Joanne's face, but Cutter didn't rise to the bait.

Cutter was enjoying Grace's temporary silence. In fact, Grace had been awfully quiet in the car. Then she asked, "How long have you known Joanne?"

He told himself that in spite of what he knew of Grace, this could be an innocent question. "Years. A family friend," he said. "Forever almost."

"She wanted to show me houses too, but I just didn't feel..." Grace's voice trailed off. "Joanne, we... we're not soul mates. Since you started showing me houses, I've wondered if I made a mistake in listing with her?"

"She's fine, Grace," Cutter said, although he believed she'd have done better with someone who took the job more seriously, someone who knew the subtleties of the market. Still, it would be unprofessional for him to say so. And Grace would probably tell Joanne that he'd said it. He ought to be careful.

No matter how careful he was now, by the time he got home, Lynne was bound to have heard about the morning's mishap. Embellished. And filtered by Ruth. That is, if Lynne were answering the phone. He couldn't do anything to forestall it.

Lynne was putting the phone receiver back in its cradle as he walked into the kitchen. "Nice day?" she asked without offering who'd been on the phone. Cutter didn't want to ask. If Ruth had called, carrying news from Joanne, he'd prefer putting off hearing about it. And he and Lynne hadn't resolved the morning's unpleasantness.

"Not exactly," Cutter said. He launched into a description of his morning at Grace's. No use in trying to hide what had happened. After all, he was coming in with a stained shirt and, possibly, the nasty effects of a narrative that had preceded him. He tried to emphasize the slapstick elements of the accident, playing down the French bedroom farce.

Lynne looked amused.

Cutter said he was going to go get some Tylenol, pleased that his storytelling had the effect on Lynne he'd wanted. He was in such trouble when he'd left that he didn't want to add to it, and the Grace-thing as he thought of it, could be trouble, too, big time.

"That's what she said you should do," Lynne said, grinning.

"Who?" Cutter was genuinely puzzled. Ruth was a great one for medical advice. Had Joanne already called her, and she'd phoned Lynne? That's record time.

"Your number two fan."

"I'm glad you're having fun with this, Lynne," he said. "But I'm having a difficult time..."

"Don't you want to know who your fans are, Ely?"

"Only one. And I hope that's you."

"Oh, yes. I'm number one. Longevity."

"So?"

"Number two? Once that would've been easy. Poor Eleanor," Lynne said.

"What are you talking about? 'Poor Eleanor.'" Cutter began to pace. "Who phoned?"

"You know I hate that. It makes me feel like I'm at a tennis match trying to talk to you."

Lynne paused, took a deep breath and said, "It was Grace. We had a nice long talk."

Grace was one surprise after another, Ely thought. She must have phoned here right after I dropped her off. What is she doing—checking up on me to see if I'm home? "It couldn't have been that long. I just dropped her off."

"It's all relative, dear. It seemed long to me."

Lynne tapped her index finger on the table. What was going on? For Lynne, finger tapping wasn't a habit; it was a signal of her mood, like the twitch of the end of the cat's tail before it pounced.

"Good thing we don't have any pets," she said.

"I don't get it, Lynne."

"This Grace of yours, she seems like a bunny boiler."

Pounce! Cutter chose his dispute, "She's not my Grace."

"Come off it, Ely."

No sense fighting it now. Make a joke. "So, what did 'My Grace' have to say for herself?"

"First, she told me about the incident—a description not very different from yours, except, of course, she went on about how awful she felt. She said to take Tylenol rather than aspirin in case you have some internal injuries. She insisted, actually. Wanted me to repeat what she'd said. Then she told me you should light a candle. Or she will, at church. For your recovery. Or gratitude that you didn't smash your head open on her floor. Something like that."

"And you said?"

"Thank you for your concern. Kind of you to call. And do light a candle. But it isn't something Jews do." Lynne paused. "She seemed rather surprised. Apologized. Said she was sorry."

"Ah!" Grace apologized too often. "I wonder..." Eli said.

"About her being sorry we're Jewish?"

"That's not what... About the candle," he said. "I'm sure we do something."

Chapter 8

That night as Cutter lay next to Lynne, she kissed his cheek and said, "Tomorrow won't be as hard."

It was more wish than promise, but Ely took some comfort in her having, at least, wished that for him. And for herself, too, probably. Lynne hadn't given up on him. She'd dealt with the call from Grace far better than he could've imagined. Grace must have been so outré that the call fell into the category of absurdity. Just as well. Lynne had been angry about seeing him with Eleanor, and that issue hasn't been resolved. Certainly, Lynne will revisit the topic.

And maybe when Ruth checked in with Joanne's report on the morning's fiasco, Lynne would take a less charitable view of Grace, adding that fiasco to her own catching him with Eleanor. Can't be helped. "Your escapade with Grace," that's what Lynne would call it. And Joanne would, too.

That damned broken glass. He'd been holding the glass to give him something to do with his hands, Grace standing so close. That's what he got for his trying to be good—shards everywhere that kept him from getting out from under Grace. If he'd had more time, he would have been able to figure out a way, but Joanne barreled right in before he could escape. Grace had been in no hurry to get off him, that's for sure. She seemed right at home, comfortable and unself-conscious, lying on his body.

If he'd had the leisure to enjoy it.... He can ask Grace what perfume she wears, buy some for Lynne.

Cutter turned on his side, his back to Lynne. He felt so

alive with Grace's small body on his, especially when she shimmied down on him with Joanne right in the next room and apt to walk in on them. If Grace had been trying to be seductive, it hadn't worked then, but now, though it was inconvenient he was entirely erect.

Quite a woman, Grace. In spite of himself, she had a powerful effect on him. Lucky for him Lynne was asleep. Thoughts might be free, but not visible arousal that he couldn't explain—for that he'd have to pay.

He woke the next morning, with a dull headache. Concussion? He got out of bed gingerly, expecting pain. No pain, but in its place, he discovered an unpleasant consciousness of his body as something he inhabited. A couple more Tylenol might do the trick.

Walking into the kitchen was like walking towards a solid wall of light. Cutter flinched and held his arms up protectively in front of him, as though he'd be meeting physical resistance. White light filled the kitchen like a substance. *Phlogiston.* He seized the word with something like delight. No, phlogiston was something else. He'd look it up once he'd had some coffee. Maybe something important had happened to him when he'd fallen yesterday; the glare from the patio had never affected him like this before. *Ether.* Maybe that's the word he'd wanted.

He turned his back to the sliding glass door, testing to see what would happen when he faced away. Everything looked normal. He looked to the left and to the right. Then a one-eighty to look out at the garden again. His old world had restored itself.

As he counted the measures of coffee, his hands shook, scattering grains of coffee on the counter. While he was cleaning up, the phone rang. Two rings and that was all. Lynne must have picked it up. Good. He wasn't up for conversation, and no one could be calling who would upset her. After all, she'd managed Grace.

Cutter had almost forgotten Ruth's connection to yesterday's fiasco.

When, balancing two cups of coffee on a tray, he reached the head of the stairs, Lynne's laughter came from the bedroom. Whoever it was on the phone, most likely Ruth, hadn't upset Lynne. In fact, she seemed to be delighted. He'd heard her hysterical laughter when she was distraught, and this was not it.

He brought the coffee into the bedroom and set Lynne's cup on the nightstand. Tears were in her eyes, and his arrival didn't diminish her mirth. If anything, his arrival had intensified her amusement. She blew him a kiss, which was followed by more laughter.

"No, no," she said into the phone, "I'm fine. He's just brought me coffee, the darling."

What was so funny? Certainly not his fall.

Ely raised an eyebrow to signal a question, but if Lynne noticed, she gave no sign, which left him holding the tray like a well-trained butler. He could get back into bed and read while Lynne was talking on the phone, or he could take his coffee back downstairs. He'd lose either way. Might as well stay. Not that forced eavesdropping was comfortable; it's been an uncomfortable situation for a long time, even before Eleanor.

If he listened to Lynne's conversation, he felt like an intruder, and, even worse, when she was in a bad mood, she'd glare at him, a look that said, "Get out of here and give me some privacy." Even when that hadn't happened, if he chanced afterwards to comment on the conversation, she was often snippy about his having listened in. Sometimes, however, he'd be in the room, paying no attention to Lynne's conversation, and when she hung up, she'd ask him a question about something she'd said on the phone. Then, when he was at a loss, she'd be annoyed at that. How could he have not heard what she was saying? When he'd reply, explaining that he hadn't been listening, she'd be cross either because she had to repeat what she'd said or because she thought he'd failed to take sufficient interest. He never knew which situation it would be.

But sometimes, before things changed, she'd talk to someone on the phone and engage him in the conversation with hand gestures, a running commentary on herself and her friend on the phone. He missed those days, and he blamed himself for their having ended.

Now it was his choice to stay or to go. He decided to stay. If he listened, surely it wouldn't be snooping if he were in plain view, not the same as if he were lurking outside the door. That's what he could do, stand outside and hear what she was saying. Surely, he'd get some hint of what was being said on the other end, and then he'd know what he could expect from Lynne for the rest of the day. So far, she seemed to be getting a kick out of the situation with Grace. But would he have to pay later?

If she caught him lurking, he wouldn't have the excuse of bringing her coffee, but he could pretend that, having reconsidered, he was returning with his own cup. He'd have to get rid of the tray in the kitchen and make it back upstairs, possibly just in time to hear the end of her conversation. If he dashed back downstairs and then up again, he'd be breathless. Ridiculous. He was making far too much of this call, and, thanks to his dithering about tactics, he'd missed what Lynne was saying even though he was standing right here in the same room.

He put the tray on a chair and sat on the end of the bed near Lynne. He patted her ankle, both to show affection and to signal that he planned to stay. If she wanted him to leave, she'd tell him with some gesture. Under the cover she waggled her foot. OK. He'd stay.

"Not really!" Lynne said. "He never said a word about that."

Cutter had never said a word about far too much. Lynne's voice changed. She no longer sounded amused. He tried to catch her eye but failed.

"What did she tell you?" Lynne said. "She" would be Joanne.

Ruth went on for quite a while reporting on his fall in the kitchen. In spite of the position in which they'd been found, even though he found Grace attractive, the incident had nothing to do with anything shameful. Ely had convinced himself of his apparent innocence. But perhaps others would see it differently.

"Good Lord!" Lynne said. "What else did she tell you about her?"

Yesterday when Lynne spoke with Grace on the phone, she seemed to have accepted the accident, had evinced only concern. After this conversation, her attitude was likely to change. He shouldn't have to be the subject of gossip. And what had Grace done anyway?

Joanne wouldn't have much good to say about Grace; nonetheless he couldn't blame her for talking to Ruth, or Ruth for calling Lynne. They must have been a sight on Grace's floor. If it hadn't been for the broken glass all around them, they might have looked as though they were working on a new sexual position with the chair as a prop.

Joanne would have dished the dirt to Ruth, and Ruth probably added her own sauce to it. Ruth was as different from Joanne as Lynne was, but the bond of being cousins kept them close. Joanne probably liked Grace's jewelry, as Joanne wore lots of clunky bracelets herself. When he'd said something about Joanne's bracelets to Lynne, she'd laughed and said they were designer bracelets, which he figured meant overpriced. Lynne said she thought Joanne wore them to look successful when she showed houses. Costuming to inspire confidence, a small step from staging houses.

Cutter believed he should look successful, but not so wealthy that his clients would start adding up how much commission they'd be paying him. Of course, Joanne's plastic-surgeon husband was responsible for the Jag Joanne drove. Focus, he said to himself, focus on Lynne's frown. Listen.

"She actually called here," Lynne said, "to tell me how to take care of Ely. Can you imagine?"

Cutter cringed. Ruth's gloss on the call would be uncertain. Maybe she'd smooth things over. No, not if she'd been telling stories about Grace, stories that came from Joanne. Joanne had always been a bit pudgy. She'd envy Grace her figure. Joanne couldn't go braless like Grace. If she'd noticed.

Lynne laughed. "And she said she'd light a candle! The little hypocrite!"

The memory of Grace in tears because she'd "ruined everything" made it painful for Cutter to hear Ruth's tone of voice. Grace had many qualities, not all of them praiseworthy, but he would have bet that she wasn't a hypocrite: Grace lacked sophisticated insightful introspection. That might look like hypocrisy. Nothing a decade or two of psychotherapy couldn't fix.

If Grace does see a therapist, with luck, it isn't anyone he knows. Grace probably wouldn't do individual therapy, but he can see her in support groups. The worst of all choices, as far as he was concerned: Grace headed down steps to a church basement where she'd perch on one of the beige metal folding chairs arranged in a skewed circle. When it got to be her turn, she'd put her yoga skills to good use, bend in half, and set to keening.

She might do no more than that for a month or so, and then she'd start spilling it. Some facilitator, some old-timer, multiply divorced, would take Grace under her wing and see to it. Yes, clutching wadded-up tissues, she would tell all, scrambling details, inventing truths that everyone, even Grace herself would believe. He couldn't begin to imagine what she would say about him.

Lynne said, "Sure, I guess I'd better. You're right. I'll ask him about that. Thanks."

Cutter waited for her to say something about the conversation, to ask whatever it was that she said she'd ask him about. Even when he knew that she wasn't angry and digging at him, he hated Lynne's questions. Lynne wasn't like Eleanor whose questions were razor sharp. With Eleanor, he didn't know he was bleeding until he looked down. Lynne used a butter knife—dull, repetitious, painful. And effective.

"So," Lynne said, "Tell me about this Grace."

Oh boy, Cutter thought. He hadn't expected one of these open-ended questions. He'd used them himself with clients, not Lynne's style. But he was stuck with it. He lobbed back, "I pretty much did."

Then he went dead silent, one of his favorite tricks.

Lynne was quiet herself for a while, for long enough for him to wonder if she was playing his game. Then she said, "That's not what I heard."

"Who said that? I don't recall that anyone was with us when you and I had our little chat." Cutter knew he was shifting the argument. It might work.

"What little chat?"

"About Grace. Didn't you ask me about her just a little while ago?"

"Well, yes." Lynne looked flustered. She reached for the phone and picked up the receiver.

Who's she calling now? Now what? But no, Lynne held the phone up high and let the receiver dangle. They both watched it spin round and round.

"Untangling," Lynne said.

Cutter grunted. Someday they'd replace it with a cordless.

He'd just wait. More would come. While he watched the phone spin, he reviewed what he'd told her about Grace. Nothing incriminating, he was certain.

"Look, Ely," Lynne said, "I don't like asking questions like this."

"*Nu*? So why?"

"That was Ruth on the phone before."

"Ruth calls, you ask questions, insinuating questions, makes sense to me." He shrugged although, in fact, it did make sense to him.

"Joanne's selling her house," Lynne said, as though that explained everything.

Cutter considered making a crack about Joanne's selling Ruth's house, but he knew that was a bad idea. Instead, he settled for, "So?"

"I don't have to tell you. You get to know your client when you're selling."

"She's been looking with me, you know," he said, hoping that would minimize Joanne's intimacy and knowledge of Grace.

"And Joanne thinks Grace is one or two cards shy of a deck. And loose." She paused, but Ely didn't say anything, and after a few moments, Lynne went on. "What was she wearing?"

"When?" Ely asked. When Lynne frowned, he continued without waiting for her answer. He was in for it. "When I last saw her she was wearing some sort of an outfit—white— looked to me like pajamas, but they probably weren't."

"Bra?"

"She was wearing a blouse, Lynne." Ely remembered his mouth inches from Grace's breast. Grace in the black tank top.

"With or without a bra?"

Without. Cutter hoped that Lynne hadn't read his mind. "This is your question? Or Ruth's."

"Joanne says."

"Joanne looks?" Cutter grinned. "I didn't know Joanne was..." he paused, looking for the right words. "...so eclectic. Good for her."

"For goodness sake, Ely." Lynne frowned again. "Was she wearing a bra or not?"

"What difference does it make?"

"I don't like it."

"Wear a bra then. In fact, I prefer that you wear one. In public."

"That's not what I mean."

"What? Grace goes braless. Therefore?"

"And Ruth told me."

What could Ruth have said? What was there to tell? "Really, Lynne. I don't know what you're talking about."

"Your promises to Grace."

He hadn't made any promises, not that he remembered. But he was certain that if he'd made them, he was about to hear a version of the truth that had gone from Grace to Joanne to Ruth and then to Lynne. He'd be lucky if it came close to whatever it was that he'd said.

"You promised you'd paint her kitchen when she bought a house."

"Does that sound like me, Lynne? When was the last time you saw me on a ladder?"

"It wouldn't stop you from promising."

"I guess it wouldn't have to," Ely admitted, "but I didn't." Then he remembered—the butter-yellow kitchen.

"You're sure?" Lynne asked, sounding to Ely equally plaintive and skeptical.

"Only one thing I can think of, she was talking about painting her kitchen, the new one in her house that she would buy—with me as agent—and she said she'd always wanted a butter-yellow kitchen. Something about tiles. She hates the tiles in her kitchen now. Counters and backsplash are terrible together. Joanne will have a hell of a time selling if anyone looks and doesn't want to..."

"You're off subject, Ely."

He was puzzled, then it struck him, "Oh. Well, I might have said something about taking care of the new kitchen once she had one. And she read into that."

"I don't know. Maybe you'd led her to believe that you would by ..." Her voice trailed off. She took a deep breath and said, "It's Eleanor."

"Eleanor? What does she have to do with Grace?" And then he flushed. She'd have everything to do with the way Lynne saw Grace. How could it be otherwise? Chastened, he apologized, first for being obtuse.

Then he said, "I wish it hadn't happened." He'd lost track of how many times he'd said that, of how many times he'd meant it, instead of only trying to mollify Lynne. Sometimes, it was a bit of both. He hated wishing he'd lived differently. It was useless. Regret made him feel as though he were cutting off chunks of his life, grinding them in a disposal and sending them down into the sewers, where they mixed with disgusting effluents and ran under the streets and out into the sea.

"You say that, Ely," Lynne said, "and sometimes I think you mean it, and sometimes…well, sometimes I think you'd go and do it all over again. That makes me crazy." She paused. "And it's not even real, so why do I get so upset?"

"I guess it seems real at the time."

"Seeing you with Eleanor having coffee was real," Lynne said.

"I explained that, Lynne. Be fair."

"I'm supposed to be fair? What does that mean, Ely? That I'm supposed to accept that because you fucked Eleanor, she has a lifetime claim on you?"

Cutter didn't answer. That is exactly what he meant, and he dare not say so. He was temporarily silenced. At least this was the method of questioning that he'd expected. He ought to have learned how to cope with it, but he hadn't. That was his punishment. That evened things out on the justice scale. He had to say something now, however: to fail to explain was a tacit agreement that she was correct.

He had fucked Eleanor, but their relationship had been more than that. As difficult as Eleanor could be, for some time he'd considered her a friend as much as a mistress—what an odd word to use; it made her seem like a kept woman, and she'd been anything but.

Nonetheless, that wasn't anything he could say, either. It would only make Lynne angry. Worse—it would hurt her.

So, instead, he said, "We're not talking about lifetime claims, Lynne. I didn't think..." He'd meant to continue, "there was any harm to be had in a cup of coffee," but Lynne cut him off.

"No, Ely. You didn't think." She laughed bitterly. "At least I hope not. It would be even worse if you'd considered my feelings and then seen her anyway." She took a deep breath and asked, "Well, which was it?"

Cutter stood and looked at Lynne, who sat propped up against the pillows. If he went downstairs, would she go too? Lynne's following him, hurling questions at him as they went, would be better than fighting in the bedroom. They'd fought in every room of the house after Eleanor, but the fights in the bedroom had been especially bitter. They'd said things, awful things to one another. He'd been ashamed of what he'd done, of what he'd said. And he'd told her so. He hoped that Lynne regretted at least some of what she'd said to him, too, but she'd never apologized, and he'd always been too self-conscious to ask her to apologize. It was his actions that had been the cause of their mutual recriminations. Nonetheless, too often he'd felt compelled to attack Lynne in what he saw as self-defense. Even when what he'd said had been true, he'd been destructive, paining Lynne and damaging their marriage.

"What do you want me to say, Lynne? What's the use? No matter what I say, I'm in the wrong."

"'In the wrong', or just plain 'wrong'? Don't blame me for your guilty conscience, Ely Cutter."

When she called him Ely Cutter, he felt like a naughty child at a loss for words. But his not knowing what to say didn't matter because Lynne kept at him.

"That is, if you even have a conscience left? Do you? Or is it entirely gone?"

"Come on, Lynne," he said, glad the trick question about "wrong" was no longer on the table. Something more damaging had replaced it. "I'm going downstairs to have breakfast now. Of course, I have a conscience. And I love you." How easy it would have been to have a roll in the hay with Grace. He wasn't sure what had kept him from touching Grace: loving Lynne, a shred of conscience, or a fear of discovery.

He couldn't use his not touching Grace as an example of anything. He'd better spare Lynne the image of Grace perched on the arm of his chair, practically in his lap. He'll have to keep that to himself. That and something else he'd brooded over, whether Lynne's harping on his misdeeds and her allegations were becoming a substitute for his conscience, destroying his own moral sense. Maybe that's why he saw the face in the sky, to get him back on track.

"So that's supposed to solve everything? A simple 'I love you'?"

"It's not simple, Lynne," Cutter said. She was puzzled; her frown wasn't angry. She was thinking about what he'd said. He'd give her a minute, then explain if he had to. Or try to explain.

"Okay, Ely. It's not simple. It hasn't been for years."

"It never was," he answered. "It's just that we hadn't paid attention to that. We coasted."

"Until?"

That wasn't a real question. He knew she meant, "Until Eleanor."

"Don't," he said, "You know what I mean." Cutter gave her a chance to push, but she didn't. She didn't make a move to get out of bed, but she didn't argue or mention Eleanor either. Good sign. He'd try again, "So what about breakfast?"

"Go ahead," she said, "I'll be down in a couple of minutes."

She wasn't moving. He didn't know what she planned, another phone call to Ruth or a shower. Whatever. She said she'd have breakfast with him, and that was good enough. Under the circumstances, it had to be.

CHAPTER 9

Parked in Grace's driveway Cutter sat in his car experiencing an unpleasant sensation of déjà vu. At least breakfast with Lynne had gone well, even when she learned that he was going to be working with Grace. He'd expected her to be sarcastic. Instead, she'd raised an eyebrow and told him to be sure to come home undamaged this time.

He approached Grace's door determined to look her in the eye, not check out whether she was wearing a bra. He'll notice, how could he not?

"Ely," she said, opening the door with such delight and surprise in her voice that Cutter wondered if he'd gotten the appointment wrong.

But no. Grace was just glad to see him. "I was so worried," she said. "I was afraid you'd end up in the Emergency Room all night, and it would have been all my fault."

"No. No…" Cutter said, in his most reassuring voice. He hoped she wasn't going to fling herself at him again. He was standing on the top step of a small landing, and if he fell backwards from here, he might smash his head open or break his back.

Grace laughed. She must have read his mind, because she stepped back into the hall, and said, "Oh, you're afraid we'll have a repeat of yesterday? I've learned my lesson, Ely. I won't be throwing myself at you—at least not literally."

He didn't want to encourage any sort of throwing herself at him, and he feared that she might interpret a simple, "That's good" as covering only the full-body slam. He looked at his watch, and said he wanted to get an early start. He had an amazing property to show her. And then he apologized because it was "too late to count as early."

"You're right on time, Ely," Grace said. "I suppose there's no time for even a quick coffee?"

"Not really, Grace."

"Well, then, I'd better unplug the coffee maker. Don't stand there in the doorway. Come on in. It's way too hot to stay outside."

"That's okay. I'll wait out here," he said, even though he agreed that it was an exceptionally hot day. "It won't take that long."

"Please, Ely. I thought I'd freshen up a bit, too."

Freshen up could mean anything from a total makeover—shower, change of outfit, hair style, new makeup – to a euphemism for a quick potty stop. He couldn't ask or even argue. It would be indelicate. He wanted to say, "You look fine, lovely." She did look fine, and "lovely" didn't begin to capture her spirit or style.

Not a drop of shade in the driveway. Hot as hell. Might as well be practical. It would be nice and cool inside. Besides, nothing can go wrong, not like yesterday. He'd just make sure that his feet were on the ground and that he kept his center of gravity low. Or at least, that he maintained his balance.

He followed Grace into the kitchen. Her back was towards him as she stood at the coffeemaker. She didn't turn to look at him, but she was pouring a cup of coffee. She grasped the plug and pulled it out of the wall. Good girl, not to tug on the wire. The coffee smelled delicious, and he regretted having said that he had no time.

"I thought you might want just a taste," she said, handing him the cup. "While I freshen up?" As she was leaving the room she called back over her shoulder. "It's best with sugar, even if you don't usually…"

And then she was out of sight. Cutter stood at the island. The broken chair was gone, and other than the asymmetry of chairs, the kitchen showed no signs of their mishap. The bowl of sugar, and two spoons were on the counter. He took her advice, and poured in one, then a second rounded spoonful.

The coffee was spiced with cinnamon, cloves, and cardamom. Black pepper too, a coffee chai.

He hoped that he wouldn't be waiting a long time for Grace to be ready. He'd left the information about the first house in the car, so he'd just have to sit. He listened for the sound of water drumming on porcelain, probably in the ensuite bath. He walked down the hall to make sure, taking a chance that Grace might catch him snooping. Or, even worse, she might misinterpret his presence if she found him standing outside her bedroom.

"Well, Ely, what do you think?" Grace asked. She was calling to him from behind the closed door.

It would be absurd for him to sneak back to the kitchen without answering. After all, he'd done nothing wrong, and it wasn't as though she'd said, "Penny for your thoughts." How many times had he heard that question from Lynne when his thoughts wouldn't have been acceptable? "What, Grace? Think about what?"

The door opened. Ely half-expected to see Grace in a bath towel wrapped around her. A white Turkish towel. No. She'd changed her clothes, though he wasn't sure why. She had on loose white slacks and a pink tank top. "Can you give me a hand?"

Now what.

Grace laughed at his confusion. "It's this." She held up the necklace he'd seen her wear before. The gold cross dangled. "Don't look so worried, Ely. I'm not going to try to convert you."

"I didn't think so."

"Can you do the catch? I'm having trouble with it."

She'd worn the necklace before. What was the problem now? "I'm pretty much fumble fingers," he said.

"It's my nails." She showed him her free hand. The nails were fire-engine red. Not like Lynne's radioactive pink.

"Please give it a try." She held out the necklace.

Cutter reminded himself to breathe and took it from her. He looked at the cross to see if it mattered which side faced outward. No.

Grace stood, her back turned towards him. She lifted her hair with both hands, and bowed her head, baring her nape. A few wisps of damp hair curled under her hands.

"This isn't going to work," Cutter said. "I'm afraid I'll drop it." He tried to remember how he did this with Lynne, but his mind was blank. Almost.

"Sorry," she said, moving her arms out of his way.

He held one end of the necklace in each hand and lowered it over her head. Now he remembered. Lynne would get the necklace all but fastened, and he'd take it from there.

Once more Grace lifted her hair from her nape and bowed her head.

Cutter struggled with the delicate clasp. No wonder she had trouble with it. He felt clumsy and brutish. As he worked with the clasp, his fingers brushed against her neck, her damp hair.

"Any luck?"

"Almost had it," he said. And then he did. "Done!"

Their eyes met in the bureau mirror. "Thanks," she said, smiling.

Cutter had been holding his breath. The hot car would have been a better choice.

"So?" Grace asked.

"So," Cutter said, "I guess the necklace is on." He knew Grace expected him to do something. Almost certainly, what he wanted to do.

"And now?" she asked. She tilted her head to one side, but their eyes were still locked.

Cutter put his hands on her shoulders, one on each side. He held her still where she was standing.

Grace shook herself free. "Okay, Ely. I take your meaning."

She was facing him now, scowling.

Cutter bent forward and kissed her on the forehead. "Not now," he said. "Not now." Without being able to say where it came from, he murmured to himself the question, "If not now, when?"

"Suit yourself," Grace said. "Besides, I think Joanne might be showing the house this morning. She told me to stay out."

Cutter stifled a groan. What was Grace trying to do? Was she telling the truth about Joanne? If she were, then they would have been caught in the bedroom. Was that what she wanted? She'd seemed genuine in her concern about him when he'd fallen. He would have to be more careful.

Cutter was taken aback by Grace's sudden change in mood. She smiled at him as though she'd never been irritated, then turned to her bureau again, reached into a gold-painted basket and pulled out a lipstick. Bright orange. "My jacket's in the living room," she said. And after a pause, "Sometimes I get cold in the air conditioning."

As they walked out, Cutter watched her sling a gauzy orange jacket over her arm. Pink and orange. It's a new world.

"Your wife sounds like a lovely woman," Grace said as Cutter was backing out of her drive.

"Oh, right," Cutter said, trying to keep the stress from his voice, "you talked with her on the phone."

"Yes. A nice chat."

He must be missing something. He wouldn't call talking about getting him some medical care and lighting a candle, "A nice chat." He'd have to look into that. There were blessings for everything. There must be one about being spared. "Oh?"

"She's much nicer than that Evelyn."

Evelyn? Oh, yes. That's what Grace called Eleanor. Now Grace is making pronouncements. What comes next? No good answer to this. Defend Eleanor at Lynne's expense? That's sure to get back through Joanne. Even if Grace doesn't like Joanne, it's a sure thing that Joanne will chat her up and pry. And Grace will be happy to regale her with stories about him, embellished in direct proportion to her dislike. Maybe it's just as well Lynne had caught him having coffee with Eleanor. Hearing that as news from Joanne via Ruth would be worse—far worse when bundled with a story of the Fall, as he called it.

"It was thoughtful of you to phone about the Tylenol," he said.

"I told Lynne I'd light a candle for you. I said you should too."

She hadn't included Lynne's rebuff in her summary of the conversation. He could attribute that to a memory lapse or to a tactic.

"So," Grace said, "What did you do?"

"Nothing," he answered, ashamed.

"Oh...," she said, "well, then." A long pause followed before she added, "Then I don't understand."

Cutter didn't want to start listing all the things Grace didn't understand—those she knew she didn't understand, and all those of which she was wholly ignorant. He was sure half of them, whatever they were, she'd blame on herself, and the others, on him, and, in any case, tears would be involved. And he'd be expected to fix what was wrong. "I suppose it's a matter of perspective."

Everything he could think of was a matter of perspective. It was a perfectly good answer, or it was bullshit.

"Joanne told me," Grace said.

Joanne knew too much. She might be trading gossip in hopes of getting Grace to buy as well as sell with her. Joanne might have told her about Eleanor, but probably not. No, she wouldn't have.

"What you saw..."

"Oh, that," Cutter said. So that's why she'd asked him if he was religious. His vision. "Well, I did see it. Nothing could have been more unexpected."

"And you're still not religious? What more do you need?"

"No offense, Grace, but this isn't what I want to be talking about right now," Cutter said. "It's a nice day, and we have some homes to look at, and this is a big topic that I don't want to go into." He could hear the edge in his voice.

"No rush, Ely, you can tell me some other time," Grace said.

Would Joanne have told her about his son, too? Not likely.

Grace hadn't said anything more. And Cutter decided to match her silence with his. He would have needed nothing more to make him religious—nothing he wanted to talk about. Besides, Grace was right, the vision had done something to him. Before that, his saying a blessing over food had been rare, perfunctory, and artificial.

"It's not much farther," he said, meaning the distance to the house he wanted to show her. When he noticed Grace, beaming, he knew she'd misinterpreted his comment. He let it go. He'd found an easy way to make her happy while getting himself off the hook.

"So, how's Saint Grace?" Lynne asked without looking up from the cutting board where she was chopping tomatoes.

"She's fine," Cutter said, wanting to avoid an argument.

"So, you're not rising to the bait," Lynne said.

She knew him, Cutter had to give her that.

"I don't blame you, Ely," Lynne said, "Not this time. You get a free pass on this one. That's a pun."

She swept the tomatoes into a bowl and picked up a red onion.

"Would you like me to do the onion?"

"Thanks, I can manage."

"I just thought…"

"You'd spare me the tears?"

"Something like that," Cutter said, putting ice cubes in a glass. "Want some?"

"I'm fine, Ely, just fine."

But she wasn't fine at all. He'd have to wait to find out what had happened, why she was so upset. If he asked now, she'd just snap at him, and he'd still have to pay until she was ready to tell him, and maybe after that, too.

Ely held a glass of ice, wondering what he wanted. Not Scotch and not iced tea. Not beer or wine, he'd feel foolish dumping the ice, and he'd never acquired the habit of pouring wine or beer over ice though sometimes Lynne did, adding a wedge of lemon and seltzer to wine or, with beer, lime. He opened the refrigerator; he'd decide when he saw the cartons of juice or the pitcher of iced tea, but instead he stared at the shelves, filled with cartons and bottles and jars. He didn't remember eating any, but the jar was almost half empty.

He set the glass on the counter and took out the jar. "Lynne," he said, "how long have we had these?"

"What?" she said, turning. "A couple of weeks. I was going to make a chicken salad . . ." her voice trailed. "They've been right there," she added.

She was being defensive, as though he'd accused her of something. He hoped he hadn't been that touchy.

"I thought you'd like them," she said. "They're good."

Cutter was pleased that she was talking about food again, real food.

Then she added, "Olives are good for you, and garlic."

"How can you go wrong?" Ely said. He'd been mistaken. The refrigerator had turned back into the medicine chest again.

"Sodium."

He turned the jar to look at the ingredients. Yes, sodium. He speared an olive with a knife, removed it from the jar, and examined it before popping it into his mouth. "It's a nice idea," he said, wishing he'd spoken before she mentioned the sodium.

The overwhelming taste was brine, but the garlic had a satisfying crunch, which made him think he ought to go brush his teeth. Maybe not. Lynne had been eating these and he hadn't noticed. He put an olive into the glass with ice cubes. He'd add pepper vodka. And a twist of lemon peel. He could give it a name, after himself or Lynne. Maybe she'd like that.

"I've invented a cocktail," he said as Lynne swept the last of the chopped vegetables into the salad bowl. He held it out for her to taste.

She looked at him with what seemed to Cutter to be a self-conscious, tolerant smile.

"In the mood for experimentation?" Lynne said.

Cutter listened, but heard no invitation, but no irony either. Still, he was wary of answering. To stall, he sipped his drink. "I don't know about this one," he said, trying to contain the issue, direct the discussion away from other experimentation that might involve discussion of Grace or even Eleanor—though Lynne wouldn't be likely to consider Eleanor "experimental" at this point. Grace was another matter.

He held the glass out to Lynne. She wrinkled her nose and took a sip. "Not bad," she said, "but not my cup of tea—or vodka." She paused. "I'm sure it would grow on me. Two or three of these. . ." She drank again, then gave the glass back to Ely.

"Hand me the cornichons, will you?" Lynne asked. "And the bottle of gin—and ice."

It was his turn now to be amused. "Any glass? Or do you have something in mind?"

"And the bottle of Rose's lime juice!"

"Does that stuff go bad? After rummaging a bit in the refrigerator, Cutter handed her a bottle. "We don't use this often..."

"The gin," Lynne said, "Will kill any germs." She paused. "At least I hope so," she said walking out of the room.

She returned carrying the chrome cocktail shaker and a martini glass. "Might as well do this right," she said.

Cutter watched her fill the shaker with ice. She poured in two measures of gin and two teaspoons of the sweetened lime juice. And then shook. She poured it into the martini glass. It was the palest green gold, much less colored than a normal gimlet.

"Cornichon time," she said.

She dropped a tiny pickle into the glass and sipped. "Not bad," she said, offering the glass to Ely. "What do you think?"

"I like it better than this," he said, nodding towards the drink on the counter. "I'll bet that tiny pickle will taste great."

"If it lasts," Lynne said. "I wonder how many could be dropped in here?"

"Three," Ely replied.

"Well, you said that with authority!"

"The first, I figure, you'll fish out immediately. The other two can stay—and that way you can share."

"Unless we're both..."

"Three anyway. They're small. . . .What will you call it?"

"No clue."

"'No Clue' is a great name, Lynne. Especially since it's mostly gin."

"I hate fighting, Ely."

"So do I," he said, hoping she would let it go, and stop there.

"I know," she said. She took a sip of her drink. "It's not bad. . . but what do you expect to happen? When you..."

Cutter didn't need her to finish the sentences to know it had something to do with Grace or Eleanor, or some combination of the two. "Why are you upset, Lynne? Did something else happen?"

"Other than?"

"Other than what we've talked about already."

"Isn't that enough?"

It was enough. Plenty, and he said so. "But, still, if something's happened—something else, that is, tell me. Please."

"So you can lie to me and say it isn't true?"

"I thought you hate to fight, Lynne." As soon as he said that, Cutter knew it was a mistake. "I'm sorry. I shouldn't have said that. It was mean."

"You were mean, Ely. And not just then, either."

"I can't change the past, Lynne."

"Brilliant thinker."

Ely hated it when Lynne was sarcastic. It wasn't a quality he found attractive, though Eleanor's sharpness suited her, he'd often wished that he could file down her edges. Just as well that he couldn't. It made it easier for him to stick with Lynne.

Lynne took a drink of the cornichons gimlet. "What's upsetting me, Ely, isn't that you can't change the past, but that I'm afraid you don't want to, that, even if you could do something so that it was all gone, every sleazy moment, you'd keep it."

She was right, but he couldn't afford to agree with her. It was a shameful admission to make even to himself, but things would be far worse for him, if he told Lynne—all those times he'd said he wished it hadn't happened! Surely, she must know the truth, but why is she bringing it up to him now?

"Did you know that you can bite through a glass like this? Bite it, not break a tooth, and break the glass?" She held the glass up in front of her face and swirled the liquid. The cornichons shimmied in the bottom of the drink.

"Not and live."

"Oh, yes. Not even be cut."

"What are you talking about?"

"It's quite simple, actually… It doesn't require much force, but you do have to be rather careful not to swallow the broken glass… Rinsing your mouth out a couple of times seems to be quite effective."

She leaned forward. "Would you like to try?"

He held up his hand as though he needed to keep the glass at a safe distance. "How do you know so much about this?"

"I could say 'reading.' Or 'word of mouth.' But, actually, it's personal experience."

"Experience!" Cutter searched Lynne's face for distress. None. And she'd said "actually" twice. Cutter paid attention. Lynne had a tic of saying "actually" when she felt stressed and wanted to seem in control.

Her tone was brittle, "I don't tell you everything either. Each of us has secrets. That was one of mine. Your turn."

"But when? I had no idea…"

"Why should you? A broken glass, one more or less glass on the shelf. You don't count them—how would you know? And it wasn't as if anything happened . . . to me."

Cutter took hold of her shoulders. "Lynne, I love you, but I don't understand what you're doing with this glass thing."

"This glass thing?" Lynne laughed. "Is that what you call it?"

"I don't know what else to call it. Experiment, was it? Come on, Lynne. If you've been trying to kill yourself…"

"I told you I rinsed my mouth out. If I were going to kill myself, is that how I'd do it?"

Cutter was abashed. He'd never thought of Lynne as someone who would kill herself. He had never imagined her biting through a glass like that. At best it was dangerous. He shuddered to think of having a mouthful of broken glass. Had she been drinking?

Lynne twisted her body away from him, "Don't," she said. "Not now."

Cutter let his arms fall. She'd made him self-conscious about his hands. It had been a long time since she'd told him not to touch her. And then she had had good reason. Eleanor. It must be Eleanor again. It made perfect sense. All of it piled together, first spotting him at the bookstore tête à tête and then having to deal with Grace. The idea of Grace, mostly. He'd have to find some way to make it up to Lynne, but how?

All he could do was to be irreproachable in his behavior, and that would take months to have any effect. And these last times, he'd been innocent, innocent as any man could be.

He wanted to leave, take a drive, walk, jump into the Delaware River, and swim upstream.

Cutter was pondering his options when Lynne said, "Oh, never mind. It's not your fault this time. Let's forget it, can we?"

What did she mean by that? If it wasn't Cutter's fault, then whose was it? Eleanor's? Grace's? Forget it? And how was he supposed to forget about Lynne chowing down on the glass?

"Sure, Lynne. Sure. Why don't I set the table, and maybe you'd make me one of those 'No Clue' gimlets?"

"What about your own drink?"

Cutter looked at it. The ice had melted. He took a sip, fished out the olive and ate it. "The olive's good. Maybe you could add a few to our salad? Maybe the excellence of the olive and garlic will cancel out the evil sodium." Speak her language, he told himself, maybe that will help smooth things over, whatever there is to smooth. "Maybe without the melted ice, this would be good, he said, but as it is. . . "He poured it down the drain in a gesture which he thought epitomized the conversation they'd just had.

Lynne laughed. He took that as a good sign.

"I suppose that settles it," she said, "One cornichons gimlet coming up. If you'd chop up five of those olives for the salad, that should be fine."

Cutter silently corrected "cornichons gimlet" to "No Clue." How did she come up with the numbers? He looked at the jar to see serving size. Nothing to do with it, maybe volume. Or maybe, more likely it was one of the ways Lynne kept her world under control. He wanted to ask her, but settled for "Coarse or fine?"

"Large enough pieces so that we can tell what they are. But not so large as to overwhelm the other ingredients."

The politics of salad, Cutter mused. He fixed his mind on cutting the olives to please Lynne. To give her a sense of control, which would make her easier to get on with. Self-interest. And it gave him something manageable to think about. He hoped he'd turned off his cell phone. The last thing he wanted now was a call from Grace.

CHAPTER 10

The red light on the answering machine was blinking. Ever since Grace had spoken to Lynne, Ely didn't know when she would take it into her head to call again. If it's Grace, I can erase it, he thought. With any luck Lynne won't have spotted a message. However, if she's noticed the light before he's had a chance to erase the message from Grace, he'll have to explain. And if he doesn't erase it, he might have to explain that, too. Bother, he thought, feeling quite like Winnie the Pooh. He said it aloud for the fun of it, "Bother." What nonsense.

Caller ID, unknown caller. Could be one of those solicitations. They still got those calls in spite of the Do Not Call List, although now they were disguised as "offers."

He was making far too much of this, he scolded himself. He'd just play the message.

"Hey, Dad, it's me," the voice said. The voice was that of a young man who sounded as though he were about the age Isaac would have been.

In spite of his knowledge that this was a wrong number, Cutter felt light-headed. "Dad!" Cutter mused, and he missed the next few words. He'd play it again.

"Shit. I hate this new machine of yours. At least you could record a simple 'Thank you for calling.'" The voice had taken on an edge, which Cutter didn't like. "Finding a phone around here, it's not easy." The voice grew softer. "Well, tell Mom I love her," he said. "You, too, Dad." A pause. "Look, I'm sorry. Really."

Then a someone put a hand over the mouthpiece, muffling

the man's voice and a woman's, as they continued a quarrel. Cutter didn't need to hear words. He recognized the tone, which was all too familiar. Whatever these two were arguing about, it was no business of his.

"OK. I'll try you again. 'Bye."

And that was it. Cutter replayed the message. He considered erasing it, but decided he wouldn't. He'd tell Lynne. Why not? She could decide for herself if she wanted to listen. He wished he could fix it so the light would blink. That way he'd be off the hook. If she listened… If he told her the whole story, she'd think he was crazy. Maybe not. Maybe good old Lynne would surprise him.

No sense upsetting her, he told himself. But when Lynne came home, she asked if there had been any calls she should know about. That covered more ground than if she had asked if she had received any calls. If Grace had phoned would that call have fallen into the category of "a call she should know about"? Not to him, but Lynne would probably put it there.

"What do you mean?" he asked.

"Just, you know, a call."

Good, he thought, listening for the tone and not hearing one that reeked of Lynne's dislike of Grace or Eleanor.

"A wrong number," he said.

"Really?" Lynne said, "So?"

Now he'd done it. Instead of just shrugging it off, he told Lynne about the message, what it said, how he'd replayed it. "So I know it was a wrong number…I don't know why I was so upset."

"Ely, you've been off balance ever since you had your

vision," Lynne said, "Maybe even before. Maybe that's why it happened in the first place."

"I know what I saw," he said.

"I have no doubt that you saw it. I'm saying that just because you saw it doesn't mean it was there."

This was going where he didn't want it to go. He'd rather hear her sniping about Grace.

"I saved the message," he said, sheepish, "just in case."

"In case? What? We're getting calls now from Heaven?" Lynne said, "Really, Ely."

"No," he said, "not that. . . Not exactly that. But, you know, I thought you might want to hear it."

"What for," Lynne's voice had nothing of a question in it. She might as well have put her hands on her hips and glared at him.

"I wanted you to . . ." Ely began.

"You wanted me to listen," she said. "And then what? To listen and to feel the same way you did? Miserable and shaken. Because a wrong number calls you 'Dad'?"

"Well, Lynne," he said, "That's about it. Yes, I wanted you to feel like I did."

"You want me to be miserable? Why?"

"No, not miserable... But I did want you to feel something. It would be something we would feel together. I wanted us to feel the same thing." He paused, thinking, "for a change." Anything other than irritation and anger. He continued aloud, "So?"

Cutter looked up at Lynne. She hadn't sat down through this, and he hadn't risen. "So will you?"

"Feel what you felt or listen?" Lynne said. "I'll listen if that'll make you feel better."

"I'm not sure I want to," Cutter said.

"We don't have to," Lynne said. "I thought it was important to you."

"I mean," he said, "that I'm not sure I want to feel better."

Lynne stared at him, incredulous, waiting for an explanation.

He got up and said, "This is an easy feeling, Lynne. Grief. It's one I know." Cutter turned away from his wife. Maybe he didn't want her to know about this, after all. It was over, he'd believed, not gone, but it had been years since he'd felt the loss of his son with this intensity.

"Oh, Ely," Lynne said, putting her hand on his forearm. "I'm sorry. I apologize. I shouldn't have . . ."

Maybe not, but you did, he thought. Aloud he said, "Now what, Lynne?"

"Now we listen to the message. Or I do if you don't want to. I can come back in after?"

"No. I want us to listen together, and then we can erase it." He put his arm around her and realized he hadn't done that in a long time. "Let's go, Lynne."

She'd developed a frown line just like her mother's, and her mother had never seemed happy. Was Lynne unhappy? Why shouldn't she be, he chided himself, with all that's happened—with what he'd done. Still, he hadn't been as bad as all that. There were men far worse.

"Okay?" he said. His finger hovered over the button.

"Just do it, Ely. This is killing me."

Cutter was relieved. Lynne's overstatements never signaled real trouble, just annoyance. But then she hadn't had his experience. Lynne couldn't have. It had all been addressed to him, to the mysterious missing father, not to the mother. Except for, "Tell Mom I love her." So where was his mother and why wouldn't she have been there to listen to the message herself?

"Too bad," Lynne said.

"What?" Cutter said, knowing, that for him, the phrase "too bad" did not apply. It was so far beneath what he was feeling. He'd underestimated Lynne. She wouldn't have said that about their son.

"Somewhere," she said, "there's a father who just got an apology and he doesn't know. Play it again."

"Again?" The repetition was dulling his feelings. "Okay."

"Listen to the end, where he pauses before he says, "I'm sorry."

That's what he'd done, listened to the pause. They both thought it was important.

"What do you think happened?" Lynne asked.

Ely shrugged in resignation.

"Who do you think she is, that woman?"

"We'll never know."

"He's not very happy, is he?" she said.

"I've been very lucky," Ely said, then added for emphasis, "I am very lucky."

A shadow settled on Lynne's face.

"I haven't made you happy, Ely," Lynne said. "I tried. I really did. If you'd been happy—with me—you wouldn't have." Her voice dropped. "I'm sorry, Ely. I shouldn't have said that. Not now."

"Thank you," Ely said, then added, partly to change the subject, partly because it bothered him. "That pause. I thought it was something important, too."

He hadn't explained, and he was glad when Lynne answered, "Yes, and maybe it had something to do with that woman . . ."

"Whatever it was, it's too bad we can't pass the message along."

"No," she said.

"And it sounded to me like this was the first call he'd made since whatever it was happened."

"Happened? Ely, you're letting him off... This thing he's apologizing for didn't just 'happen,' I'll bet it was something he did, deliberately, too."

"You're probably right, Lynne. And, worse." He paused. "Even though he said he would, I don't think he's going to..." He said with an emphatic tone, "I think he won't call again. Not any time soon, anyway."

Would his own relationship with his son have been any better? He sighed. "He doesn't say it often, does he?" Lynne would know what he meant—he could count on her for that.

"I don't think he does," she said. "Do you want to erase it, Ely? Or would you rather I did?"

This was like removing the *yahrzeit* candle they lit on the anniversary of Isaac's death. "I'll do it," he said. He looked at the machine, the rebuke of the steady red light, and added, "Later."

"No," Lynne said. She leaned over and pressed the first button. The message began to play, "Hey, Dad! It's…" and she pressed the second button.

The mechanical voice said, "No old messages."

"I had to, Ely," she said. "One of us had to. And this time it was easier for me."

"Okay, Lynne." He wanted to listen to the recording again. "Hey," he started.

He wanted to say, "He loves you." Instead he said, "I love you."

"I love you too, Ely," Lynne said.

And Cutter knew that, in a way, both of them were telling the truth, or, at least, neither of them was lying. For now, that was just as good, or, anyway, it would have to do.

"The Feng Shui is all wrong," Grace said after Cutter closed his car door.

Cutter was tired of hearing this, not from Grace, who had invoked Feng shui just this once, but from other women who had too much time on their hands. Time to worry about placement of doors and windows and mirrors and light instead of sensible things like closets. Or that's what it seemed like, though he had to admit he hadn't heard too much from Grace on the subject.

Grace must have just read a magazine article on Feng Shui. For months after such a publication, he heard from those newly conscious of that ancient art. Or was it a science? He wasn't sure, even after having read a book so he wouldn't seem foolish.

He was able to nod, agree and even make a suggestion, one that didn't involve too much expense, something that would remedy the problem. He prefaced all of his comments on this topic with, "I'm not an expert, of course, but I've done a little reading. . ." No matter what happened with that property, he'd forged a bond with the woman. Important in this business. "I don't want to overstep my bounds," and then he'd be invited to speak. He was sure that he'd saved at least one sale like this.

Sometimes they brought in a Feng Shui expert to look at a house before they put in a bid. Over the years, two of them kept coming around: One, a woman who always wore the same outfit, a gray skirt and a black tailored jacket with a white blouse with floppy bow. She teetered on heels in a way that it suggested to Ely that she never wore them except on occasions like these. The other wore a succession of linen outfits, flowing skirts and tops, slacks and tunics, always white in summer, black in winter, beige in spring and fall. He wondered what they charged, and whether their charges were based on some official organization through which they were certified.

"What?" he said, suddenly conscious that Grace had been going on and he hadn't been attentive.

"Oh, never mind!" Grace laughed. "You weren't paying a bit of attention, were you?"

"I'm sorry, Grace."

"Well, you should be sorry, Ely Cutter," she said. "For no other reason than it's good salesmanship to pay attention, or at least to seem as though you're listening."

"No excuse," he said. "None whatsoever." He stopped

short of asking her to repeat herself. It was likely that she could, word for word. "It's the Feng Shui. 'All wrong,' I think you said. I confess, after that I got lost." Easier that way than explaining the whole thing. He didn't want to denigrate something she held dear. Better than saying "you lost me." Take responsibility, he told himself, it plays better, especially with Grace. At least today she wasn't bursting into tears. Her crying spells are, he thought, without much consequence, but damned inconvenient.

"Seriously, Ely, you haven't been yourself today." Grace said.

Careful, Cutter warned himself. He hadn't realized he'd been so thrown by yesterday's phone call. He couldn't make himself think of it as a wrong number and nothing more than that. "Sorry, Grace. I let my mind wander, that's all. It's the Feng Shui." Better that route than the direction she's going. "I've read up on…"

"Poppycock," Grace said. "How do you like that, Ely? It's what my grandfather used to say when he was angry. Or 'Horse feathers!' Much nicer than bullshit, I think, but that's the proper term for it. Bullshit, Ely. I don't believe you. What's wrong?"

"Nothing's wrong. I honestly was thinking about Feng Shui."

Grace waved her hand, making the gesture he was coming to associate with her, so dismissive for such a diminutive woman. Perhaps she'd learned to be that way, a defense because she was so tiny. Or maybe women didn't think like that. It would be true if she were a man. Cutter continued,

"And the experts who were brought in to look at houses." He paused. "Are you planning to do that, Grace?"

He didn't want to step in it any more than he already had.

"No. It was a joke. You would have known that if you'd been listening."

No wonder she sounded peevish now. No woman wants to feel as though she isn't being heard. Even less when she's a paying customer. Or will be if she can find a house to buy.

"I'm sorry I missed it then. For more reasons than it's being good 'salesmanship.'"

Cutter smiled, his best trust-me-I-have-your-interests-at-heart smile. It had taken him years to get it right; he hated the oleaginous smiles at car dealerships. He was aiming for something from an old-fashioned hardware store, where someone named Ed greeted customers with a comment about the weather. Something male, that wouldn't be threatening or subservient. But he had to be careful with Grace. She was too quick to get ideas, and he couldn't afford her ideas now.

"So, what's wrong, Ely?"

"Let's go, Grace. We have another house to see, and then we could stop at the office and review what we've seen so far. I want to make sure I understand what you want."

"You're in the driver's seat," Grace said. "Literally. Besides," she added, "you know what I want. Or I think you do. That's all right, isn't it?"

Cutter turned the key and listened to the motor. He hadn't quite turned off the radio although the volume was way down, and, if he focused his attention, he could hear the announcer's voice. It gave him something else to think about besides

Grace's perfume—gardenias, jasmine, and roses—which, today, he found too strong—and the jangling of her bracelets; nonetheless, he found her attractive. The Feng Shui must be right, he said to himself, pleased with his private joke.

"Grace," he said, "you know I'm a married man. You spoke with my wife."

"A lovely woman," Grace said.

Though he'd listened for tone, Cutter could detect no irony in her voice.

"Yes," he said, "my wife is a lovely woman. I've always said so."

"Have you? That's not what I think."

"What you think? Grace, this isn't a fruitful topic. It can't go anywhere good."

"Good for me or good for you?" She chuckled. "Your choice of words is amusing, Ely. Was it good for you?"

Cutter had thought he was past embarrassment with Grace. Maybe he could get out of this by pretending he didn't understand her double entendre—or would it be better to be urbane? He hadn't had much luck with pulling the wool over Grace's eyes. He didn't want to upset her. "As for marriage, good is what you make it, Grace. I've chosen to make it good."

She was quiet. He looked over at her to see if he'd been successful. When their eyes met, she said, "Touché."

Was she going to cry again? "I don't want to hurt you, Grace." What was he doing? Wasn't he taking this, taking her, far too seriously? Nothing had happened that should have precipitated his saying this. He wasn't about to take her to bed. That's when he should be saying, "I don't want to hurt you, Grace," not after he's said he's a married man. Cutter winced as he realized that it was all too appropriate, that the juxtaposition of "I'm a married man" and the statement, "I don't want to hurt you" was tantamount to a proposition. He hoped Grace didn't misunderstand him. Or understand. He was almost confused himself.

"Don't worry, Ely. I'm a big girl."

"You're barely five-two." He'd try shifting the conversation, making a joke.

"Five four—in heels, thank you." Grace reached over and set her hand on his leg.

On the finger where a wedding band would have been she wore a large clunky silver ring, modernistic, what could be seen as an anti-wedding ring. No mistaking it. Ring finger. A statement.

He'd have to get her hand off his leg. He put his hand on hers. What a tiny soft hand! He squeezed it gently, hoping that the gesture would be received as reassuring, and friendly rather than as a come on.

"That hurts, Ely. The ring cuts into my fingers, when you do that..."

He let go and put both of his hands on the steering wheel. She was massaging her hand as though she wanted to rub away the pain. That wasn't what he'd planned, but at least her hand wasn't on his thigh. "I'm sorry," he said.

"You're apologizing a lot today, Ely."

"Oh? I guess I am."

"What's wrong? What happened, Ely?"

"Nothing, Grace. It was nothing."

"It?"

Cutter felt like a mouse in the talons of a hawk. He might as well be with Eleanor. Even Lynne had become aggressive in questioning him. Something must be in the air. "Look, Grace. I don't want to sit here in this car with you, discussing what happened or didn't happen. I want to show you a house…"

"You mean you want to sell me a house?"

Cutter was indignant. He was about to protest, but, yes, of course he wanted to sell her a house. He was a real estate salesman, after all. If he didn't want to sell her a house they wouldn't be sitting in his car in the Ehrlich's driveway, freshly blacktopped to encourage quick sale of the property. Nothing else would have brought them here together. But he had to say this with tact. He'd already showed her almost a dozen houses. If she walked now, went to someone else, he would have lost all this time. Someone else would get the sale; she was determined to buy. He'd done a good job of qualifying her. But he hadn't counted on Grace being so difficult to predict, so difficult to handle. "It's my job, Grace. That doesn't mean I don't like you."

"Oh, Ely, I know you like me. It's not that." Tears welled up in her eyes and slid down her cheek. "And I know Lynne is a good woman. I'm sure you're a happily married man, and I'm just a fool."

There it was. The perfect trap. If he says he's happily married, she's a fool. And if he denies that she's a fool, then by extension he's not in a happy marriage, and she'll consider him fair game. Open season on Ely, he said to himself. "You're no fool, Grace, but I am happily married." Ely paused, then added with all the contrition that he could muster, "I'm afraid it doesn't always show."

"She's a lucky woman," Grace said.

Before Ely could say anything, she added, "and I'm lucky, too. Our relationship doesn't have to touch your marriage, Ely. And it shouldn't. I trust you to see to it. If I thought we'd hurt Lynne—or anyone, I'd back off."

"Backing off is a good idea," Ely said. "I think we should both do that."

"Let's go into the house again, for just a minute. I want to splash some water on my face. I feel all messy."

"You look fine," Ely said, "Just fine." She did, too. He hadn't noticed before how that color—did they call it coral or peach—looked so good on her. And it was unheard of to use someone's bathroom to freshen up. He'd have to stop that. "I'd tell you if you were a mess."

"Would you even notice?"

Another puzzler. Did she want him to say that he had? She certainly had been a mess at the bookstore, and he was sure that anyone looking at her would have known. Maybe he could pretend not to have heard. This was no time to take her to look at a house. Buckingham Palace would seem cramped to her while she was in this mood.

"I guess that wasn't a fair question." She sighed, "Now it's my turn to apologize. I'd like to look at the kitchen and bathrooms and closets again. I promise I won't use their plumbing."

"Fine, Grace. We'll go back in. We might have to reschedule the other place. What do you think?"

"Reschedule, then. It makes sense to see this one again while we're here. I can't use those diagrams you give me."

He'd make a joke, find a light tone. "You promise you won't be checking for Feng Shui?"

"Feng Shui?"

Cutter could tell by her tone that she was puzzled. "You'd said it was 'all wrong' in this house."

"I said I was joking. I never joke about joking." She paused, then said, "We have so much to learn about one another."

He'd have to get this situation straightened out sometime soon, but, as they were about to go back into the house, it would have to wait. Good Lord! How could he be planning to negotiate a breakup with a woman he wasn't seeing?

While he was unlocking the box to get the key, another car pulled into the drive, and parked next to his. He hoped it wasn't the owners. Owners always made looking at a house difficult; no matter how much they'd been told, they tried to sell the place, and they did it all wrong.

"Ely!"

Wonderful. It was Joanne; he looked to see who she had with her. Yes, the same couple who'd been with her that awful day at Grace's. It hadn't been that long ago, though it seemed like weeks to him. Of course, it made sense that they should see this place. It had some of the same features as Grace's house.

"How are you, Ely?"

Joanne punched the 'are' too much so that she missed the sincere tone he knew she was going for.

"I'm just fine, Joanne. And you?"

"Oh, Ely. I'm always fine."

She laughed and put her hand on his shoulder. Joanne was a tall woman, and she was wearing heels. It disconcerted Ely to look at a woman straight on. Women could get away with anything. If a man did the things Joanne and Grace did …

The husband nodded at him and gave him a sympathetic smile. It was getting worse and worse.

"Yes, how are you?" the wife asked. "We hoped you hadn't been hurt."

"I'm fine, thanks." Hadn't she heard him tell Joanne? Well, it was a topic of conversation, he supposed. Wouldn't you think she'd understand that it was embarrassing? Women were supposed to know these things. Joanne had been needling him, but this woman was pathetic in her attempt to make small talk. He wondered if she'd be different in twenty years.

"You're finding something, I hope?" Get the topic onto real estate. Property. Back away from the personal and onto real estate where he was comfortable.

"Yes, we've seen a number of very nice houses," the woman said. Turning to Grace, she added, "I really liked your house," she said.

"So did I," Grace said.

They might've been two women at a party. Listening to Grace no one would believe that it was her choice to sell. And maybe it wasn't. He had only her word to go on, and she might not have wanted to tell him the financial arrangements associated with her divorce. Maybe the woman did have limits, after all. Cutter was cheered by the thought.

"Let's all look, then, shall we?" Joanne said. "Is it all right with you if we start with the downstairs?"

"I don't like her," Grace said when they were back in Cutter's car. "I think she knows what she's doing, but … there's something I can't put my finger on."

"Don't try, Grace. Joanne's selling your house. She's not your tennis partner."

"Do you want to be my tennis partner, Ely? Do you play tennis?" Grace laughed. "I don't. Not a bit. Not ever."

Cutter played tennis, and he had a partner. But he had no desire to share this information with Grace. She was full of questions, and each time he answered, she made it into another rope binding them together.

"I'll let you know when I get an appointment for the other house," Cutter said. "Are any days better for you than others?"

"They're all the same, Ely."

"Okay, then I'll shoot for Thursday, see if I can put together a couple of properties that we should look at, based on your preferences, then."

"So, you're not going to tell me, are you?"

"What?" Cutter was off-guard.

"Why you're not quite yourself today."

"I am myself, Grace. Very much so." Cutter bristled. He didn't like being pushed. Yet, at the same time, he wanted to tell someone about the call. And he couldn't tell Eleanor. It was too close to their meeting, to what Lynne called their date. Eleanor would think he wanted to start all over again. "I'm fine."

"I can wait," Grace said. "We have plenty of time."

CHAPTER 11

And then one day as Cutter was weeding the pole beans, he cut through an earthworm with his trowel. The two parts continued to move. He felt revulsion as he watched the slimy writhing creature, even while he pitied it. The earthworm had every reason to be where it was. He should have been more careful digging, but how?

He stood up, feeling unwell—somewhat nauseated and dizzy. He was almost overcome by the intense smells of vegetation, compost, and freshly turned earth. It was the heat, he was sure. Lynne was right: he should wear a hat in the sun. The sky was so pale it might have been bleached.

He was startled when Lynne asked, "What are you looking at? Is it up there again?"

Ely's grip loosened when he turned his attention to what Lynne was saying, and he dropped the canvas garden gloves and trowel he was holding. They fell on the small pile of weeds he'd managed to remove from the dry soil. He'll have to water later in the day, be careful not to get the leaves wet, he reminded himself. He couldn't do anything these days without thinking about it; when he didn't stop to think, his clumsiness left a trail of pain and brokenness.

"Are you all right?" she said.

"Just a little dizzy. I stood up too fast."

Lynne handed him his glove but kept the trowel.

"Thanks, Lynne. You startled me."

"You looked like you were in another world. . ." Her voice trailed off.

Cutter laughed. His laugh sounded phony to him, but Lynne didn't remark on it. Maybe his perceptions were skewed today. "I'm right here. In the garden. And I have a pile of weeds to prove it."

"Today they're weeds not salad greens. That's encouraging."

"You liked the purslane, didn't you?"

"It must be an acquired taste, like okra. It wasn't bad. It's more the idea of it."

"These are weeds, no way around it." He paused. If he said what he wanted to, Lynne would be annoyed. He'll take his chances. She's his wife, and he's not talking about another woman. Just some wild greens. "No purslane here." There, he'd done it.

"I suppose you could ask Sam for some. He'd probably be glad for you to 'harvest' it. He'd like help with the weeding."

"I might just do that. It won't upset you, will it? What Ruth says?"

"Ruth? If the only thing she can find to talk about is your wanting a few clumps of purslane for a salad, we'll be just fine."

"What has she been saying?" Cutter was alarmed. What had he gotten himself into? Was Joanne stirring up trouble?

He didn't remember Grace saying anything outrageous while Joanne was in the house. Still, she needn't have heard anything awful. She could have taken something innocent and embroidered it. Not that Grace was innocent. But he was. At least he was so far.

"Oh, nothing, really. I shouldn't have said that," she said.

Cutter did a quick translation. Lynne had just said, "I don't want to tell you, either because 1. it would upset you or

2. put you on your guard." He couldn't tell which.

"Water might be a good idea," he said.

"For you or the garden?"

"Both. I'll start with myself."

"I'll get it," Lynne said, and, despite Cutter's protest that he could do it himself, she went to the house.

Cutter stared at the sky, looking for the face. He was sure he hadn't imagined it. Even now with his eyes closed he could see the face, with rays emanating all around. Or maybe it was Sam and Ruth's garden ornament that he was seeing now in his mind's eye. Couldn't he tell the difference between a garden ornament and God's face?

" . . . all right?"

Cutter looked at Lynne, puzzled.

"You didn't hear me before," she said and handed him the glass, filled more with ice than with water.

"I must have been daydreaming," Cutter said. He didn't want to tell her what he'd been doing. If she asked him why, he wouldn't be able to give her a good answer, not even one she'd settle for.

"Thank you, Lynne," he said.

"Don't thank me, Ely. I didn't make the water—I just brought it to you. Your Friend in the sky made it."

"Maybe I should be thanking both of you."

Cutter stared at the water in his hand. He was thirsty, but Lynne was right, and he should be thanking God for the water, saying some sort of blessing. Brings forth fruit from the tree, brings forth fruit from the earth, what for water? Water from the earth? It is from the earth, but from the sky, too. He'd have to look. For now, he said a silent thanks and drank.

Later he had the answer to his question about the blessing for water. Cutter said to Lynne, "It's 'Blessed are You, *Hashem*, King of the Universe, by whose word everything comes to be.'"

"What?"

"The blessing for water. You said I should be saying one. I looked it up."

"This is something new that you're going to be doing?"

"I might," Cutter said, uneasy, looking away from her. He wasn't sure that he wanted to commit to doing it. If he told Lynne he would, she'd be watching. He wondered if God cared about gratitude or about manners. Maybe the blessings are supposed to remind you that you're grateful—or should be. So many things he should have done and didn't, so many he ought not to have done but he did. Saying a few blessings would never make up for everything he's done wrong.

Still, when he took a drink of water after having worked in the garden, picking tomatoes and beans for dinner, he said the blessing to himself and to Whoever Else would be listening.

"Ruth called," Lynne said. "I invited them to come for dinner, potluck."

"I have an appointment to show a house late this afternoon. . ."

"I told them six-thirty. Not too late an evening. Is that all right?"

"Sure," said Cutter. "I can be home by then."

And if Grace hadn't had a meltdown he would have been.

"Well, Grace, what did you think?" He was not hopeful. Maybe she was in a bad mood, but she didn't even like the sunken tub with the Jacuzzi.

"An accident waiting to happen," she said, "and so much hot water. It's not very green, is it Ely?"

"There's a regular shower, too. Look, it's large enough for a shower bench if you want to sit down."

"You mean when I get old!" She smiled at him and tilted her head. It looked to him as though she wanted him to kiss her.

"You have a long way to go," he said, although that wasn't accurate for either of them. They were both skidding down the last steep slope of middle age. He didn't know what he'd be meeting on the way down, but he'd be having a bumpy ride. Everyone did.

"It's large enough for two. Ely," she said, "do you want to try it out? We can check the water pressure, see what all those hoses and nozzles do."

"It does look like a carwash," he said, peering at the array of nozzles. If he could keep the focus on the shower, he might be able to navigate away from this situation. "'Custom tile work. Glass mosaic tiles.'" he read from the sheet. Large ensuite bath designed by. . .' Are you up on local interior designers of baths?"

"Not now. I might be by the time we find a house."

Cutter noted the pronoun. She's made this a joint venture. In a way she was right, they were both looking. But he hoped she didn't intend their finding to be followed by their moving-in.

"Do you realize how many bedrooms we've been in, Ely?"

"I haven't counted. I guess it's like the old joke, but instead of dividing, multiply. Which ruins the joke if you haven't heard it."

"Divide by four," Grace said.

Cutter smiled, "Good. I don't know enough jokes to lose one like that."

"My house, my current house, counts too," she said, frowning. "So many bedrooms ..."

"Sometimes it takes a while to find the right place, Grace. It's too soon to give up."

Grace looked in the mirror. "The light in here is terrible," she said.

He was about to say that the light was good, and then he realized that what she meant was that the light wasn't flattering. He had to admit that she was right. In this light, angled as it was, they had both aged five hard years. Cutter wasn't one to stare into a mirror, and he was surprised at his wrinkles, his age-splotched skin. You had to have a strong ego to face yourself in this mirror every day. No wonder there was a Jacuzzi and a fancy shower. You'd need one after you'd taken a good look at yourself. Aloud, he said, "I suppose you could use a lower wattage."

"Oh, Ely! This isn't what I wanted for myself!"

The vehemence with which she spoke startled him, and then he realized that she wasn't talking about the house. Of course she wasn't. Who would want to be on the wrong side of 50 and looking at a life alone? He and Lynne have had their rocky moments, to be sure, but their worst of times together is better than the life he'd have without her.

Here he is with Grace, both of their reflections in the mirror with its too bright lights. Grace made no attempt to wipe away her tears as she stood facing the mirror. Rivulets of black eyeliner ran down her cheeks. Her eyes got smaller as her eyelids puffed up. He had never seen such a rapid disintegration of an attractive face. Her arms hung limp at her sides, and her shoulders began to shake as she sobbed.

Cutter had no tissues. He should have made a note to carry them when he was with Grace. I hate to do this, he said to himself, but this situation is no good; Grace's eyes were streaming, and her nose probably about to run. No one will ever know, he thought, so he leaned over and pulled a tissue from the Alabaster box on the vanity. It was the last one, and the hole in the top of the container gaped. He hoped Grace wouldn't notice.

"I wanted an ordinary life," Grace said, still snuffling. "I just wanted to be a housewife. I shouldn't be here like this."

Cutter nodded. He didn't know what to say to her.

Then she added, "I tried so hard. Nothing I did could make it right."

"I'm sure you did try, Grace. Sometimes there's nothing we can do. We can't change the way other people feel. Sometimes people can't even fix their own emotions." He couldn't.

"It's not fair, Ely."

"Even so, Grace, I'm in no position to be giving you advice about accepting the way things are."

"What would you change? You told me you were happy. No, not happy, content."

Cutter thought she was less incredulous than accusing. "I am. Mostly."

"It's none of my business, but if you ever want to talk. I'll be there for you," Grace said before she burst into tears again.

Cutter felt trapped. Instinct would have him put his arms around her to comfort her, but that would just lead to more trouble.

Before he could do anything she looked at him and said, "And what will happen when I find a house? Will you still see me?"

"Let's not worry about that now."

"That's easy for you to say."

"Not so easy, Grace. Life is complicated, isn't it?" He was being deceitful, but he wanted to buy some time until they were out in public again.

Although they were alone in a stranger's "super-luxe bath," at any time someone could walk in on them. With his run of bad luck, it would be Joanne and the young couple he was calling the Joneses, for the pleasure of saying the phrase, "Joanne and the Joneses." Now playing. Limited engagement. It was evident they were looking for a place in the same range as Grace. For them it would be a starter house. These days people started bigger than they used to. And that was fine with him.

Grace threw her arms around him and gave him a hug. She buried her face in his chest. When she pulled away, she looked up at him and said, "Not everything is complicated. Some things are plain and easy. This is one of them, or it can be."

"I don't think this is the time or place to be having this discussion, Grace," he said, self-consciously pompous.

"If not now, when, Ely?"

"Grace, I don't want to be having this discussion at all." Yes, pompous and even a bit self-righteous. What did he offer a woman his age who was like a young girl—impetuous and un-affected.

"I don't want to be having it either, Ely. I'd rather just be playing it by ear, doing what comes naturally for both of us." She paused, as though waiting for a response. When he didn't fill in the silence she asked him, "You do find me attractive, don't you?"

"I'm not going to say any more, Grace." If he did, he'd have to admit that he found her more attractive than he could have imagined, even with her face puffy and her eyes and nose reddened by tears.

"You don't have to say anything, Ely. I can tell you do." She nuzzled into his upper arm. "We look cute together, don't we?" she said looking into the mirror.

And, in spite of himself, even in the merciless mirror, Cutter agreed that they did, indeed, look cute.

"What's that perfume, Grace?"

"It's my secret scent. I'll never tell. I use two perfumes together to come up with this so no one will ever have it but me. Maybe someday I'll tell you what they are. You like?"

"It's distinctive." He looked at her to see if she was about to cry.

"That's okay, Ely. I'll try something else if you think this is stinky."

Cutter laughed. She could be amusing. When she wasn't crying.

"Can you picture me in this shower, Ely? Does this look like it should be my house?"

Cutter didn't want to picture her in the shower. "How can I tell you what house you should buy? That's not a decision I can make for you. I can tell you generally what the positive features are, what the drawbacks might be, but what's right for your personal lifestyle, only you know. What's an advantage for someone else might be a negative for you. And vice versa." He could give this speech in his sleep; he'd done so on other occasions, less emotionally fraught.

How clever she'd been to ask him to picture her in the shower. He couldn't look at her now except to imagine her naked body in the blue tile shower. Though he didn't know much about her, he knew that this house offered many of the same features as her current house. And this one came free of memories.

Cutter hoped she wouldn't cry again. The accusing void in the tissue holder limited his options.

"It feels good. I don't know why, but this house feels very good. Right somehow."

Cutter could have told her why, but he knew that if he did, she'd turn her back on this place. She wanted to leave her house; however, in choosing this one she was choosing her house all over again. Maybe it was like a spouse. He'd heard that people choose the same person over and over. That was one thing he didn't have to worry about. He had Lynne.

"That's a good thing, isn't it?"

"I suppose, I wish I knew that we'll keep seeing each other."

Now it was Cutter's turn. "I hope you'll forgive my feeble

attempt at humor, but I think I need to say, 'we can't keep meeting like this.'"

When Grace laughed, Cutter was relieved that she'd appreciated his joke.

"Not unless this is my place," she said. "I guess we won't be using your house. That would be mean."

"Let's go, Gracie." Nothing he could say after that would be acceptable. Cutter looked at his watch. He was late for dinner. He'd be explaining not only to Lynne, but also to Sam and Ruth. At least he could say that he's probably making the sale. Lynne will be glad when he wraps up this one.

"I wondered when you'd call me that!"

When, not if: Cutter registered his dismay at having been pegged as someone who'd do that. "Does it bother you?"

"I like it when you say it. It sounds kind of sweet and old fashioned." Grace squeezed his arm. "Do you know how old fashioned I am at heart?"

"I'll take that as a rhetorical question."

"Are we going to celebrate my finding a house?"

"We can do something to celebrate once you have a bid accepted." Or not, he added to himself. Maybe by then you'll be over this silly crush. Was he talking to Grace or to himself?

Cutter left Grace smiling.

Too bad he was late, he thought, but Sam won't hang me out to dry. He might even put in a word to smooth things over. They'll need smoothing, too. Lynne was generally easy going, but not when it entailed waiting at dinner time. Cutter was rarely late. In his business, he had to be punctual, and it was a habit he'd cultivated. He'd learned to check his watch without making a show of it, unless he was using the gesture as a device to get free. Some people who weren't committed to buying were a waste of his time. Tonight, he was late, and though he was risking Lynne's wrath, it had been worth the risk.

He took a deep breath before turning the key in the lock. "Sorry I'm late!" he called out as he stepped into the living room.

When he heard Lynne's voice coming from the dining room rather than the den, he knew he was late past her endurance. Only once before had she served dinner before he'd come home. He hoped she wasn't remembering that occasion, associated as it was with his relationship with Eleanor.

He bent down and kissed the top of Lynne's head, and said, "Darling, I'm sorry I'm late." Smiling at Ruth and Sam, he added, "I'm glad I didn't keep you waiting."

"You did keep them waiting," said Lynne. She wasn't about to cut him any slack.

He looked at the table: chicken salad, a cold green bean and potato salad, sliced tomatoes. Nothing that would have been ruined had she waited for him to come home. Still, he was more than a half an hour late.

"I should have called," Cutter murmured to no one in particular.

"Is everything all right?" Lynne asked.

Cutter knew she was talking to him by her tone, a frosty concern.

"Fine, dear. Again, my apologies."

Cutter wished that he'd told some story about traffic and a dead cellphone. He could have managed that by plugging in his cell phone to charge, turning it off in order to circumvent an unfortunate call. He'd done that more than once when he'd been with Eleanor. That had been a difficult time for all three of them. He'd never imagined how complicated things could become with the simple addition of one person to his life.

Lynne had made one of his favorite summer dishes, marinated green bean and potato salad with onions and black olives. It wasn't one she, herself, liked. No wonder she was so piqued. He looked at his watch again to see if he'd made a miscalculation: seven-fifteen.

"We waited at least half an hour for you to get home. I finally gave up and started dinner," Lynne said.

"I'm glad you didn't wait any longer. I should've called." He changed his tone, trying to sound like someone making a proud announcement not a sorry excuse, "I'm on the edge of selling a house," he said, adding, "to Grace." He turned to Sam Ruth, "Grace is…"

"They know who Grace is," Lynne said.

Of course. He'd forgotten Ruth's calling to tell Lynne about the Fall. Cutter would have liked to tell the story of being knocked over backwards. In his telling it tonight, he could have stripped the anecdote of any sexual overtones. Lord knows what Joanne had said about the incident and, especially, about Grace. The two women weren't fond of one another and their being bound together by the contract to sell Grace's house opened some not-so-pretty possibilities for interaction. And if his sale moved towards closing, that would ramp up the pressure for Joanne. Grace didn't strike him as one who was willing to take a loss to limit the potential for even greater losses. He'd better remember that.

"We heard about your accident," Sam said. "Maybe we need to amend the helmet law to include sitting on kitchen stools."

"That's not a bad idea," Cutter said. "Or raise insurance rates for people who own them."

"Invent a whole new area of liability."

"What do you think the warning label should say?" Leave it to Sam to lighten the mood.

"Yes, Ely's given unprotected sex a whole new meaning," Lynne said.

Had she said "it's" and not "Ely's" that wouldn't have been half as bad, maybe even amusing.

"Lynne," he said, trying to mask his annoyance, "I've already apologized. I can't turn back the clock to make it six-thirty."

"You'd have to turn it back farther than that, Ely," Lynne said, and then changed the subject by offering more wine.

The wine bottle was at Lynne's end of the table, a by-product of his having been late. Pouring wine had always been his job. That must be one of the things Grace had to get used to. So, now he was reframing things in terms of Grace. He'd have to watch that, or it would get out of hand—if it hasn't already.

"Grace sounds like quite a character," Ruth said.

For a moment Cutter worried that he'd said something aloud instead of thinking it. Thoughts still were free, weren't they? Maybe Ruth was trying to defuse the situation by opening it for discussion, as though there were nothing taboo about it.

"A real firecracker," Sam said.

"Is she, Ely?" Lynne asked, "a firecracker?"

He wasn't sure if Lynne was putting him on the spot or letting him off by giving him a chance to address the issue. After her crack about unprotected sex, he was afraid she meant to skewer him.

"It depends on how you mean 'firecracker,'" he said.

""What the meaning of 'is' is?" Lynne said.

Cutter got the reference and didn't like it. "Not at all like that," he said.

"Don't be so huffy, Ely. You asked for it."

It wouldn't be possible for Ruth or Sam to say anything now. Who knows what they'd been talking about? Ely saw only one way to get out of this trouble.

"Lynne, I've apologized for being late. I should have phoned, I know. I thought I'd get here earlier."

"You're never late, Ely. You know to the minute how long it takes to get from one place to another, adjusted for traffic at the time of day." Cutter was dismayed at the scorn in Lynne's voice.

"Yes, you're right. That makes this all the worse, I admit it. I am sorry." He hoped he wasn't putting too much emphasis on "am."

"What are you sorry about, Ely? Being late, or what made you late?"

"I'm sorry we're having this discussion in front of Ruth

and Sam," Cutter said, surprised at himself. "I'm not sorry for what made me late. As I said, I was close to closing a sale."

"So," Lynne said. "That's your story?"

"That's my 'story,' Lynne. I'm sorry if you don't like it, but that's the way it is," Cutter said, "And now I think we should move the conversation along before we chase our friends away."

Lynne stood up and went into the kitchen. Sam and Ruth looked dismayed. Now I've done it, Cutter chided himself. He left the table without apologies and followed Lynne.

His wife was leaning against the counter, wiping away tears. Two crying women in one day! Cutter put his arms around Lynne.

She pulled away and said, "I don't know what perfume that woman wears, but it's far too strong, Ely. You stank of it the day you fell, and you stink of it now."

"She was crying, Lynne."

"So you tried to comfort her, the way you did with me just now? That makes me feel wonderful."

"No, that's not the way it was."

"So, how do you account for the smudges on your shirt?"

"I told you she was crying."

"Makeup doesn't fly through the air, Ely, just because a woman's crying."

"I never said it did. We were standing in a bathroom, Lynne. She leaned against me, sobbing."

"She's taking this house thing, hard, I suppose."

"It's not just the house thing—it's the divorce thing. That's mostly it."

"You expect me to understand? It's your job to sell houses, not to comfort divorcées—you're a real estate salesman, not a gigolo."

"Why are you doing this?"

"You come home late, humiliating me in front of our friends. They know all about your Grace. Ruth heard about her from Joanne. She has quite a reputation, your firecracker."

"I didn't call her that, Sam did."

"You didn't take issue with him, did you? I'm surprised you haven't taken to defending her."

"I don't think Grace needs defending," Cutter said. "I'm selling her a house, not playing house." He took a deep breath. "It's you I love, Lynne. Just you."

"I hope you're telling me the truth, Ely," Lynne said, adding, "or I'll make you pay."

"If love is our currency, you already have all I have to give," he replied. He was surprised at his own hokey eloquence. He hoped she would fall for it. When she did, he felt relieved and, to his surprise, vindicated.

CHAPTER 12

Cutter didn't want to re-open the discussion in front of Ruth and Lynne, but he was taken aback when Ruth said that Grace had "quite a reputation," and what did Sam mean, anyhow, when he called Grace a "firecracker." He couldn't ask Sam without risking his telling Ruth, and he couldn't ask him not to. Sure disaster. Sam would tell Ruth that he'd asked him not to tell her, and she'd go straight to Lynne. They were all good friends, but Cutter was bumping up against the limits of his friendship with Sam.

It was unlikely that Sam meant anything sexual. He wouldn't have put him in such an awkward position. Did everyone in Cherry Hill know that Grace was unstable?

When the time came, if it did, he could use Sam to get the word to Lynne that everything was on the up and up. He'd do that only as a last resort. He could use Sam to convey a lie once, and when—if—he did, he'd endanger their friendship. It was a real pickle.

No one brought up Grace's name for the rest of the evening, and Cutter was pleased when neither Ruth nor Sam suggested that they leave right after dinner. Manners aside, if they'd been uncomfortable or if they'd sensed that Lynne needed to thrash things out with him, they would've left.

But when they said goodnight, Sam, who resorted to Yiddish when stressed, said with an emphasis uncommon to their usual good-byes, "*zei mir gezunt.*"

Cutter hoped Lynne hadn't made the connection, and, if she had, that she wouldn't say anything. "You be well, too, Sam," Cutter said, patting him on the forearm.

And then he was alone with Lynne. The best way to deal with Lynne's distress was to disarm her by talking about Grace, saying only what was true. It was true that Grace was on the verge of buying the last home he'd showed her. It was true that he was pleased that the sale was so close. It was true that Grace wanted Joanne to do a better job of selling her house. It was true that he thought little of Joanne as a real estate salesperson. And it was also true that Lynne was aware of his disdain even though Joanne was married to Ruth's cousin. Cutter determined that he would start with the least threatening of these.

If he had to have recourse to a partial truth, he would have laid the foundation to support it with solid, good, full truths.

Cutter began. "Thank you for making that green bean potato salad, Lynne," he said. "I know you're not so fond of it yourself." That was the truth, the whole truth.

"I'm sorry I almost ruined dinner by being so late." The truth. "I ought to have called." More truth. And then he shut up.

"What's going on with Grace?" Lynne asked.

"I'm selling her a house." He held up his thumb and forefinger, "This far away from her making a decision."

"Personally, I mean."

"Personally, she's a mess," he said. He felt loyal to Lynne and disloyal to Grace. He had no time to brood. "It's what I said before. She's shell-shocked from her divorce, which, I gather from her, was not what she wanted. That's why she's trying to get out of her house and into another one.

"Situation normal. She needs to sell if she wants to buy. So there's some tension between her and Joanne?" he finished, using the inflection of a question to bat the ball back to Lynne.

"You heard what Ruth said. What do you think?"

This was where it got touchy. "Joanne's one of these women who 'do' real estate. They give the pros a bad name. Don't get me started on the subject. You already know what I'm going to say." And she did. She'd heard his diatribe many times. He went on anyway. It was a safe topic. He needed safe.

"It's the women who get caught with them. They meet another woman, feel some sisterhood, kinship—whatever you want to call it—sign up with them and then complain because they're stuck with a dilettante. The same things that attracted them in the first place, it's what they end up complaining about."

"You don't like Joanne."

"You know how I feel about Joanne."

Lynne nodded. "Yes, but she's not that bad."

He shrugged. "I'm sure she can be very nice," Cutter was treading on dangerous ground. Keep it true, he told himself. "I'm just saying I wouldn't trust her to sell my house." That was true. "I've seen her do too much damage with her lackadaisical attitude." True again.

"She doesn't much like Grace."

"So I gather. She doesn't have to like her, just sell her house."

"Why do you think Sam said Grace was a firecracker?"

"Beats me."

"But you agreed!"

"What was I going to do, Lynne? Disagree? Already I was

late for dinner. Was I supposed to pick a fight with Sam, too? And over what? It's not up to me to defend Grace now, is it, just because I'm trying to sell her a house?"

He hoped he wasn't overplaying this. Stay true, he told himself. "She's got a stormy disposition. Bursts into tears like this," he said, snapping his fingers. "I put it down to the divorce. It's a phase. A lot of women go through it." He saw Lynne's face and amended his statement, "so I hear."

"I just don't want another situation," Lynne said.

Cutter knew she was talking about his affair with Eleanor. If Lynne had been trying to be delicate, she hadn't been delicate enough. Cutter winced, hoping that Lynne hadn't noticed his reaction. Then he said, "Any man who gets involved with a woman like Grace is asking for trouble." He paused for emphasis. "Even I know that." And that was true, too.

It took as much will power as Cutter could muster not to flinch with Lynne staring at him, peeling back protective layers to uncover the one truth that he was trying to keep hidden among all those that were harmless.

Lynne said, "I hope you remember that."

And then it was over. Lynne was in the shower, and he was in bed, waiting for her, hoping she wouldn't want to make love. He wasn't sure he could manage it, and he was sure that tonight Lynne would take his failure as a rejection, or as evidence that he had, in fact, been unfaithful. He felt sorry for Lynne, with full knowledge that he had himself to blame for her unhappiness.

He wanted to turn out the light and close his eyes. Block it all out. He had to wait for Lynne, or he might as well hand her his signed confession of infidelity. He couldn't forget what he'd said: Any man who gets involved with a woman like Grace is asking for trouble. Now that sounded less like an excuse to Lynne than a warning to himself.

Lynne came to bed, leaned over, and dropped a kiss on his cheek. "I hate fighting," she said.

"Yes," Cutter replied, hoping that would be all.

And it was.

Cutter had just opened Grace's car door for her when she said, "Let's do it, Ely! Let's put in a bid on the house."

After she finished her crying, she was in a good mood.

"Does the house make your heart go pitter-pat?" he asked.

"You make my heart go pitter-pat," she answered, "but the house is me."

Cutter smiled. Of course it is. The overdone bath was the equivalent of her bangle bracelets. "You like to garden?" he asked.

"Do you?"

Cutter wanted to take this next turn on all four wheels. "This home has especially nice landscaping," he said. "You'll want to maintain it." He found it useful to introduce a note of moderation at this point. It was a good way to test enthusiasm. And if the client pushed past his mild reservation, he was home. Or they were, which was the same thing.

"We can find out who does their work, can't we?" Grace asked, frowning.

"I'm sure we can. A simple matter."

"I always wanted a butter-yellow kitchen," Grace said. "And now...I don't."

"After you've lived with the kitchen the way it is for a while, you can decide if you want to change the color." Cutter said. "The walls are in good shape. Painting won't take but a day or two."

"You're right—again. You will help me with this, Ely?"

"With everything I can," Ely said, feeling like a weasel.

And then, without thinking, he kissed her.

Entertaining this memory, Cutter wondered who had seen him kiss Grace and if someone asked him, what plausible explanation he could offer. He had none. What was worse, had anyone been watching, the likelihood would be that speculations rather than questions would follow. He'd have to be more careful.

If Grace is a firecracker, how long and how slow burning is the fuse that he'd lit with that kiss?

Now when the phone rang, Ely checked the caller ID or waited for the answering machine to pick up. He hoped the young man would call him—his father—again. What was happening to him? How was he? Had he smoothed things over with the woman? Why were they at odds? Now that he'd apologized to his father, had he been able to move on with his life? Would he come home?

When, for the third time, Sam ribbed him about screening his calls, Ely decided to explain himself, not with an excuse, but with the truth.

"So, Sam," he concluded. "Am I crazy, or what?"

"In general, or about this specifically? In general, yes, of course, definitely *meshuggah,* in specific, with this, you're fine. Anybody under the circumstances... You're not made of stone, Ely."

"So, Lynne hasn't told Ruth," Ely said. "I don't know what to make of that. I expected that she would. Maybe to her it wasn't such a big deal."

"The kid was talking to his dad," Sam said, "So it would be natural for it to get to you, less for her. Too indirect, maybe. And besides, you're the one who heard the message first. That would make a difference, too."

"You think that if she'd heard it first, she would have erased it and not told me?"

"Maybe. She'd want to protect you."

"From what? A ghost?" Ely winced at his own words.

"Or she wouldn't have thought anything of it."

Ely told him about his questions, how he imagined a number of scenarios, each more outlandish than the one before. "I get into this whole South Seas thing, tropical breezes, the pounding surf, a thatched roof outdoor bar on the beach, the woman with a pink hibiscus flower in her hair—an older woman, maybe she has ten years on him, someone I didn't approve of."

"His father didn't approve of?" Sam said, correcting him.

"Ah, Sam. You caught me there."

"Don't take it like that," Sam said.

"No, I understand."

"I mean only the best for you."

"I know, Sam, I know." Ely paused. "Look. I feel a little silly about this. If you have to talk about it, tell Ruth. But otherwise, can we keep this between the two of us?" Cutter knew as he spoke that it was more request than question.

"This call, Ely. It came after you saw the face?"

"After. Definitely after. You think there's maybe a connection?"

"Everything's connected. It's all one big system. The butterfly effect. The I Ching—it's all connected."

"E what?"

"Ching. Fortune telling with yarrow sticks."

"You lost me."

"You need to do more crossword puzzles. They're a great civilizing force, crossword puzzles." He laughed. "You're fine, my friend."

"You too, Comrade," he said resorting to their ongoing joke. If he was not yet, in fact, fine, he was confident that he would be soon.

"So, why I called," Sam began, and they set up a time on the weekend when they could play tennis at the city courts.

Ely leaned against the doorframe, near where Lynne sat in the den, working on a needlepoint pillow. She often did needlepoint when she was upset. She's probably worried about Grace, and what she's about to hear isn't going to make things better. "Bad news, Lynne."

She looked up but didn't say anything.

"The house Grace was interested in buying is under contract. It went like that," he said, snapping his fingers. "I can't believe it."

Cutter tried to read Lynne's face, but it was impassive. "So much for being 'this far' from closing," she said, holding up her thumb and forefinger. "Now what?"

"Now I have to get in touch with Grace and let her know."

"How do you think she'll take it?"

"Tears," he answered. "I'm doing this one on the phone."

"You don't usually do that."

"I don't want to deal with her tears."

"She won't cry if you're on the phone?"

"I didn't say she wouldn't cry, just that I won't have to deal with it."

"You'll hang up on her if she's crying? I find that hard to believe, Ely."

"I hadn't thought about that," he said. "You have a point there. I guess either way I'll be dealing with her tears."

"She's manipulating you, Ely. And you let her do it."

"What can I do, Lynne? I'm trying to sell her a house. Do you want me to drop her, suggest that she work with somebody else for the rest of the process?"

"You could."

"Of course 'I could.' Is that what you want? What am I supposed to say to whoever's going to get her? 'My wife didn't like my working with her'?"

"I'm sure you could come up with a better story than that if you wanted to. You just don't want to let her go."

"'Let her go'?"

"Exactly." Lynne looked down at her needlepoint and made several stitches, then said, "Well?"

"I'm sorry I told you. You make me sorry."

"It's easier when I'm in the dark. Or when I keep quiet," she said before she returned to her needlepoint. "The sky is easy. Do you want me to put a face in it?"

His wife made several more stitches. Her voice had been shaky at the last. Was she going to cry? "I don't want to upset you," he said.

"I don't like being upset. And I'm not going to be. Not this time."

"I'll try not to give you anything to be upset about."

"Yes. 'Try,' then."

"That's all I can promise to do," Cutter said. This had spun out of his control without warning. And he still had Grace to deal with.

"I have an appointment tonight."

"I'm sure you do," Lynne said without looking up from her needlepoint.

"It's not with Grace," he said. He felt as though his answer was unfortunate: ineffective and at the same time inflammatory. Less is more, he counseled himself.

"Suit yourself, Ely. I'll put some dinner aside for you." She looked up from her work.

Cutter stopped himself from replying, "Suit yourself." Instead, he offered a simple thank you.

"Thank you for telling me it's not Grace," she said.

"It's okay," he said. That was as close as she'd get to apologizing. He crossed the room to bend to kiss the top of her head. He looked at his watch. He'd better phone Grace and get it over with. He'd call from the office. He didn't want Lynne walking in on the call.

"It's not that bad, Grace," he said. "All this means is that we keep looking. You'll find another place." Cutter offered her a tissue. He'd stuffed his pockets with them before leaving the office. Ridiculous. She'd be in her own house. Surely a woman who cries as often as she does has her own tissues!

His evening appointment had canceled, maybe just as well. Cutter decided he'd swing by Grace's house on his way back home. He'd told Grace he had something he wanted to discuss with her, and she'd brightened, asking if it was about "their house." He'd put off the news until he arrived, knowing Grace's reaction.

"At least I know I'll be seeing you," she said, dabbing at her eyes. "I look like a mess again, don't I?"

"Don't worry about how you look, Grace," he said. "You look fine, considering how upset you are."

"Anyone would be upset, losing a house."

"That house is gone, but we'll find one you like just as much, maybe even more."

"It's going to take forever," Grace said. "And what if nobody wants to buy my house? I'm counting on that money, Ely."

"Nothing takes forever, Grace, even though it might seem like it," Cutter was afraid she would think he was being condescending. He'd have to take care of that, so he added, "Everyone worries about the same things." Of course, not everyone was working with Joanne, so Grace had more to worry about than she knew. If she were lucky, Joanne's social calendar would be empty in the next month or two and she'd devote substantial time to business—the amount it deserved from a professional. He wondered what sort of contract they'd signed.

"Are you this nice to 'everyone'?"

Cutter pasted on a smile. He hated trick questions. He was at least this nice to everyone, but Grace wouldn't want to hear him say so. And he wasn't about to say that she was getting special treatment.

"I'm glad you think I'm being nice," he said instead; that was true, but not likely to get him into more trouble than he was already in.

"Do you have more of those tissues?"

Without saying anything, he handed her another one. She placed all the wadded-up tissues she'd used so far in a huddle on the end table next to the empty ashtray and the candy dish.

She blew her nose, and said, "I'm going to have to buy more of these. I don't know how I ran out."

Cutter knew how but didn't offer it.

Grace smiled. When she was smiling, she looked just fine, more than fine, in fact. It was a pity she was so insecure. How long had she been like this? Had her neediness driven her husband away? Funny—he was assuming her husband had wanted the divorce.

The first time he'd been here, she'd practically read his thoughts. Either he was being more guarded with her, or maybe they were on such different wavelengths now that she no longer knew what he was thinking. The light in the garden was almost gone. The shadows had vanished. It was getting late. He hadn't expected to be here this long; he'd figured he'd be just a few minutes. Instead, it had stretched out into more than an hour. Grace kept going over the same ground with him.

"A penny for your thoughts," Grace said.

"It's time for me to be going."

"That's what you were thinking? All of it?"

"Pretty much," Cutter said.

"I'd bet it's the rest of it that's really interesting. Even if that's most of what you had in mind, and the rest is just a teensy part…that's the part that matters, that smidge."

Cutter shrugged. "I couldn't say," he said, dropping his voice.

"You could, you just don't want to."

Cutter felt uncomfortable, pressured. As much as he was attracted to Grace, he was also put off by her constant plucking at him.

"But that's all right," she added.

Maybe she wasn't so bad.

"Stay for a light supper?"

"Lynne's expecting me to be home for supper," he said. He didn't mind stretching the truth.

"But you told me that you were supposed to work tonight."

"Yes, I had an appointment."

"—which got canceled?"

"Which got canceled."

"So, you're not expected to be home, after all. And you're free! Perfect!"

"I'm not exactly free, Grace."

"But you're free for supper, Ely. Come on! Why not?"

"Only free for supper, not really free, Grace. We've been over that."

"I thought we got past it."

She leaned forward towards him, and Cutter found himself

looking down her blouse. She wasn't wearing a bra.

"Then why did you kiss me?"

"I think I shouldn't have done that." He hated being wishy-washy. Maybe she hadn't noticed what words he'd used.

"I think you should have," she said over her shoulder as she walked into the kitchen.

Cutter heard the clink of ice cubes, and then, while he was trying to figure out whether he should follow her, she returned.

"Here," she said, handing him a glass.

"What?"

"We'll have a drink, eat a light dinner. What's the harm in that?"

Cutter looked at the floating ice as though he could find an answer. He sniffed the glass, trying to be unobtrusive. Vodka.

"*L'chaim!*" Grace said. "To life! I love that toast."

Cutter looked at her quizzically.

"What's the matter? Didn't I pronounce it right?"

"Just right, perfect, Grace." Cutter raised his glass, "L'chaim."

CHAPTER 13

Cutter took a tentative sip of his drink. He thought the ice would have melted somewhat, but the vodka was full strength and syrupy.

"I keep it in the freezer," Grace said.

He'd read that alcoholics did that. He nodded, resolved not to drink but half, and then not until after the ice had melted. Maybe not even half.

"Is there anything you can't—or don't want to eat?"

"No ham or shellfish," he said after a moment's consideration.

"So, the scallops wrapped with bacon and broiled are off the menu? Just kidding." She laughed. "You can come into the kitchen and keep me company—if you don't mind taking your chances on one of my three stools."

"I'll live dangerously," he said, but when he got to the kitchen, he changed his mind. "Can I give you a hand?"

"Another time, Ely, when you know where things are. It'll be faster now if I do it myself.

"Dinner's mostly pre-fab anyway."

Grace moved from refrigerator to chopping board and back. She cut up an avocado, some scallions, a jalapeño pepper and put them into the blender with some cream and ice cubes. It made a dreadful racket. "Chilled soup, avocado, OK?"

"Sounds great," he said, half-expecting her to explain the nutrients in avocado.

"It's yummy, even if I made it myself," she said. And added, in a voice that seemed to him to have something of a dare about it, "There's not such an awful lot of cream in it.

"I think we'd better eat in the dining room. You don't look too eager to sit here."

"I feel like a big baby," Cutter said.

"Don't. It took me three days before I'd sit on one of those chairs, and it's my kitchen!"

Cutter agreed that the soup was probably going to be "yummy," but Lynne wouldn't let him cook with cream. He opened his mouth ready to say so and realized he couldn't.

"I hope you like cucumbers," she said.

"Yes, thanks," Cutter said, but then he found himself staring into a dish of cucumbers and onions. He was going to reek. He'd have trouble explaining the onions and even more trouble if his clothes smelled like Grace's perfume. He'd gone out of his way to tell Lynne that he wasn't going to see Grace. He'd seem like such a liar.

He'd have to keep his distance tonight if it wasn't already too late. He remembered with chagrin the hug she'd given him when he came into the kitchen.

He'd worry about that later.

"Is something wrong?"

"Not a bit," he said, lifting a spoon of the green soup to his mouth.

"Haven't you forgotten something?" Grace said.

"Many things," Cutter said, "But none that I can think of. If I could, then they wouldn't be forgotten, would they?" It was an old joke, one that he and Lynne and Ruth and Sam used with one another—and with increasing frequency.

"The blessing before food?"

Cutter shook his head. "Sorry," he said, "We—I don't usually say them." He didn't, anyway. Not all the time.

"Them?"

"Them." He hesitated, unsure of whether to say, "we have or "Jews have." He solved his quandary by a half-sentence: "Different blessings for different foods."

"What's the blessing for soup? Avocado soup?"

Cutter was embarrassed. "I don't know. I'm not that observant."

She looked puzzled, and he added "religious."

"I have a one-size fits all," she said. "Mind if I do it?"

"I can't say, 'Be my guest,' or I would," Cutter said, self-conscious about trying to be amusing. Maybe this was how people felt on dates. Awful! He was glad he was out of all that nonsense.

Grace held her hand out for him to take. It took a beat before he realized that her head was bowed, and her eyes closed. Grace, saying grace, he thought, of course.

"Lord," she said, "bless this food to our use and us to Your loving service…"

Cutter, who had not bowed his head or closed his eyes, saw her lips moving after she'd finished.

She didn't squeeze his hand, just let it go when she'd finished.

"Is that all?" he asked, knowing it wasn't.

"No," she said. She was blushing. "There's more, but I didn't want to say it aloud."

"Oh, I see," Cutter said. He was uncomfortable. He'd liked the first part just fine.

"So, it's not quite one size fits all," she said.

"You're religious?"

"Not conventionally," she made a moue that reminded him of a little girl. "Does that mean I shouldn't thank God for things I'm grateful for?"

Cutter shifted in his chair, uncomfortable again, unsure. It was a larger question than he could consider while spooning the soup to his mouth.

He wasn't surprised when she told him she hated cooking for herself, that it seemed like a waste of effort, and how happy she was that he was here, that she could cook for him, how she looked forward to doing that again, to cooking with him, which she thought would be "fun."

"But you made this cucumber salad for yourself," he protested, "and it's great." And filled with raw onions, he thought, tasting the thinly sliced cucumbers and onions in vinegar.

"I didn't say that I don't do it, just that I don't enjoy it."

Cutter felt helpless as he searched for an appropriate response. Everything he thought of saying was a terrible cliché. Widows and divorcées had this sense of loss in common. Why had Grace and her husband split? Why should it matter to him?

"Will you teach me, Ely?"

Now he was flustered. He hadn't the slightest idea what she was asking him to do. Lynne hated that. Once she'd said, "You think too much," and they'd both laughed. If he did confess to having gotten tangled up in his own thoughts, he'd risk another offer of a penny, and this time it would be hard to get out of telling her. What could he say? I was wondering why you'd gotten divorced? It was none of his business. And this way, he'd never have to answer Lynne's question. He could continue to say he didn't know.

He shook his head. "Don't get old, Grace. Don't get old." He was being disingenuous. She wasn't his age, but she was close to it. When he first met Grace, her slender body had misled him into thinking she was much younger.

"What choice do I have? You lead me to a grave decision, Ely," she said, smiling.

Her smile was without mirth. Ely shuddered: for a moment, instead of her face, he'd imagined a grinning skull.

"What's the matter?"

"No matter," he said, shaking his head. Maybe he did need to see a shrink. First God's face in the sky, and now this with Grace. "I'm fine. What was it you wanted me to teach you?"

"Tennis. I've always wanted to learn to play."

"Then you want to take lessons."

"I want you to teach me."

"You said you want to learn to play? Learn from someone who knows how to teach it, who knows the right way. If I try to teach you, you'll learn all my bad habits."

"All of them? Or just those on the courts? What are your bad habits, Ely?"

She was flirting again. "I'll never tell." He stopped himself from saying, "You'll have to make those discoveries for yourself." He had no right to say anything like that.

"Then I'll just have to find out for myself, won't I? Isn't that what you were thinking?"

"You're quite a woman," he murmured.

"I'll take that as a compliment," she said. "Thank you."

She looked stricken.

"Why, Grace, what's wrong?"

"Everything's wrong. You belong here, Ely—or in whatever place we find. And I'll always only have half—sometimes the larger half, sometimes the smaller—I know, half is half—but you know I'm right."

"You have all of me now, don't you?" Cutter was appalled at what he'd said, but he couldn't take it back.

"If your way is right, then later when you've left to go back to Lynne, when you've gone home, what will I have then? Nothing…not any part of you."

"That's the way it is, Grace. That's the way it would have to be." He'd gone too far.

"All right, then. If those are your terms…" she said.

What was she saying? If those are your terms, this is it? Over, *fini*, before they even got started? Cutter found himself at a loss. How could this be? Grace was "breaking up with him," he thought, amazed that he saw it like this. He was a married man. He didn't see how she could break up with him when they'd never slept together, and yet that was what had happened. She was leaving him, calling it quits, and he was dazed and bereft.

Grace looked miserable, but she wasn't crying. "I guess I don't have much to choose from. But I'd rather have all of you part of the time, than never have you at all."

She took a deep breath. "Okay, then, that's the way it will be."

"No," she said, with a half-smile, "That's the way it is."

He'd gotten it all backwards—or she'd done an immediate turnabout.

She was out of her chair and standing by his side, holding her hand out to him. "I don't want to waste my time with you—our time together."

Cutter took her hand and stood up. "I don't want to be unfair to you." He was going to have to find a graceful way to leave now that he was on his feet. She shook her head. "You're not unfair. Besides, I know what I'm doing." She put her arms around his waist and laid her head on his chest. "I can hear your heart," she said. "It's strong and fast."

His arms fell limp at his side, but she made no move to let him go. He sighed and folded his arms around her.

"That's much better, isn't it?" she said.

Cutter didn't answer with words, but he stroked her hair. It was so soft; he was used to Lynne's hair and Eleanor's. They both used spray or gel.

"I'm so nervous," she said, "Isn't that silly?"

He wouldn't have used "silly" to describe how he felt: he was disconcerted by how fragile and vulnerable she was when he held her in his arms. Even when she was not crying.

She was too short for him to rest his chin on her head. He found himself staring at their image in a mirror over the sideboard in the dining room. Grace's head was turned away from the mirror, which removed one possible source of self-consciousness. He would have welcomed her saying that they looked cute. The tumult he was experiencing wasn't cute.

"I have to leave, Grace."

"Now?"

She didn't pull away to ask her question, and Cutter wasn't sure if she'd asked "How?" or "Now?" He didn't want to ask her to clarify, so he searched for a phrase that would suit both, and he settled for repeating his comment, "I have to leave."

"You mean you want to leave," she said.

"Yes," he said after some deliberation, what seemed to him a too-long silence, "I suppose I do."

When he got home Lynne's car wasn't in the drive and the house was dark and quiet. She hadn't said she was going out. Well, he thought, why not? After all, I said I'd be working late. She probably didn't expect him to be home for hours.

Good. I'll have time to shower and change my clothes, he told himself.

He was getting too old for shenanigans, although if he could relegate what he'd done—what he was doing—with Grace to shenanigans, he'd be fine. Shenanigans. He said the word aloud. It seemed to echo in the white-tiled bathroom he shared with Lynne.

He thought, as he lathered himself, that it was too bad that Grace had lost the house with the amazing bathroom. She was right. The house was her. Maybe if he asked her to stop wearing that perfume, she would. He washed his hair, wishing it wasn't gray and thinning.

While he toweled himself dry, he examined his body in the mirror: the hint of a paunch, his arms going somewhat slack. He sucked in his belly. Not too bad. What did Grace see when she looked at him? Was it different than what Lynne saw—or, for that matter, Eleanor?

He picked up his shirt and underwear from the bed to drop it in the laundry basket. Did it smell like Grace? Not that he could do anything about it. He held his shirt up to his face. It did!

Roses. Maybe gardenias. Heady stuff. A bit too much, but that was Grace.

He was inhaling her scent, when Lynne's voice sliced into his reverie about Grace, "Does it pass the sniff test?" She sounded amused. "Really, Ely, just toss it into the laundry. You don't have to wait until it's rank."

He was relieved that she sounded amused rather than curious.

"Sure. Of course," he said.

Lynne stretched out on their bed. That's not like her, he thought. "Are you all right?"

"If you keep frowning like that, you'll get lines," she said. "And then you'll always look worried or cranky. And then no one will buy houses from you, and then you'll really be worried and cranky."

He sat on the bed next to Lynne. He reached out to brush the hair from her face with his fingertips. She flinched when his hand was about to touch her face, and he left the hair on her face. Were those tears?

"Do you want to know where I was?" she asked.

He smiled. "If you want to tell me. It sounds like you do."

She nodded. "I was running an errand. For you."

"For me?" He was puzzled. He couldn't think of anything that had needed to be done that would have required an errand.

"Where's your cell phone, Ely?"

"In my jacket, I guess."

"Call it." She sat up, lifted the phone from the bedside table, and handed it to him.

It wasn't like Lynne to play games like this. Had he left his phone at Grace's? If he had, had Grace answered a call from Lynne? Was Grace that foolhardy?

He didn't like this game. He could tell from Lynne's face that in this round he was going to be a big loser.

He heard the phone ring in Lynne's pocketbook.

"Thanks, Lynne," he said, trying to sound casual. "Where was it? Obviously, I hadn't missed it yet."

"You're usually so careful. You don't lose track of it— sometimes I think it's attached to you by a steel cable. But today..." Her voice trailed off.

While Cutter searched her face for a hint of what bad news was coming, he tried to mask his own discomfort.

"So, you went to pick it up for me?" Even to him his voice dripped with false cheer and heartiness.

"Well, I couldn't call you to tell you to get it," she said. "And I know you need the phone. You didn't miss it?"

"No," he said, glad he could talk about something safe, something about which he could tell the truth. "I didn't."

"You didn't think it was odd that you weren't getting any calls?"

"I didn't notice." Was this getting to dangerous territory? When had he last used his cell phone?

"Your phone rings all the time."

This was an issue. Now that he had a cell phone, he was getting calls often. "I didn't know it bothered you."

"They're business calls."

Why was she emphasizing business so much? Had he left the phone at Grace's? He kept returning to the worst possibility.

"I never minded those. I get to see you as much as any woman sees her husband—although it's true we miss a lot of weekend time." She seemed to be drifting off, lost in her own thoughts.

"Why the mystery?" A good offense is a good defense, or something along those lines. He must be upset if he can't even remember a bromide. His memory wasn't that bad.

"No mystery from my end. Not at all. Jenna called to say that it was on your desk. She called here because she was under the impression—you'd given her the impression—that you were on your way home. You'd left, and she was passing your office when your phone rang. She thought you were home, would have been home awhile.

"You get the idea."

Lynne's voice grew stronger as she talked.

"So, I waited for you for a while, and then I drove over to your office to pick up the phone. Marvelous invention, the cell phone."

"Better than sliced bread," Cutter said, knowing more was coming.

"In some ways I have to admire you, Ely, sitting there so cool, in nothing but your bath towel."

"Shall I get dressed? That's what I was going to…"

"What you were doing when I came in? No, what you were doing was smelling your clothes to see if they smelled of that woman. Really, Ely. You must think I'm both blind and stupid."

"Neither, Lynne," he said in a soft voice. He did not ask who she meant when she said, "that woman." Or why his clothes might have smelled like her.

"Are you going to make me ask you? Or are you going to be decent about this part at least?"

"I don't know what you want," he said. He was miserable, and she was too angry now to be unhappy.

"All right, then, I'll have to ask: Where were you, Ely?"

He took a deep breath. She was watching him, and the longer he took to answer her, the less she would believe. He'd have to tell her the truth now: or the part of it that he thought she could stomach.

"I went to Grace's house to talk to her about the house that she wanted—the one that somebody else snapped up?"

Lynne nodded, but that was all.

"She was about to have dinner, and she asked if I'd have something to eat as long as dinner was on the table."

"Dinner was already on the table? She eats early."

"Figuratively speaking on the table."

"Very eloquent, Ely. Is it a metaphor or a simile?"

"What?"

"You said, figuratively speaking. Never mind."

"And that's all. Dinner, pure and simple. She served cucumber salad with onions. Would I have eaten onions if I'd wanted to hide this from you?" He congratulated himself for turning the onions, which had worried him, to his advantage.

"That would depend on whether you thought you could get

away with it. For all I know, maybe you'd planned to say you had a hamburger with onions."

"I planned nothing of the sort. She was upset about the house, 'losing the house' as she puts it."

"And you had to comfort her?"

"Reassure. It's my job to reassure. To keep the client in a comfort zone. What would you expect me to do?"

"This isn't a good time to ask that question. My expectations right now are low, Ely, very, very low."

"Aside from the soup, you'd approve of the dinner: cucumbers, onions, salmon. The soup was avocado—with cream. Quite good, but too rich, actually. I didn't eat the whole bowl of it." Maybe he could distract her.

"Do you want a gold star for your virtue? You'll have to try harder.

"What wine did she serve?"

"No wine. A cocktail. But I didn't drink mine. A sip to be sociable, non-judgmental. She might be, I think, a shikker."

"And this is supposed to make me feel better?"

"I'd like you to feel better, but it's not supposed to make you feel better. It's just the truth. That's all."

"The whole truth?"

"There's nothing more that I can tell you." That was true, he couldn't tell her more, though he certainly had more to tell.

"Can or want to?"

There it was again, can or want, twice in one evening. "There's nothing. Wait. It was whipping cream. There, that's it," he said, holding his empty palms up in front of him in a gesture of surrender.

"You're telling me there was no…"

Cutter watched Lynne flounder as she looked for the right word. He would have helped her, but he didn't want to give her the opportunity of later accusing him of limiting her question to deceive her.

"…hanky-panky."

"That's what I'm saying."

"Can I believe you?"

"I'm hoping you can. We'd both be happier."

"Okay, then," she said.

He waited far too long for her next sentence. "Do I owe you an apology?"

Not at all," Cutter said, shaking his head, and then nodding. "I should have phoned you to tell you what was going on. I didn't give it enough weight. So it's my fault." He had given it enough weight, but he was convinced he was right. They'd both be happier if she believed him. It was a win-win situation he told himself.

While he was dressing, he wondered what fell into the category of "hanky-panky." Would kisses count? He had a nagging, sick feeling that anything he wouldn't want Lynne to see would be hanky-panky. In that case, he'd been deceitful in answering her most significant question.

He replayed their kiss at the front door, which was, technically, a series of kisses. The first of them, the first several, had been tentative. He searched for a description: they were like picking up leaves that were floating in the middle of a fishpond, leaning over, being careful not to fall in. He chuckled at his efforts, which he took as proof he couldn't become a writer.

He couldn't find other words to describe them. Grace, she seemed so pliant, so without resistance to his embrace, that it was as though she had no bones at all. He could have done anything with her, and not needed further permission.

At the time, he'd marveled at his rising passion and her response. Even Eleanor had not yielded like Grace. Strange, Grace was so…aggressive…and yet, like this, so tender. He couldn't remember the last time he'd kissed Lynne like that. And that was how he lost his place, so to speak, with Grace.

Grace pulled away from him. "What is it?"

"Nothing. Why?"

"Ely, don't tell me it's nothing. Where did you go? First you were with me, really with me, and then, poof! —you weren't."

"I'm sorry, Grace," he said. He was sorry, too.

"What about? Drifting away from me, or the reason you drifted?"

"A little of both," he said. "I'm out of practice. This isn't something I'm used to." He was being ambiguous. If he were lucky, she wouldn't ask him what he meant by "this." After all, he couldn't very well tell her that he was out of practice in having an affair. It wasn't a matter of practice, was it? From his experience with Eleanor, he'd learned that the first few times with her were more grating to his conscience than those that followed. And by the end, it was less his conscience troubling him than the increasing inconvenience of trying to keep the two women happy. Keeping two women happy was impossible. For him. Other men seemed to manage.

He wasn't eager to suggest that Lynne and he didn't have a good sexual relationship, but that was the impression that he would leave. It was the lesser of two evils, and he'd be faced with that choice, or its reverse, whenever he had to choose between pleasing Lynne or Grace. "It's my problem," he said, "not yours."

Grace raised a single eyebrow. "I find that difficult to believe."

Cutter smiled and said, "Frankly, Grace, so do I."

Grace laughed. "I'm glad to hear that. It gives me some hope that you're an honest man."

"An honest man in this situation? No wonder you find it difficult to believe me."

"Promise you won't lie to me. Ever."

"I'll try not to," he answered. "Whatever it's worth, I give you my word."

"I'll make an honest man of you," Grace said, laughing. "Or die trying."

"I hope you won't have to go as far as that," Ely said. He took her in his arms again, and, catching sight of the two of them in the hallway mirror, he was surprised again at how old he looked, how worried.

utter's strong point had never been returning Sam's overhand, but, on the whole, he felt he'd given as good as he'd got. Besides, if Sam won one week, he'd have his chance another.

"Someone's waving," Sam said.

"Who?" Cutter said, glancing in the general direction towards which Sam had nodded. At the far edge of the courts, in the shade of the old oaks, a woman in tennis whites stood waving, her arm making a large arc.

"She's on a mission," Sam said.

Cutter shrugged but looked again.

"It looks like she thinks she knows at least one of us," Sam said. "Though at this distance, I'm not sure how she can tell." He looked over his shoulder, "Nope. Nobody else in this direction."

Cutter held his hand up and shaded his eyes. The woman in tennis whites waved again. Cutter waved back. "I don't know," he said in a soft voice, as he turned towards Sam. "I might know her. So many people over the years. A small town. I keep meeting people I've sold houses to."

"Ely!" she called. She was off the bench and walking towards them now.

Grace. Of course, he should have known her, even from the distance. Now it would seem to Sam that he'd been prevaricating. Cutter was puzzled.

She was beaming and continued waving as she walked from the benches. "Ely!" she called again. She held a racket in a cover tucked under her arm. "What a surprise!"

She has hair in her eyes. Cutter stopped himself from reaching over just before Grace pushed the damp hair from her forehead. It would be a gesture like that, a casual touch that would announce his relationship with Grace to the world. No, the world wouldn't care. To Sam. He'd notice, and he'd care.

"I thought you didn't know how to play tennis," Cutter said. He made the briefest of introductions. Together they walked back to the benches in the shade, headed towards the parking lot. After an hour on the court, Cutter welcomed the shade, and he was sure Sam did, too.

Grace leaned her racket against the bench.

"I've always wanted to learn," Grace said. "Why not now?"

"Sure," Sam said. "Why not?"

Sam sat on the bench while Cutter and Grace remained standing. Sam rested the tip of his racket on the ground and spun it as if it were a top. That was uncharacteristic of him. Maybe it was related to his having called Grace a firecracker.

Grace was asking something about lessons and the bulletin board, and Sam wasn't buying in to this conversation.

Cutter explained that he didn't know anything about the local tennis coaches, but she would be able to find one. He pointed out a lesson on one of the courts and suggested that she talk to the woman being taught. Or she might be able to decide by watching.

"How can you tell? What should I watch for?" Grace asked.

Cutter laughed. It was a conundrum. How would you tell the difference between the results of a good teacher and an apt pupil? "Anything would be better than nothing, Grace."

"You're not available?"

He glanced at Sam, who seemed to be studying his racket. "Not today, not at all, really." He stopped short of saying that it wouldn't be a good idea. No, he wasn't about to wrap himself around her on these courts.

She made that moue again. Something new and unattractive. With luck, Sam hadn't noticed. No matter, it was better than her bursting into tears.

Grace placed her hands on her hips and faced Sam. "Your friend Ely helped me find the perfect house," she said.

"Oh?" Sam said. "Congratulations!"

"He's a wonder; amazing, incredibly helpful," she said, smiling.

Her tone of voice, Ely thought, was like one she might have used talking about Mother Teresa. He wished she wouldn't.

"But no congratulations. The house got snatched up by somebody else."

"You'll find something," Sam said.

"I'm relying on Ely."

"Yes," Sam said. "You can do that. He's as reliable as they come."

"I know," Grace said.

To Cutter's dismay, she slipped her arm through his and patted his bicep with her free hand, looking up at him with an adoring smile.

To disengage himself, Cutter rested his hand on hers, gave a quick gentle squeeze, and stepped back, trying to be casual, conscious of Sam's appraising gaze, "I'll do my best not to let you down, Grace."

"All right, then, Ely. I'll check the boards—find a great teacher and challenge you to a game. Nice seeing you, Sam," Grace said. She rested her tennis racket on her shoulder as a young boy holds a wooden musket, nodded to both and walked away, leaving Cutter and Sam an awkward duo.

Cutter looked at Sam, questioning.

"Not here," Sam said.

In the car, Cutter turned the air conditioner to the coolest it would go.

"Nu?" Cutter said, "So?" Sam, usually relaxed, was looking out the window.

"It was a long time ago, my friend."

Cutter didn't have to ask him what.

"Ruth knows. I wasn't able to hide it."

"Lynne never said…"

"Ruth didn't tell her—as strange as that seems." Sam turned towards Cutter. "In case you're wondering, before Eleanor."

Cutter was wondering. "Good," he said. As though it might be catching.

"The firecracker?"

"I shouldn't have said that. It was unkind. Indiscreet and unkind. Ruth gave it to me when we got home. She said, heaven help me, that I wasn't being a gentleman."

"No kidding?"

"It—I—raked up the whole thing all over again."

"I had no idea," Cutter said. He found it difficult to drive, thinking about Sam and Grace.

"You weren't supposed to."

"And now? Why are you telling me now?"

"What should I have done? The firecracker remark I could blame on Joanne. I would have, too, if you'd asked."

"Right," Cutter said. He felt grim. "But I didn't."

"No, and I hoped you wouldn't. It would have started up the same old series of lies all over again. I suppose it was the 'nice seeing you'?"

"That and the rest."

"I was that transparent?"

Cutter smiled without mirth. "Just the rest, all of it."

"Are you okay with it?"

"You're asking my permission for something that's done and over." Cutter paused. "Done and over, right?"

"I told you. Before Eleanor."

"Is that how we're marking things now? Before Eleanor. After Eleanor."

"In this context I thought you wouldn't mind."

"You thought right."

Neither man spoke, and after a full minute of silence, Cutter said, "You know, I felt like you were judging me, back then. And I was afraid you'd be judging me again. With Grace. That's funny, isn't it? But the joke was on me."

"I didn't intend it to be like that."

"No. It wouldn't be something you planned."

"Hardly. She's something though."

"I suppose," Cutter said, wary.

"She told you, I suppose," Sam said.

"What, about you? You know she didn't."

"No, no. She wouldn't do that. About her son."

Cutter searched his memory for whatever Grace might have said about children. Nothing. Wait, some passing remark about their absence.

"There was a falling out between him and his father, something about a girl. One of those things you read about where both the father and the son are doing the same woman," Sam said.

"Tabloid, movies. Not real life."

"That's what I thought, but Grace was torn up about it."

"Revenge?"

"I don't like to think of it like that."

"Who would? Nobody likes to be used."

"It happens all the time," Sam said in an even tone. "The transitional man?"

It's a warning. Sam had turned his attention to the side window as though the familiar streets had become spectacularly fascinating.

Maybe Sam could be right. He could be just that, transitional. Of course, he was. What else could he be to Grace? One way or another, their relationship would end, would have to. Or his marriage would, and Lynne knew him as well as he knew himself, maybe better. They'd shared everything, good and bad since they were kids. Without her? But for Grace, the timing was convenient for Grace.

"Not consciously," Sam said. "I don't think she's using you like that. She's not that sort."

"What sort is she then?" He was walking along the edge of a precipice in this conversation, he told himself: this friendship, his marriage, and his self-image. Following this line, he was endangering all three.

In some ways he felt protective of Grace, and Sam did, too. But he wanted the advantage that Sam would—or could—give him.

"Grace is what she seems," Sam said, and held his hands out palms up. "Just that. What you see is what you get."

"What I see keeps changing," Cutter said. He felt like a whiner.

Sam turned to him with a smile, "Then you'll have to keep looking, or look in another direction. The ball's in your court." He paused, but before Cutter could reply, added, "For now."

"So, how's Sam?" Lynne asked, looking up from the tomatoes she was slicing.

Cutter laughed. "He plays a good game."

"So do you. I can't keep up with you on the court," she said. "I've given up trying."

"It's exercise," he said with a shrug, "and more fun than a treadmill."

"I worry about you out there in this heat, especially now."

"Why now? I'm in fine shape. Great numbers at my last check up." He gestured at the cutting board. "We eat right."

Lynne pointed at the sky.

Was she saying God had it in for him? That's not her style.

"The face," she said. "What you saw."

"Nice," Cutter said. "I'm glad you know I didn't imagine it."

Lynne frowned. "I don't know that at all. I meant that you're seeing things, so I worry about you."

"Once. I saw it once. That's all. You make it sound as though it's an everyday occurrence."

"You haven't given up on it."

"I know what I saw, Lynne."

"That's why I worry, Ely."

Cutter opened the freezer and dropped some ice cubes into a glass. "I'm getting some ice water. Do you want any?"

"You and Sam didn't go out for lunch?"

Cutter murmured the blessing for water and drank. "Next time. He had things to do. And so do I. We ran into Grace."

"I don't follow the logic of that series."

"It's not a straight line. Each item's discrete," he said. That was a poor choice of words, a Freudian slip.

"What's she doing these days?"

Cutter shifted the meaning of his wife's question. "I don't have anything for her. When I do, I'll set something up. She told Sam she'd found the 'perfect' house and somebody else got it."

"Why on earth would she tell Sam, a stranger, about that? She's not very appropriate, is she?"

Cutter couldn't explain that Sam wasn't a stranger, that she had every reason to tell him about the house and about more than that. Instead, he said, "Sam was with me. I think it was her way of making conversation, to say something nice."

"So, how was that nice?"

"That I found the perfect house for her."

"I thought she said she found it."

"She did—effectively, if I found it, she found it."

Lynne tilted her head and asked, "So, how does she play tennis wearing all those noisy bangles?"

Deciding to ignore the sarcasm, he answered, "Beats me. I

didn't notice if she was wearing them." He grinned and added, "They make a racket, but she couldn't play tennis with it."

"You're in fine form, Ely. But even with all your jokes I don't trust her."

He wanted to say, "You don't have to trust her. You just have to trust me." He didn't dare remind her. In fact, she didn't trust him. Why should she? He barely trusted himself.

"What do you say about inviting Ruth and Sam for supper tomorrow? Barbecue?" Lynne asked.

That sounded like a terrible idea to Cutter. He wanted some time to come to terms with the news Sam had given him. Until he'd managed that, Ruth was one person he didn't want to see. That must be how people had felt about Lynne. He'd never know how many invitations Lynne didn't get because of him. He hadn't had any idea of all the ways Lynne could be hurt. Now he did—or anyway he was learning—but if he continued in the direction he was headed, he'd be doing it all over again. And this time he wouldn't have the excuse of ignorance.

"Why not?" he said. This was his problem. He wasn't going to make it Lynne's. Not if he could help it.

All through dinner Cutter alternated between being self-conscious and curious. He kept losing track of the conversation, because he was stuck on something Sam or Ruth had said. When the conversation moved forward, he hadn't moved with it.

He was startled when Ruth said that she and Lynne "were in the same club." Had she decided to announce Sam's affair at the dinner table? Cutter glanced over at Sam, who showed no emotion at Ruth's statement, and Lynne was laughing. They must have discussed this before, but she wouldn't be laughing like that if it had to do with affairs.

"Aren't you going to ask what club?" Ruth said.

Cutter struggled to produce what he hoped would be perceived as a self-deprecating smile. "I was wondering whether it would involve weekly meetings that would result in Sam and me cooking dinner?"

"Close," Lynne said, "We're both going to try yoga."

Sam said, "I've been reassured that we'll still have red meat from time to time. This doesn't mean a switch to nuts and berries—not that there's anything wrong with that."

"In the fall," Ruth said.

"After the holidays," Lynne said.

"We've signed up for the beginning class. For seniors, can you believe?"

"Seniors! Anyone over fifty-two is a senior, now."

"Maybe they'll go easy on us in the beginning," Ruth mused.

"It's just for women," Lynne said.

"Is that legal?" Cutter asked.

"I'm not sure, but that's what they've advertised. Why? Do you want to come?"

"You sound scandalized," Cutter said. "Is it the thought of me in tights?"

"I'm pretty sure you wouldn't have to wear tights, that is, if you really wanted to go."

"At the Y," Sam said. "Twice a week, six weeks."

"It will keep us flexible," Lynne said.

"I'm sure it can't hurt," Cutter said. "Why not?" Beginner's yoga. Good. Grace wouldn't be in a starter class, so they won't be running into her on a regular basis. Wouldn't that be something, all three of them in the same room. Grace would be the only one who wouldn't give a damn, not judging by the way she phoned Lynne to talk about my fall! Lynne wouldn't be so nonchalant. And Ruth? Ruth is fine with Grace. Now.

"That Grace does yoga, doesn't she?" Ruth asked.

Cutter was startled. Had she been reading his mind? And who was she asking, anyway? Him or Sam? And what for? He looked over at Sam who seemed to be oblivious to the question. Or perhaps not. In spite of his having once called Grace a firecracker, he looked as though he had no knowledge of her at all. That's the ticket, Sam, Cutter thought, blend into the wallpaper on this one.

Should he lie? Was it worth lying about this?

"She said something about it once. No details."

"It was Yoga or Pilates," Lynne said.

Cutter caught Lynne's switching topics. She didn't believe him.

"Pilates. Not long ago I didn't know how to pronounce it, and now it's everywhere," Ruth said.

"It's like anything else," Cutter said. "I never thought I'd be eating tofu. In soup, maybe."

Or that Sam would have been *shtupping* Grace. What a word. Didn't Sam and Ruth have a perfect marriage—as perfect as any, that is? Sam was his best friend. If he'd known, he wouldn't have gotten into this fix. It would've seemed wrong.

Regardless of Sam, this was wrong.

"I'm sure it will be good for us," Lynne said. "What do you think, Ely?"

He hoped she was still talking about the Yoga. "I'm sure it will," he said.

"So, you don't mind?"

That was tricky. "No," he said, "it's fine."

When Sam and Ruth left, Cutter thought that Sam rested his hand on him just a moment too long, that his thank you was a bit too earnest. Cutter wanted to say, "It's all right," and he imagined that Sam wanted to say that and more.

But it wasn't the time, so, instead, he pecked Ruth on the cheek then put his arm around Lynne who seemed to be both surprised and happy at his affection. No sooner had Cutter allowed himself to relax, than Lynne stiffened and pulled away from him.

"What's wrong?" he asked. For once, he said to himself, he didn't know the answer when he asked that question.

"It's Grace, isn't it?" Lynne asked.

"Grace?" Cutter was puzzled. Of course, she might be upset about Grace, but he'd tried to assuage her concern. What now?

"You and Sam, all night the two of you were acting…," she paused.

Cutter kept himself from jumping in to supply the word she was searching for. He was uncomfortable with what came to mind: "suspicious."

"Like you had a secret."

She never finished that sentence, but instead she said, "You told me that you ran into Grace yesterday."

Cutter waited.

"He knows you so well."

"He's a good friend."

"He knows, doesn't he? He saw you and Grace, and he knows. That's why the two of you were acting like that all evening. Cagey. Too clever by half."

Cutter was stumped. He couldn't tell her the truth. If Ruth had told Lynne, well, she would have. And that would have been that, but it would be wrong to violate Sam's confidence.

So, here he was, caught. He hated secrets. He'd do his best to keep Sam safe without hanging himself. "There's not much to know, Lynne. He was here the night I was late to dinner, and he heard Grace asking me to teach her tennis."

"And you said?"

"I told her to look on the bulletin boards. That's where she could find a teacher."

"That doesn't sound right, Ely."

Cutter shrugged. "That's all that happened."

"You mean it's all you can tell me about."

"I don't know what else to say, Lynne." That was true. He didn't know what else he could say without betraying Sam. Looking back, he realized that when Grace had taken his arm, she'd been pushing Sam's buttons. And, as their affair preceded Eleanor, Grace would have been married at the time. All that post-divorce wounded innocence and virtue didn't seem like an act, even in light of what he'd learned about her relationship with Sam.

"Something about this doesn't fit, but I can't put my finger on it," Lynne said.

"It's not worth trying, I promise you. You don't have to worry about Grace."

"I wouldn't have to worry about Grace if I didn't have to worry about you."

"Don't, Lynne." Cutter himself wasn't sure if he meant that she should be quiet or that she needn't worry about him. But he was relieved when she sighed and said she was tired of arguing and just plain tired, that she wanted to take a long cool shower and go to bed.

CHAPTER 15

Cutter walked into the kitchen grinning. He dropped a plastic bag on the kitchen counter and announced "Dinner." Then he waited for Lynne's response.

"Is it a secret?"

Cutter emptied most of the bag. He'd taken care to remove the roots from the leaves and to wash off all the earth. He thought of it as earth, not dirt. Dirt is on weeds. Earth is on vegetables. "Not a secret, but maybe a surprise."

Lynne wrinkled her nose. "Weeds!"

"They're good as spinach," Cutter said. "Maybe better. Sam doesn't put pesticides on his lawn. These will be just fine." He paused, waiting to see whether Lynne had anything more to say. When she didn't, he said, "Chickweed, plantain. Chicory. Kept the chicory separate. You put the roots in coffee."

"I like the coffee just fine the way it is. I want the coffee plain, Ely. Don't get any ideas about the coffee. Please."

He was surprised at the vehemence of her protest. "You won't have to drink any, Lynne. I thought it would be fun to try it." Cutter reached into the bag and pulled out a clear plastic container with blue flowers. "I thought you'd like these anyway."

"For goodness' sake, Ely. What am I going to do with those?"

"Chicory flowers. We're going to put them in ricotta cheese. I got the reduced fat kind. I thought you'd rather..."

"I'd rather you were normal again. That's what I'd rather."

"Things are what they are. I am who I am."

"I'm not sure who you are, anymore, Ely."

Ely let the cold water run for a bit, and then he filled a glass. "Want some?"

"No, no. What I want. . ."

"I know, Sweetheart," Cutter said, "In lots of ways it was easier before."

"Well, that's good," she said, "That's a good start, anyway."

"Easier isn't always better." He paused and murmured the blessing for water, then drank. He'd begun with that and had kept it up. "Nothing easier than instant mashed potatoes, for example."

"We're not talking about mashed potatoes—or I wasn't. I was talking about—"

"—our life together?" Cutter had heard exasperation and pain, not anger in her voice.

"Yes, and..."

"That's all there is, Lynne." Cutter rested his hands on Lynne's shoulders. He lifted her chin with his right hand so that he could look her in the eye. "That's all there is."

She pulled away from him. "It's not going to work."

Cutter felt himself panic. Was she leaving him? Now? What for? She hadn't left before, and all that had been far worse. "Of course it will," he said. "We can make it work. I'll try harder. I promise." He made a sweeping gesture towards the counter. "We can forget about all this."

"It won't work," she repeated. "You can't sweet talk me into forgetting about it.

"Everything's upside down," she said. "Weeds on the kitchen counter. They're a symptom."

Cutter kept silent. Silence had its uses, and he'd already finished one of Lynne's sentences, to no good end. At least now he knew what she said wouldn't work, and it wasn't as bad as he'd feared. He wouldn't try more honey.

"Ever since you had that vision, it's been all mixed-up," Lynne said. "On the one hand, you're praying all the time, and, on the other, I have Grace to contend with."

Lynne was being melodramatic. He was hardly praying all the time. Not at all if he looked at what he might be doing. Besides, in actuality she'd had to contend with Grace just that once when she'd called the house. But if she was worried that he was getting involved with Grace, which she was, then she was being less melodramatic than understated. He kept quiet because he had nothing to say. Cutter had abandoned strategy.

"Aren't you even going to deny it?"

"I can't deny that Grace upset you. I'm sorry for that, Lynne." Sorry, but not repentant.

"What does she have that I don't?"

"It's not what she has, Lynne, it's what she doesn't have." Cutter thought about the list: thirty-seven years of marriage with me; a dead child; sagging flesh; graying hair kept unnaturally bright; nails painted radioactive pink; and, most important, a righteous sense of grievance directed at me.

"What's so important that she doesn't have then?"

"It's simple, Lynne. And it's why I keep seeing her and calling her."

"You look so smug," she said.

Cutter had to admit to himself that her accusation was on target: he did, indeed, feel smug. "She doesn't have," and here he paused. The grimace of pain on Lynne's face jarred him out of his sense of self-satisfaction. He hated feeling cruel.

"What she doesn't have that you do is a house. One that she wants, anyway." He went on, piling up the details. Making it real or trying to. He wanted Lynne to believe him, not to make it easier for himself, but to make it less painful for her.

"She has one she's trying to sell, and there's the house she's looking for. And that's why I call her, why she calls me, and why, tomorrow, I'll have to spend three hours with her opening and closing drawers in kitchens and checking out closets in hallways and bedrooms."

What already had happened with Grace couldn't be changed, and what would happen with Grace, that he didn't know. But he wanted to leave Lynne out of all of it.

Lynne looked skeptical. "Is that all? Is that the whole truth?"

Cutter reviewed his real list of what Lynne had that Grace lacked, no part of which he could tell her, or anyone: not Sam, not Grace, not even Eleanor. He was in enough trouble without adding Eleanor to the mix even in his thoughts. And then he had an idea. It was perfect. Inspired. He beamed with a smile so delighted—though, in fact, it was joy at his finding a clever way out—that he was sure his smile would allow him to get away with his deception. "What you have, and Grace doesn't, Lynne, isn't just this house, it's me."

He recognized that his logic was imperfect, but he'd found the required palliative.

He knew he'd succeeded because Lynne returned his smile, then held up a long limp strand of chickweed and said, "Well, Maestro, what do we do with this?"

The rest was easy.

"It's not what you think, Ely," Grace said as a greeting.

Cutter wondered what had happened to "hello." He longed for the small comforts convention could provide. Surely, he hadn't forfeited his right to a little comfort: He thought not, but here he was anyway, with Grace in her gold bangle bracelets. She was wearing another black tank top. Perhaps yoga would fix Lynne's saggy arms.

"I'm sure it isn't what I think," he said. "I've learned that almost nothing is what I thought it was. It's one of the penances—or pleasures—of age, owning up to your failure to understand."

"Don't change the topic. You know what I mean. He told you, right?"

Cutter felt caught again, not knowing how much he was supposed to know. Grace would never believe that Sam had told him nothing.

"I know you weren't strangers," he said with a shrug. Noting to himself that neither one of them felt it necessary to use Sam's name.

"Good," she said. "And what else?"

"Let's not play games," Cutter said, purposely including himself. "What do you want to know?"

He studied Grace to see if she looked like she was about to burst into tears. Not a hint of it. She looked tired, but not puffy.

"Sam's okay," Grace said.

Cutter found himself irritated. He didn't need Grace to grant approval of his best friend. But then he realized that wasn't what she meant. It was her way of saying she knew Sam had been what one used to call a gentleman. Cutter could let down his defenses. About this.

"At the least."

"That's not in question," she said. "But?"

"I think I'm the one who should be asking."

"I thought you didn't want to play games."

"Right."

"So, what is it now, a 'but'? or 'and'?" Grace asked.

"You don't play tennis, but I feel like I'm on the court with McEnroe."

"What?"

"Never mind. Can't you just tell me whatever it is you want me to know?" Cutter said. He was nearing the end of his patience.

"Don't you think I've done that?"

"Sure. I thought you were amazingly without pretense. Direct."

"That's past tense, Ely."

"You want to know what I know. I take it that means you have something specific in mind." He paused. He didn't want to say anything more direct. Make her tell him, then they could get on with business. Or whatever else.

"What do you mean by 'It's not what I think'? How do you know what I think, anyway?" he said.

"I thought you didn't want to play games."

"I was out of line, Grace. Apologies."

"Accepted. It's just that it was all so. . ."

Cutter wasn't going to complete her sentence. All the words he could think of were grotesque clichés.

"You're not going to help me out here?"

"I'm not finishing that thought for you, Grace. How can I?"

He searched her face for a clue. On some level he did want to help her, but, even more so, he wanted to hear what she had to say. He'd learn something he might be able to use. "I can't presume that I know where you're going with this."

He was almost certain that she was talking about the mess with her son and her husband.

"I had a minor role in a bad remake of a Greek tragedy."

"You want to tell me about it? Maybe it's better if I don't know."

She laughed. "No doubt. It would be better if I didn't know, either, but I do. And I think Sam probably said something, assuming I'd told you myself."

"So?" If she was talking about what Sam had said about her son and her husband, she had more than a minor role.

"When I say minor, I don't mean that I escaped. I didn't. I suffered plenty." She paused.

She was showing less self-pity now, telling this story, than she had when she heard she'd lost the house with the extravagant bathroom.

"But it was everyone's story," she said, "We were all victims."

"Innocent victims," Cutter said, hoping to prompt her into a revelation that would explain everything, especially her neediness, her wanting to force him into the role of protector and lover: a bedmate, a chopper of vegetables, and a painter of kitchens. She might say something that Sam hadn't told him, maybe even something that Sam himself hadn't been told.

It would be satisfying to be in possession of something Sam hadn't got. Cutter wasn't proud of feeling this, but it didn't diminish his desire for dominion, however proscribed by the circumstances of his relationship with Grace.

"Not one of us was innocent, not even me," she said. She laughed. "And I was The Wronged Wife, the one in the movie who wears the modest dress and sensible shoes. Though not unattractive."

"A modest dress in a Greek tragedy?"

"I said it was a bad remake."

Cutter wanted this part to be over. It was too late now for him to speak up, to tell her that he knew about her husband and son. She'd hate him, and he'd miss out on what might be the best of the story. If he had to, he'd trick her, force her to tell him.

Maybe it would be good for her to get it out. If she told him about it, maybe it would turn into a story for her. Just a story. Even now she was getting into it, and he began to wonder how many times she'd recited these descriptions. Maybe it already had become that for her, a story. Everybody had one; he'd heard dozens of them over the years, what with selling all those houses, or trying to.

He was rationalizing, and he knew it. He wanted to save face for not speaking up before, and he wanted to get something from Grace. It was all at her expense. He was doing this for himself, not protecting Sam from being seen as a betrayer of confidence, as a gossip no better than an old woman.

"You don't have to tell me any of this, you know," Cutter said.

"I don't have to do much of anything," she said, "But this is important. If you want to know who I am, you ought to know this."

Grace leaned towards him. He tried not to look into her cleavage. He forced himself to concentrate on what she was saying, amazed that Grace still unsettled him.

"Well, of course I want to know, Grace. But not everything. A sense of mystery..." Cutter didn't want to declare too much.

"Mystery? I'm offering to stand naked and you're handing me a fig leaf?"

Mystery, mastery. Cutter hadn't engineered anything. This is what Grace herself had wanted—she'd maneuvered him into this position. It was one thing for him to know the story, the skeletal facts, another for him to admit that he wants her to open the vault.

"Come on, Grace. You're not being fair. I'm trying to be considerate."

"I don't think so. I think you want to get everything and pay nothing."

"If I wanted everything, why wouldn't I want you to go on?"

"You want it for free." She paused, but when Cutter didn't add anything, she continued, "You pretend to not want to hear, and that way you can avoid all responsibility for what you might learn about me."

"Oh..." Nailed! Grace knew him better than he'd thought.

"Don't worry. You don't have to hold my hand, and if I cry, I won't ask for your handkerchief," she said.

Cutter refrained from asking if she'd started carrying her

own tissues. It would do him no good to be snide; she was a client, whatever else she might be. He raised both his hands in the classic gesture of surrender.

"Where should I start?" she asked.

This must be a rhetorical question. As far as Cutter was concerned, she'd started some time ago, when she brought in Greek tragedies.

"Pick it up wherever you're most comfortable."

"Then there's no good place to start. The short of it is that my husband, soon to be ex-husband after years of his indecision, not letting go, but not really staying—my husband and my son, our son, that is, were both seeing the same woman. More than seeing, actually."

"Complicated. Awful, of course, especially for you."

Grace waved her hand, "Awful for all of us. It comes of having a common last name. If it had been Stepanowicz, the triangle might not have happened. She had no way of knowing until, of course, she was brought home to meet Mommy and Daddy."

"He didn't call you that?" Cutter was taken aback by his own foolish irrelevant question. What was there that he didn't want to hear?

"Of course he didn't. Oh, when he was seven, but not then. I said it as a manner of speaking." She frowned, and Cutter felt chastised.

Cutter tried to imagine the introductions, but his imagination failed him. He had impressions of French farce, a maid in one of those ridiculous uniforms with high heels and a frilly white apron. Not tragedy, even a bad remake. But, of course, this was not his life.

"She came for dinner. Robert was late, working late. For months he'd been working late often. He'd phoned to tell us not to wait dinner. Everyone was agreeable. The sweet young thing appeared to be not at all offended. Robbie was smitten and cared for nothing as long as she seemed happy. And she was. I found her charming. She was fresh-faced and wholesome as a milkmaid, a milkmaid who'd been to good schools, mind you. We'd had a round of drinks. Two rounds, in fact, and had moved into the dining room.

Dinner was on the table—beef Wellington. I'd gone all out, to please Robbie, to show his young lady that this was an occasion. It was in the days when serving red meat was still considered festive, rather than homicidal. The beef had been served, as had the asparagus and glazed carrots. The cabernet glowed in three of the four glasses. Laughter tinkled and earnest discussion was swirling around the centerpiece of roses and freesia and baby's breath. The sweet young thing and Robbie glowed in the candlelight. I dare say I was glowing, too, and then, into this image of perfect hospitality, walks Robert, fully prepared with an apology and welcome, a welcome which he had rehearsed with me that very morning."

He'd been right. This wasn't the first time Grace had told this story. He had a difficult time reconciling what he was hearing with the blubbering woman in the bookstore.

"Did he ditch the speech?"

"Not at all, though he barely touched his wine. I thought he was going to make a toast with just the barest hint of a wedding, but, instead, he raised his glass, locked eyes with each of us in turn, and said '*Prost.*' I'd never heard him use that toast before—or since, for that matter.

"I must say, the conversation didn't lag, contrary to what you might have expected. Perhaps Robert's familiarity with the sweet young thing actually had facilitated conversation. But she whispered something to Robbie after dinner and not long afterwards they left. I assumed, well, young love…"

"It didn't strike her as odd that two men had the same name? Come on."

"Oh, Robbie always went by his middle name, Bruce. He hated the junior thing. I called him Robbie but nobody else did, not since he started high school. And every third girl her age is a Jennifer."

"Your husband said?"

"Nothing that night. Danced around, not answering straight when I asked what he thought of her. He talked about the dinner, the flowers, about me, about everything else. I knew something was wrong, but not what."

"I expected Robbie would call the next day, but he didn't, and he didn't answer my calls, not for a whole week. And then he was odd. Off."

Cutter tried not to snicker. Odd. Off. To find out the old man's been boffing your girl. He supposed the boy would be sounding odd.

"It was over, right?"

"Not exactly. Jennifer figured she had to make a choice, and she chose, well, not the married man. By the way, Robert hadn't told her he was married."

"She should have known, no home calls. The rest of it," Cutter said.

"She should have. Maybe she did, but she told Robbie she hadn't known."

"He believed her."

"Sometimes men believe what they want to believe, I suppose. Women certainly do," Grace said. Cutter listened for a trace of irony but heard none.

"But Robert wanted to keep seeing her. She told Robbie, and Robbie confronted him. I walked in on it. Robert's nose was bleeding. He had a bloody paper towel with an ice cube in it up to his face, dripping blood and water on the kitchen floor."

"No kidding."

"Right. No kidding. And that's how I found out. Robert didn't deny it.

"Robbie told me I should leave."

"He and Jennifer?"

"Stayed together. Maybe they still are, for all I know. He said he wouldn't speak to me unless I left Rob. He was furious. Especially that his father didn't want to stop. He'd told Jennifer that if she wanted to break it off with Robbie, he'd do what he could to make it up to her. But if she wanted to see both of them, that was all right with him, too."

"Maybe they are? You don't know?" And then he remembered what Sam had told him. How could he have forgotten? He'd been accidentally cruel again. But it was a natural question. Spontaneous, impulsive, thoughtless.

"I tried, but he didn't want to talk to me. And one day his phone was disconnected.

"Robert and I stayed together off and on for a few more years. He replaced Robbie's Jennifer with other Jennifers or Megans. I didn't know their names. He was ..."

"He wasn't Sam," Cutter ventured. It was the least he could do. He felt queasy. What a story. How much of it was true, or what passes for truth? He chided himself for his skepticism. A man who sees God's face in the sky should lighten up in the disbelief department, he told himself.

"No. And Sam wasn't Robert, so he listened, and a little more, but...Anyway, he was kind, very kind at a time when I needed someone to show me some compassion."

"You've looked for Robbie?"

"He doesn't want to be found. And even if I found him, what then?"

"You're divorced, divorcing, so..."

"You don't understand. He lost respect for me. He doesn't want to see me, talk to me, certainly not to talk with his father. None of that. When he does, well, he'll call me. Us. Robert and me. What was us. You know what I mean."

"I do know." He nodded, "I lost a son, too, you know."

Grace was still, so still she might have been holding her breath.

"Someday," he said, "someday I'll tell you about it. All about it maybe."

"Even after everything I've said, you won't talk about it?"

"Even after Greek tragedy. Especially not after." Cutter took a deep breath. It wasn't a sigh, just a good, long breath. He changed his mind and went on with what he had to tell.

"What can I say, Grace. First Isaac was, then he wasn't. We don't have any stories, Lynne and I. An album. Small, almost empty. That's it. And each year a candle. You know all about candles."

"It's just as well we don't know when we're young," she said.

"We don't know a lot of things when we're young, but why just as well?"

"I'm not talking about what we don't know because we're inexperienced. I'm saying it's just as well we don't know the future."

"We never know the future, do we?"

"We don't know the middle, but we know the end," Grace said. "And the middle gets shorter and shorter until eventually the end is the only clear thing ahead."

Cutter thought about the face he'd seen in the sky. He used to be certain about death. Now he was asking questions again.

"You think that's it?"

Grace laughed. "I'm sure that it's not all. But what I meant to say is that if we knew what the future held for us, most of us wouldn't be able to stand it."

"That's bleak. You don't think some people are happy?"

"I think you're happy, Ely."

He felt himself blushing and wondered why. "I suppose I am, at least sometimes."

"Right. And suppose when you were crazy in love with Lynne, you'd known what would happen with your son, with Isaac. What then?"

Hearing Grace say "Isaac" was jarring. He wished she wouldn't call him by name. But he felt it would be petty, if not mean to tell her not to. Instead, he said, "I would have married her anyway."

He hoped it would appear that he'd paused to give the

question the deliberation it deserved. He had been crazy in love with Lynne, though he didn't know why Grace had assumed he had been.

"But would she have married you? Knowing, I mean. Knowing it all. Every shitty thing. Would she have? Be honest, with yourself at least."

Cutter said that he understood tornadoes, but he didn't get erosion. "And look at the Grand Canyon."

"Don't try charming, Ely. Not now."

After Grace's set piece? "Why the double standard?"

"Charming is over. I'm finished with charming."

It sounded to Cutter as though she meant it, but he didn't understand.

"What are we going to do now, Ely?"

What did she mean by that? When she'd mentioned "Every shitty thing," had she intended to include what already had, what might happen between them?

"I know what we were supposed to do," he said, "We're on the calendar to look at a split level on a cul-de-sac in the Pines. You know the area?"

"Isn't cul-de-sac a fancy name for a dead end?" she said, teasing.

"In real estate there are no dead ends, just cul-de-sacs, and turnabouts. They're very quiet. Almost no traffic, but not a dead end. Once you find your way in, you just go around in a circle, retrace your steps, and go back."

"Unless you decide to stay."

"Of course. You can always decide to stay."

"Forever?"

"It's a house, Grace. Not a cemetery plot." He was appalled at what he'd said, but to apologize would call attention to his gaffe.

"Then I suppose I can furnish it however I please," Grace said, which Cutter took as permission to move on.

"As long as your bid's accepted," he said.

"That's what I'm hoping for, Ely. No, that's what I'm planning. To make the winning bid."

"When the place is right and the price is right," he said.

"That's what you're here for, isn't it? Why we're doing this together? After all, you've qualified me, haven't you? Isn't that what you call it?"

"That's the term, all right. But right there besides place and price, there's time. It has to be the right time."

"Timing's everything, isn't it?" Grace asked, almost as though she'd never heard the cliché.

"It's important, yes."

"And this is the right time, Ely. For both of us."

"I admire your optimism, Grace. Your optimism and your candor."

"What about you? Does that mean you're not optimistic? or honest?"

"I'm honest," he said, "but sometimes it's difficult to be candid without being hurtful. And I'm not optimistic, but I've managed to remain hopeful."

"That's good enough for me."

"It's generous of you to say so. For me, at least, it's sufficient, sufficient to the day."

He did not hear Grace murmur "unto," and if he had heard, he would not have understood.

CHAPTER 16

Even before he got the key out of the lock, as he stepped into the house, Cutter heard the sound of falling water. His notes hadn't said anything about a fountain, but here it was, the focal point in a center hall as large as many living rooms: a blue glass wall of water with a raised garden and a huge pool at its base. Fifty gallons, maybe more. A skylight lit the pool during the day, and track lighting assured that it would be spectacular after dark. He walked over to look for pot lights in among the plants. A water garden, complete with small white and orange koi. He'd never seen such small koi. Grace was going to love this.

What would happen when she found a house? Cutter had no ready answer for himself. He'd given those to Grace. He took no pride in being glib, and he had been slick.

"Ely, you never said a word!"

Cutter was jarred, but he reminded himself that Grace was talking about the fountain. He shrugged, but was pleased that he'd avoided a gaffe, making something she'd said more personal than intended.

Cutter steadied himself as she rushed over to where he was standing. If she'd been a child, she'd be skipping. "Fish!" she said.

Now what? Was she going to throw her arms around his neck and tilt her head back for a kiss or snuggle her head against his chest? He'd gotten used to both, so much so that he'd almost lost his fear that someone would walk in on them.

As for flinging herself at him, once had been enough. After

it had become clear that he hadn't suffered a concussion, Grace had stopped fussing over his health. Had she ever worried that he would sue her? Now Grace teased him by telling him that even Joanne knew she had fallen for him.

Sometimes he'd respond, equally flirtatious, knowing it was wrong, and attempt to undercut his own emotion. He'd tell her that she knocked him over, so they'd both laugh.

Nevertheless, now he braced himself for impact, just in case Grace hurled herself against him in a further expression of delight. He half-expected that she'd push him backwards into the fish pool, crushing the plants. Cutter imagined that scene: there he'd be, sitting in the pool with startled, curious koi swimming around him and between his legs. Or the pond destroyed, water all over the floor, and koi flopping around gasping. That'd be a scene for Joanne to walk in on. He'd dealt with her amused looks all summer. She'd always been a borderline bitch.

This time Grace didn't fling herself against him.

"Two of them," he said. He peered into the pond. "No, three."

"They grow, don't they?"

"Yes, I believe they do," he said, knowing that they can grow to 3 feet—under ideal circumstances, which this was not.

"What happens if they outgrow the pond? And how can you tell?"

Now she sounded anxious. Maybe she would change her mind about "Fish!"

Aloud he said, "I suppose you can give them to someone

else who raises them. Or sell them. They can be quite valuable. Something about desirable patterns.

"They live a long time," he said. They might outlive us, he thought. That was something he ought to keep to himself. He peered into the pond again. "These look pretty young."

"Do they come with the house?"

He looked at the sheet again. Rooms, square feet, fireplace, sunken tub. Nothing about a fountain. "The fountain itself, most likely. And depending on how the water garden is installed, that too." He looked at it, walking around. "It could be hiding a problem with the floor."

"Or making one?"

"Right. And if it's removed, you couldn't tell which came first, the water garden or the problem. They'll leave it."

"A liability?"

"A delightful liability at worst."

"Like the cathedral ceiling?"

"Your call," he said. He waited in the archway that led to the living room.

"You know I never wanted one," Grace said.

Cutter knew. It was something she'd said she definitely didn't want. That and a picture window facing the street. This house had both.

Grace stood in the middle of the living room in front of the black granite fireplace. She leaned backwards, looking up at the Sputnik-style chandelier, and Cutter worried that she would fall, but he told himself that the yoga probably gave her balance. She wasn't showing off. He'd already seen her show off her yoga.

"This is huge." She made a sweeping gesture. "I'll bet there's an echo in here."

"Is it too much for you?" Cutter already knew the answer. "Do you want to see the rest of the house, or..."

"Or make the offer now?" Grace said, grinning. "It's nothing like I wanted, and it's perfect."

Cutter didn't want to be led into a serious discussion about their future. He just wanted her to buy this house. He'd show her the rest of this place. First things first.

"Grace is on the phone," Lynne said. "She sounds agitated."

Cutter sighed. Was Grace back to her old ways? He'd thought she'd calmed down over the past weeks. She still burst into tears, but not in Barnes & Noble. Of course, they hadn't been together in Barnes & Noble since that first evening.

They hadn't been anywhere, really, except for other people's houses. And his car. They'd spent hours in his car, riding or sitting parked in one driveway or another.

The summer was almost over. Grace was in a bidding war for the house, and she was probably going to lose.

At least Lynne wasn't upset, Cutter consoled himself. He wouldn't have privacy unless he took the phone upstairs. and that would be a mistake, certain to upset Lynne.

"Your cell was turned off, and you were on voicemail at the office," Grace said, "so I called your home phone."

Be nice, Cutter told himself, and don't snidely articulate the obvious. He aimed at a droll tone allowed himself to say, "So I see."

"I'm sorry, Ely, really I am. I hope Lynne isn't angry with you because I called you at home."

Lynne will be angry with me, Cutter thought, if I stay on for a long time and she can't hear my voice, the sound of it anyway. She won't care about the words. He didn't want to sound guarded. Guarded would be terrible.

"No, no," he said, "It's fine."

He didn't know what else to say. Why are you calling? What's wrong? What do you want? None of them was right. What's up? That would never do. He hoped she'd just come out with it, that she would be brief, that life as he'd known it in the last three hours—peaceful, sunlit, almost loving—could continue when he went back to the room where Lynne was waiting for him.

"You know I wouldn't have called," Grace said, "if it weren't an emergency."

Cutter frowned, glad that Lynne could see him—and that Grace could not. Almost anything that had to do with him was an emergency to Grace. It was probably the house. "But, Grace, you might not hear anything for a few days."

"This isn't about the house. Not about any house. Oh, God...it's too much."

She's been drinking, Cutter told himself. If I'm patient, she'll tell me, and I won't have to ask questions.

"I need you to come over here, Ely."

What now? "Sure thing, Grace, I'll be glad to come over." He reviewed his schedule in his mind. Tomorrow was open. "Is late morning good for you? Are you free then?"

"Not good. Tomorrow's not good. Please, Ely, can't you come now?"

"I'll shift my appointments around to fit your schedule.

What's the best time for you?" Cutter wanted to sound accommodating. It was an old rule of salesmanship. He'd passed that approach with Grace, but he still had to manage her. Or try to.

"You don't understand. I need you here now."

Lynne came in, carrying two glasses of white wine. She handed Ely his and put hers on a table. Ely nodded his thanks and took a sip, feeling hypocritical drinking wine a moment after thinking that Grace drank too much.

He was annoyed and distracted when Lynne started writing on the message pad next to the phone, but he didn't want to turn his back on her. She held it up: a big question mark. Lynne handed the black sharpie and the pad to him. He took it, underlined the question mark, and wrote a tiny one next to it.

"What's going on?" Grace said.

Ely was at a loss, unable to calm down Grace when she panicked like this. Not with Lynne at his elbow.

"Why don't you answer me? You don't understand..."

Lynne sitting at the table just a few feet away would hear everything. He hoped Grace wouldn't say anything that he couldn't explain.

"What am I talking about?" Grace demanded.

Cutter thought he heard her laughing at him, but he wasn't sure.

"You can't understand, not unless you hear it for yourself." Cutter held the phone away from his ear.

"Then tell me. I can listen," he said.

"I'm telling you, believe me, I need you here. Really."

Grace sounded increasingly desperate. He wanted to help, but he'd learned to be wary of her when she was flailing. She was likely to get both of them into trouble. Or try to. He was in a bind.

"I don't ... Grace, it's not a good time," he said, hoping both women would be understanding. At least if he put up a fight while Lynne was listening, maybe Lynne would see that he tried. Maybe tomorrow she wouldn't be upset when he went to help Grace with whatever emergency Grace had created for herself.

"Please, Ely. I'll explain to Lynne. Please. Put Lynne back on the phone."

"If you can explain to Lynne, then you can explain to me." Cutter believed this.

Lynne held up the question mark.

Cutter pointed to her and then to the phone. Lynne frowned and shook her head "no," but she stayed right where she was.

"I don't think Lynne can come to the phone now, Grace."

Lynne blew him a kiss.

"It's Robbie," Grace said.

"Robbie? What about Robbie?" Maybe this really was an emergency, one that he would recognize. If he could explain it right, Lynne would understand.

Lynne held up the pad with the question mark. Cutter shook his head no, and held his free hand in the air, in a plea to wait. Lynne didn't know about Robbie. He was sorry now that he'd never told her the story. He hadn't wanted to answer Lynne's questions, and she would have been full of them. If he'd refused to answer, she would have known he was holding back. That would have led to other problems. But maybe it would have made this situation tonight easier. One more regret, either way.

"He phoned," Grace said, "but I wasn't here."

And now Cutter was sure that she was laughing. She hadn't quite reached hysteria, but she was teetering on the rim of its abyss.

"He left a message on the answering machine, Ely. That's why I want you to come over. I want you to listen to it."

"OK, Grace," he said. "I'll listen."

"Good," Grace said. "I'll see you soon then." And she hung up.

Why hadn't she understood?

"I don't know what happened, Lynne. You heard what I said, every word of it. She thinks I'm on my way over there now. Something about a message her son left. She wants me to hear it: to listen to it right there, tonight. What for, I don't know."

"I didn't know she had a son," Lynne said.

"She does. But it's a story. A story like no other." He made a grand gesture, as though pointing to a theater marquee quoting a positive review. The gesture was one of a repertoire of their private jokes that Lynne was certain to appreciate. He felt ashamed for his making light of Grace's situation, but he was at a loss for a better way of telling Lynne. What he did say was that the outline of what Grace had told him was so improbable that to summarize it would have made it seem ridiculous, more far-fetched than any soap opera.

"I'm sure it is, Ely. And you would know."

He didn't know if she was referring to his vision or to his relationship with Grace. In either case it wouldn't do to get into it now, but, at least for the time being, he was off the hook with having to tell Grace's story.

"You don't mind if I go?"

"I do mind," Lynne said, "But go anyway."

"It's a mitzvah," Cutter said. Even to him, calling this a good deed sounded like a rationalization.

"Oh, please, Ely. You're leaving me to see her. Go if you want to, but don't pretend! If your motives are pure tonight, it'll be the first time."

"It was business, Lynne. You know that. I've always had to work weekends." She was probably thinking of the night he'd almost missed dinner and all those times with Eleanor. She was mixing them together into a poisonous brew.

"Just go. Why did you ask me if I mind, if you don't care whether or not I do?"

"I do care..."

"About who? Grace? Or me?" Lynne emptied the glass of wine. "Or about yourself? Is that it? Ely does 'me, myself, and I' and pretends he's being selfless. Please, Ely, spare me."

Ely was caught between two women saying "please." Maybe Lynne was on target, and this was about getting what he wanted, not about doing what was right. He wasn't sure what right was, anyway, not in this context.

"I do want to spare you," he said. He meant it, too. Sparing her was sparing himself. He could have said, truthfully, that she's his life as much as his breath, although Lynne would not have believed him. And now a look of pure rage flickered across Lynne's face. He'd made an awful mistake.

"Oh? And what exactly do you want to spare me from?"

He ought to keep his mouth shut because he didn't get any credit for trying. But he did want to spare her, and he'd always wanted to. If he could have spared Lynne the pain of learning about Eleanor, spared her from her suspicions about Grace, he would have. He tried to but failed. If he could have spared her being the subject of gossip, he would have, and spared her from people turning away because they didn't know what to say to her, he would have done that too—though he hadn't even imagined that possibility until he wanted to avoid Ruth. He wanted to spare Lynne from being married to someone who didn't know how to spare her from anything important. And that brought him to what he wanted most of all.

Most of all, he didn't want to lose her, and in response to her question, clumsy and inarticulate, he said, "Everything." He might as well have said, "Nothing."

So, flummoxed, he wasn't surprised when his wife turned from him, and, without a word, walked into the garden and slid the door closed behind her.

Cutter considered following Lynne and trying to set things right. She wouldn't be able to hear him unless he opened the door. He put his palms flat against the door, like a mime in his invisible box, and peered out into the darkness. She hadn't turned on the outside lights before she'd gone into the garden. He looked for Lynne, but he couldn't see her. He imagined her striding down the path, past the ripe, bursting tomatoes, past the pole beans where he'd had his vision, slowing to admire her moon garden, and walking even more slowly back to the patio. Maybe she'd come back in while he was still home.

He stood waiting for what seemed to him a long time, long enough, he was sure, for Lynne to return. He would try to kiss her, and, if she let him, certainly if she kissed him back, he would stay home. Grace would get on without him for the night. She would have to. Lynne would come first. But if not...

Cutter caught sight of his reflection in the window of the closed door. How spiteful he looked, how confused, how frightened, how old!

And then he left without saying even one word more, not even goodbye.

Grace had turned on every light in the house as well as the lamp posts at the foot of the drive and next to the flagstone path that led to the front door, which was wide open. Jazz came from the house, a female vocalist. Cutter didn't know Fitzgerald from Holiday, even though Grace was in the habit of changing the radio in his car to listen to one jazz station or another, depending on the time of day. The first thing he did after he dropped her off was to tune it back to where it had been.

Cutter paused in the open doorway, considering whether to knock while calling Grace's name. The distinction was too unimportant to parse, but it seemed essential to get it right tonight. He'd left too much to chance, if not to fate. And to Grace.

He expected Grace to answer with his name or some greeting, and, when he got no response, now standing in the foyer, Cutter tried calling her name again. Again, nothing. Crickets and katydids filled the night. Moths fluttered around the light fixture next to the door: they flung themselves at the light. He pulled the door shut behind him.

He called to Grace again as he walked down the hall to the kitchen. Lined up, the three tall chairs that had survived the accident divided the breakfast bar into perfect thirds.

The music came from the living-room. Not much was different from that first night, except now Grace, dressed all in white, lay on the white sofa, motionless, her eyes closed, and next to her on the glass-topped coffee table sat a tumbler of clear liquid, probably vodka, with a few slivers of ice. It wasn't that hot in here, so he guessed that it must have been full about the time she'd phoned him.

With all the lights on, standing close to her, Cutter didn't have to think twice about it: Grace was fine—that is, still breathing.

He'd considered the possibilities on his way over here. She might have been planning a suicide event, might have done something to herself before she called him, drugs and alcohol. Maybe that's why she'd been so insistent that he get there right away, why she'd left the door wide open. If not Cutter, a neighbor might have found her—if not tonight, then before it got too messy.

Cutter felt like a motorist trapped in crawling traffic, a casualty of gaper delay, the wreckage of the horrific accident in plain view, and the last victim being lifted into the remaining ambulance after the others have sped away carrying whoever and whatever they could get out of the smash-up.

"Ely?" Grace spoke without opening her eyes.

"Yes, I'm here." Cutter was both annoyed and frightened

that she kept her eyes closed. What was wrong? He'd seen this behavior before only in the very ill.

"'fraid you wouldn't get here."

If his earlier worries are on target, he has to figure out something to save her. He was glad that Lynne knew where he was, what had happened. At least he didn't have to worry about her.

"You sure left on a lot of lights."

"Mmm," she said.

Cutter waited, but when she didn't say anything else, he asked, "Grace, are you all right?" "All right" could mean almost anything.

"Turn off the music, will you? It's over..." she made a feeble gesture with her hand.

Cutter knew where it was from other visits; her gesture told more about Grace's condition than about the location of the stereo.

Without the music, the house was silent. Blazing bright and silent. With the windows and door closed, the crickets and katydids vanished.

"Just us now," Grace said.

"I told Lynne I..." Cutter had been about to say "wouldn't be long," but he changed it to "was coming over."

"Gotta..." Grace said.

Had "gotta" referred to telling Lynne, or something more personal to Grace, something more urgent? That was too complicated a question, so instead he asked, "Can you open your eyes?"

"Have to?"

"Yes," he said.

He wasn't sure why, what he was supposed to do if she didn't. Had she taken anything with the vodka? He'd seen movies of people holding up a staggering friend, making him walk, not letting him sleep. If she couldn't move, maybe he'd have to call 911.

Grace raised her eyebrows but didn't open her eyes. "There," she said

"Try again," he said.

Her eyelids fluttered open. "'kay?"

"Good girl!" Cutter said.

"Puppy," Grace said, closing her eyes. "'Not a puppy."

Cutter was embarrassed. He had been talking to her as though she was a puppy being paper-trained.

"Did you have anything besides this vodka?"

"Vawdka," she said, "Vawdka. Not vahdkah."

"Did you?"

"Vawdka. ...*Njet*."

Was that yes or *njet*? Why was Grace speaking Russian?

"Grace, did you take any pills, please, English."

"No pills. Vawdka with vawdka."

"Okay, Grace, we're going to sit up now," he said although he didn't know how "we" were going to do anything. It was the only remedy that he could think of. "Take it slow, swing your feet down to the floor."

She didn't move.

"You can do it, Grace. Do you want help? You have to sit up now."

"...shist," she said. She struggled into a sitting position.

Grace had called him a shit. He'd proved that he had the capacity for it. Then he realized, "Fascist? You're saying I'm a fascist for making you sit up."

"Yes," she said. "I'm fine."

She did sound much better. Maybe she'd been sleeping when he came in. He'd never seen her asleep before. He sat on the couch next to her, and when she reached for her drink, he put his hand on her arm and said, "I can get you some water. I can make coffee."

"I'm sure you can. Doesn't make you sober. Just nervous." She held out her glass, waggling it before him in an invitation, "Want to catch up?"

"Can't," he said. "You're too far ahead of me." You always are, he thought.

She was crying, but this time, she wasn't asking him for anything beyond what he'd done already by coming here. It would be so easy to take her in his arms, and, this time, maybe, even an act of kindness. "Ready?"

She began to get up, lost her balance, and landed back on the sofa. "Sometimes I don't know why my parents named me Grace."

Cutter stood and held out his hand. She'd slurred her words enough to make his offer more than a gallant gesture, "Where is this answering machine?"

She shook her head. "Give me a minute."

He sat in the big armchair. Safer, unless she came and sat on the arm of the chair again—or in his lap.

"I don't understand what he said. It doesn't make any sense. Maybe you can. It's in the den," she said. "Let's go."

"Here it is," Grace said, pointing to the answering machine, which was the same as the one Cutter had at home.

"I kept the voice message that came with it," she said.

"We did, too," Cutter said. He was uneasy. What did Robbie sound like? Had it been so long, was he so far away that Grace had trouble understanding him?

"Here goes," she said, and pushed the button:

"Hey, it's me. Christ, I hate this machine. Sorry for swearing. This call should be easier, but it isn't. Anyway, I'm still fine. Are you both ok? Oh. I'm not with Jen now. We're having what we called a trial separation. And we're not even married. Funny, huh? After everything, you know. I'll try calling again sometime. Love ya."

Cutter was almost certain. "Play it again?"

CHAPTER 17

He'd asked to hear it again just to make sure. That was the same voice, all right.

"Do you think he'll call again, Ely?"

"Absolutely, Grace. No doubt about it."

"You're not saying that to make me feel better?"

He hesitated, then told her about the call he'd found on his answering machine, how he'd played and replayed it, and everything he'd heard. "I kept thinking some parents would want to know their son was apologizing, but I didn't know who, where to start..."

"Why did..." Grace stopped short. "Isaac?"

"Crazy, right?" He hadn't told her all of it. But Robbie's fight had been with his father. Grace was collateral damage, so maybe she wouldn't be hurt if he told her. "It was how the call started, he said, 'Hey, Dad, it's me.' The 'Dad,' it got me off guard. It wasn't all that long after seeing His face, and I..."

"Had a fantasy?"

"I suppose it was, but when he said, "Finding a phone around here, it's not easy.'..." Although he couldn't figure out how to end the sentence, Cutter felt less sheepish than he'd expected he would.

"I want to hear the message," Grace said.

Cutter heard her tone, not whining or wheedling—but peremptory.

"It was erased," Cutter said, choosing the passive to avoid blame.

"How could you, Ely?" Grace said, "Or was it Lynne?"

"It doesn't matter which of us, Grace," Cutter said, recognizing that it was true; he was glad he hadn't told her whose idea it was to erase the message. "It's gone. But I know it by heart."

He didn't wait for Grace's response, and he launched into his recitation, "'Hey, Dad, it's me. Shit. I hate this new machine of yours. At least you could record a simple 'Thank you for calling.' Finding a phone around here, it's not easy. Well, tell Mom I love her. You, too, Dad. Look, I'm sorry. Really. OK. I'll try you again. Bye.'"

"You're sure that's how he said it?"

"Oh yes. Exactly." Cutter chuckled. "I thought he should show more respect. But he made up for it, I guess."

"The woman, you said that she interrupted, but when?"

"Right after he apologized and said 'Tell Mom I love her. You, too, Dad.' That's when he must have put his hand over the phone, and I couldn't catch exactly what they were saying, but it wasn't what I'd call friendly. Now that you've told me what happened...no wonder she was mad."

"I'm not erasing this," Grace said.

She sounded defensive, but she was almost sober, or seemed to be. This wasn't the truculence of Grace, drunk. Maybe she couldn't have been as far gone as she had seemed to be when he walked in and found her on the couch. Had it been an act, a set-up? Even the thought put him off.

"No reason you should." He meant it. Now that he knew who it was, he wished he still had the message that had been on his answering machine. Even after his common sense told him it wasn't Isaac calling, he'd liked hearing, "Hey, Dad. It's me." It was too late now, though.

And then Grace asked, "What about Robert?"

Of course, Robert. It took him a few moments before he could say, "Yes, Robert." He tried to keep his voice so neutral that when Grace heard it, instead of knowing what he thought, she would project her own feelings onto it. Anyway, his thoughts were a jumbled heap.

"Are you saying I have to do something about him?"

"You'll have to do something—not telling him is doing something, too, isn't it? And he is Robbie's father, isn't he?"

"But what should I do?"

"Grace, I can't tell you that," he said, although he thought that his questions had revealed his opinion almost just clearly as if he had been explicit.

"But, Ely, I rely on you."

"Not for this, you can't." If this were his son, he wouldn't want someone like him giving advice to his ex-wife; nonetheless, he said, "If he got the call, would you want him to hide it from you?"

"Is that what you think I'd be doing?"

Ely shrugged. But he'd never felt less casual.

The phone rang, and they both jumped. Cutter leaned forward to see the caller ID.

He had trouble reading the screen in this light, but there it was: Unknown Name.

"How many rings is the answering machine set for, Grace?"

"Four."

"This is four coming up. Aren't you going to answer?"

"He'd leave a message, wouldn't he?"

"Pick it up." And when she didn't move, Cutter grabbed

the receiver from the cradle. He held it towards Grace, but she shook her head and folded her arms across her chest.

"Hello," he said, wondering if he should add, "Cooper residence."

He heard a buzz, and distant voices, and then a woman asking to speak to Mr. Cooper.

"May I ask who's calling?" he asked, trying to sound like someone whose business it might be to answer the phone.

"No, not really," he said and hung up, adding, "I took the liberty of saying you don't want to lower your heating bill by installing new windows." Took the liberty, now he was talking like a butler in a forties movie.

He smiled, feeling foolish at the urgency with which he'd answered the phone. After all, it wasn't his son.

"I told you," she said.

"I'm going to freshen up my drink," she said, as she headed out the study door. Looking over her shoulder she asked, "What can I get you?"

Cutter looked at his watch. It wasn't all that late. Altogether he'd only been gone about an hour. It would take longer than that for Lynne to calm down, unless of course, she'd been building up a head of steam, in which case, she'd be worse off. And so would he. He could call and tell her he's...what could he say that would make it better for Lynne?

He wanted to say vawdka and make Grace laugh. But he didn't want to drink vodka the way Grace did, syrupy from the freezer over ice. One drink the way she poured, and he'd be blotto. He experimented silently with ways of saying "water" that might amuse her.

"Well?"

He must have taken longer than he thought to answer. He smiled at Grace and said, "Surprise me."

"Gladly," she said. "It's my ambition."

He had surprised himself once more. But what harm could there be in his having a drink with her?

Cutter had just begun thinking about the answer to his own question, when Grace called to him from the kitchen, leaving him no time to wallow in the possibilities of everything that could go wrong. "I'm on my way," he said.

He felt like an obedient, elderly dog. He wondered if Grace had Lynne or Eleanor to thank for his complaisance. In either case, no matter, Grace was the beneficiary tonight.

Grace had hung her white linen blouse on the back of one of the stools, and she was wearing only her white tank top with her long skirt.

"I should have told you before. You look like Emily Dickinson all in white," he paused, "It's all I remember about her from high school, that she wore white. Funny."

"Have I spoiled the effect?"

"Oh, and "Because I could not stop for Death," something, something."

"He kindly stopped for me," Grace said. "Morbid stuff."

She used her index finger to stir a drink, then put her finger in her mouth. She repeated the two gestures, and removing her finger, said, "Don't worry. That was my drink."

"It hadn't crossed my mind," he said. And it hadn't. He'd been thinking about her finger in her mouth, whether she was conscious of her teasing.

"So, tell me, have I?"

"What?"

"Spoiled the effect."

"I can't imagine her wearing a tank top,"

"Or not wearing a bra."

"Am I supposed to say I haven't noticed? Or that I have?"

"That depends, Ely."

"On?" He expected her to answer, "On what you want."

But she said, "On whether you haven't noticed. Or whether you have?"

"Well, Grace. You have surprised me."

"You ain't seen nothing yet," she said, laughing. "I have something very special for you."

She was laying it on a bit thick. "I'd ask what you have up your sleeve..."

"But I don't have sleeves," she said delighted, triumphant.

She held a drink out to him. A double highball glass, frosted. He couldn't tell what was in there.

When he reached for it, she said, "Just a minute. Close your eyes."

"What?"

"Just do it."

And he did. When was the last time he and Lynne had flirted like this?

"OK. Now I'm going to hand you the glass and guide it up to your mouth for you to drink."

"You won't spill it?"

"You mean, you won't."

What was this anyway? The glass was cold and wet, and

Grace's hands on his were cold, too, probably from holding the glasses. Or maybe she was upset, still, about the call. He was unsettled, which is not what he would have thought his response would be to solving the mystery of the call. But the business wasn't over yet. Far from it.

"Inhale, a deep breath. Now hold your breath," she said, and brought his hands up, guiding them with hers. He felt the glass against his lips.

"Wait!" he said, and murmured the blessing that would cover water, or liquor. He was sure this wasn't wine.

If this was pure vodka, he'd be in trouble, depending on how much she had him drink. And he should be driving home at some point. He was in no hurry. "Exhale, drink," she said, tilting the glass so the liquid ran into his open mouth.

"Water!"

"I told you I had a surprise for you. Disappointed?"

"I'm not sure," he said. "Not with the drink."

"Feeling let down? I can do something about that," she said.

She was standing so close to him that he told himself to back away. At the beginning, he would have stepped back by now. He caught himself using the phrase, "at the beginning," and wondered what had begun, and if this was no longer the beginning, was he closer to the middle or to the end.

As Cutter drove home, he pondered what he would tell Lynne. He settled on what he hoped would be a palatable version of the truth; after all, nothing had happened. He had left Grace with a chaste kiss.

The moment when something might have happened arrived, and he had allowed it to pass. He recast his regret for an opportunity missed: it became satisfaction in having resisted temptation. His primary loyalty was to Lynne, but there was no denying that he found Grace loveliest when she was vulnerable, as she was this evening.

Sam must have felt that. He'd tell him Robbie had called; Sam would want to know.

"So," Lynne said. "Is it all fixed?"

"It'll take more than I can do."

"You went over there because you thought you could take care of her."

"I love you, Lynne. And I went there because she'd got a call from her son. It was the wrong number."

"But..."

"The wrong number was when we got the call. That was her son." Cutter told Lynne what he knew, careful to stop short of telling her about Sam.

"It's too bad," Lynne said.

"People get themselves into fixes, don't they?"

"It is too bad," Lynne said.

Cutter heard the determination in her voice. He could tell she had something in mind.

"Yes, I'm sure it is," he said to be agreeable.

"Really, Ely, you don't have a clue of what I'm talking about."

Lynne was right again. He didn't have a clue, and there was no sense playing games. He didn't blame her for being exasperated with him. "So, *nu?*"

"Too bad someone else didn't get Grace's business."

Cutter opened the refrigerator to look for dinner and took out some tomatoes and Swiss cheese. "Have you eaten?"

"You're glad about Grace."

"I'm not sorry, Lynne. Maybe it was supposed to happen that way."

"Wonderful, my husband says meeting Grace is bashert. Fate brought you together?"

"You're twisting it all up," he said.

"Untwist it," Lynne said. "I'm going to bed."

"All I can do is try," he said, as she walked out of the room. She did not turn or answer.

Cutter sliced the tomatoes and onions and arranged them on a plate, sprinkling them with balsamic vinegar, and drizzling a green olive oil. A few grinds of pepper. He cut a strip from the cheese, and then another. He said the blessings for the food. Had he got them in the right order? And he ate.

Lynne would be asleep, or she would pretend to be. Just as well. That would give him until tomorrow, and maybe then he'd have an idea of how to set things straight.

Cutter woke at dawn and couldn't find a comfortable position. If he were alone, he would turn, sit up and thump his pillow, throw the sheet off, and tug the sheet back up again. He would try lying on his side and on his back with his pillow covering his eyes. Instead, thinking of Lynne's admonition to "untwist it," he gave up. Maybe he could get some work done in the garden. These would be the last weeks of hard work.

Cutter, squatting, chopped with a grubber at the ground

around the base of the pole beans. He looked at the greens he uprooted and tossed to one side—some of them could be edible. He could check the websites and his book, but he'd done such a good job of keeping the area clean that all of today's crop didn't amount to much. Not a hill of beans. He smiled at his own joke. He'd use these for mulch, not for food. Not worth the aggravation with Lynne.

Especially today.

He glimpsed something gleaming in the newly turned ground. Just a bit of it showed. He used his hands to move aside the earth to get to it. He'd worked this ground for years, and he'd never found anything valuable. He picked up the clod of earth that held this object, and broke it apart, revealing a man's wedding band. He stood up and brushed as much dirt off the ring as he could and turned the ring to see if he could find an inscription. He'd wash it off and take a better look at it when it was clean. He'd never worn a wedding band himself, though Lynne wore hers.

"Good morning!" Lynne called from the patio.

He judged from her tone of voice that she'd put last night behind her.

He slid his hand into his pocket and dropped the ring in it. "'Morning, Lynne. I thought I'd put in a bit of work before breakfast."

Lynne had brought out a tray with orange juice and a pot of coffee. "I thought it might be cool enough today..." she began.

"Great idea, Lynne. What about one of my omelets?"

"I made French toast," she said. "It's in the oven."

French toast was tricky. While Cutter had taken to saying

blessings both before and after most foods, he hadn't learned the longer prayers required after bread. And he wasn't eager to discomfit Lynne. He'd do his best. God would know his intentions were good.

"I'm going to wash up a bit," he said to Lynne, holding out his hands for inspection. he'd taken off his gardening gloves while he was unearthing the ring.

Lynne wrinkled her nose, and he waited to see if her expression would end in disgust or amusement. Either way he'd get a moment of privacy to look at the ring again. It wouldn't take him long.

He used the nailbrush to get his nails clean and debated whether or not to use it on the ring, but water seemed to do the trick.

He looked inside the band. Writing. He'd expected to find a marking for the gold, 14k, most likely. But he saw more than that—though without his reading glasses he couldn't decipher what it was. Initials, maybe a date. But whose, and what date?

If it was new, being buried had given it a patina.

Would it fit? He put it on his ring finger. It fit, a mite snug, sliding over his knuckle. He looked at his hand. He wasn't used to wearing a ring. Lynne had never cared about his having one, so the topic hadn't come up since they were first married.

"Ely?" Lynne was knocking at the door. "Will you be down soon? I don't want to take the French toast out of the oven unless you're coming down."

"I'll be down in just be a minute," he said. He wanted to take off the ring and slip it into his pocket, but when he pulled on it, the ring caught on his knuckle. He tugged: the loose flesh at his knuckle made a fleshy ridge.

Soap. He could get his finger slippery and get the ring off that way. He washed his hands and rinsed only the right hand. He dried that hand as he could on the towel nearest the sink, so he'd have a better grip on the ring. He couldn't get it over his knuckle, not even after a try with soap.

No help for it, then, he'd have to go to breakfast with the ring on, and deal with Lynne who was sure to have something to say.

By the time he got downstairs, Lynne had already taken the French toast out to the table on the patio. The orange juice glasses were beaded with moisture. He wouldn't say anything about the ring until Lynne noticed it. Cutter drank his juice and poured coffee for himself and for Lynne. He was sure she would spot the ring when he took her cup. "Full cup?" he asked.

"It's my first, Ely."

"Full up it is, then, Lynne," he said.

"What's the matter?" Lynne asked. "You're acting strange. Did something happen that I ought to know about?"

"The French toast looks delicious. You never burn it," he said. He kept his left hand in his lap, grateful that was where it belonged anyway. "And that thing you do with spices? I can never remember what you use besides cinnamon and nutmeg."

"Ely Joel Cutter you think you're too clever by half," Lynne said. "What happened with Grace that you're hiding?"

"Nothing, Lynne," he said, determined to speak only the

truth. "I swear to you, you could have had the whole thing on video." He was in the high-toned suburbs of the truth, about to head out into the wilds. "You wouldn't have seen one thing that you wouldn't have wanted to."

"Can you give me three reasons why I should believe you?"

For a moment Cutter was stumped. He wanted her to believe him, and that was the answer. He said, "Only two good ones." He paused and held out his right hand for her to take, hoping she would.

She didn't, but he kept his hand out, waiting to see what she'd do when he finished.

"One: you want to believe me. Two: I want you to believe me."

"Those are good reasons?"

"The essential ones, Lynne. If I don't care if you believe me, then I don't value your trust."

He knew he was on shaky ground with that one, but he moved ahead without a pause. "And if you don't want to believe me, you never will. So, what's the point of any of it?"

Lynne sighed. Cutter was deciding what to do or say next, when Lynne patted his hand. It wasn't what he'd been hoping for, but it was better than her ignoring his gesture.

"Sometimes I wonder just that," she said. "What's the point? Any of it."

Cutter looked away from his wife, away from the table, out across the garden with its last of summer's bounty—bursting tomatoes, zucchini and eggplant, its exuberant red and pink cockscomb and yellow and pink zinnias. He looked up to the sky, searching for the spot where he'd seen the face. Seeing it had changed his life, but maybe not enough.

"You can't even look at me?"

"No," he said, turning towards her, "I guess I couldn't. Not just then."

"And?"

"I love you, Lynne, but I understand why you'd wonder. I have, too." Was this it? After so many years of real trouble, was their marriage ending like this, on a patio, over a platter of untouched French toast?

CHAPTER 18

The ring was still on his finger. Lynne was miffed, more than miffed, and she hadn't even seen the ring yet. Cutter sighed and thought his sigh might as well have been a prayer.

He'd been offering blessings of thanks for food and drink, but how many of his blessings had been perfunctory? Not the first, certainly, and not all. But some. And often he'd said them because he'd decided to do so, not because he was supposed to. Did that matter? He hoped that he'd earned the right to petition for help—he needed it now.

If he sat here too long, Lynne might be gone. If she were still in the house, he had a chance to set things right, but if she left, when she returned it might already be too late. And it would be his fault. He couldn't hide from it. If he sat here and let her leave, he'd be to blame for what happened next. He wasn't to blame for what had happened before. He wasn't responsible for Grace's falling for him. That is, he hadn't intended for her to fall for him, and that was almost the same thing.

Cosmic questions aside, he'd better take the French toast into the house. On the best of days, he'd get into trouble if he abandoned a perfectly good platter of food to bugs.

Lynne was standing at the sink with water running, and she didn't turn when he entered the kitchen. He set the platter on the table. "I brought in the French toast," he said, wanting to sound normal, wanting to gain her approval. Pathetic. He chided himself for dipping his toe in the bottomless waters of self-pity.

He could put the slices in a plastic bag or cover the dish and put it in the refrigerator. The plastic bag would take up less room. Or he could ask Lynne what she wanted. No emotional overload in that. "I'll put the French toast in the fridge," he said, and when she didn't say anything, he added, "right after I bring in the rest of the food from the patio."

He was glad he had more to bring in, giving him a good excuse to get away from Lynne. He didn't want to lose Lynne, but it was too painful now to be in the same room with her. He would have preferred that she raise her voice. Even sarcasm would be better than this silence. Eleanor had been a master of the perfectly aimed sarcastic comment, and in these last few months Lynne had surprised him by sounding like the least attractive aspect of Eleanor. From time to time he worried that he himself had ruined Lynne.

On the patio, he tugged at the ring one more time. It wasn't so tight as to be uncomfortable, but he couldn't get it off his finger. He'd almost forgotten about it in the kitchen. Lynne wears her ring all the time. Maybe he would ask her if she ever forgot that she was wearing it. He'd have to wait to ask—unless it's already too late.

Cutter put the coffee and their cups on a tray and headed back to the kitchen, stopping before he went in. Lynne looked forlorn standing by the sink doing nothing. He wasn't used to seeing her idle.

He set the tray on the counter near where she stood. "I'll be right back," he said. He brought in the juice and the flowers from the table. They'd wilt in the heat if he left them out all day, though nights were cooler now. He could always make another trip if he got too uncomfortable.

"Finished?" Lynne asked.

Cutter looked over his shoulder at the closed door to the patio. He knew that Lynne must be able to see the dishes out there as well as he could. The edible remains of breakfast were set here and there in the kitchen.

Cutter shrugged. "There's nothing left out there that's urgent," his voice lowered, and he added, "I suppose."

"You suppose?"

"That matters."

"So, if we talk, you won't be rushing out into the garden, onto the patio?"

I'm not the one who walked away from breakfast, he thought. "Not unless you come with me. There's a bit of a mess to clean up."

When Lynne frowned, he realized that he'd been ambiguous in his answer.

"Two messes," he said. "One of them is my fault."

"And? I thought you said everything you wanted to say at breakfast. You left it up to me. As if my not trusting you is my fault."

"I can't make you trust me."

"No, but you can help me," Lynne took a deep breath. "You act like you have something to hide."

"All the time? Maybe it's just my personality."

"That's a cop-out, Ely."

"OK, I'll try to do better."

"With Eleanor? With Grace?"

Eleanor. Why was she bringing her into this? Grace he understood. But he had a good reason to be with Grace, one good one anyway. And as for the other, he'd have to deal with it. "All around. Lynne, I love you."

"And what does that mean?"

"This isn't *Fiddler on the Roof.* I hope you'd know by now." He couldn't explain it to her. He couldn't even explain it to himself. Could she, if he asked her? "I don't want to lose you. For no reason."

"I wouldn't say I don't have a reason."

"I understand. All I can do is to try."

"You've said that already, Ely. Maybe this isn't going to work."

"Can't we start over?" Cutter said. They were standing at opposite ends of the kitchen, separated by the kitchen table, but he stayed planted where he was, what seemed to him to be far away from his wife, as though he were looking at her through the wrong end of a telescope.

"I'm not a teenager anymore," Lynne said.

"I'm not either, Lynne. Besides you look even more beautiful now," he said. This was something he might have said at one time just to make her happy, but now he was surprised to find that he meant it. She did look beautiful to him. She didn't have the kind of figure that would allow her to go braless, but even if she did, he wouldn't have wanted her to run around town like some chippy. Like Grace? Did he think Grace was a chippy? He shouldn't be thinking about her now.

"I wasn't talking about how I look. I was talking about how I feel."

"We're middle aged, after all, and even a bit past. But we're not that creaky."

Lynne sighed. "You don't get it. I'm talking about starting over, not about how I look, or whether I can do some pretzel posture in yoga."

"I still don't..." This discussion was going in circles. Lynne was right about not being teenagers; nonetheless, right now Cutter didn't have any more idea about what Lynne wanted than when he was seventeen.

"When we were young, I had no idea—though I would have sworn I did," Lynne shook her head.

How was he supposed to do what was expected of him, if Lynne refused to tell him how or even what.

Then he was ashamed. He'd been the one to cheat, not her. She hadn't mentioned Eleanor for years, not until the night she caught them together at the bookstore. And everything that had happened with Grace! Nothing he could do about that now: with Grace things had been what they were. No wonder Lynne was disconcerted.

First, he sees God's face in the sky. That would have been enough to upset Lynne; it certainly upset him. And then Grace comes barreling into their lives.

Cutter wished he could put Grace away. He had to focus on Lynne if he wanted to set things right with her.

"I don't know if I have the energy to start over. Or the imagination. I'd have to make it all go away," she said.

He walked around to where Lynne was standing. That would be a good start. He reached up to stroke her hair.

She jerked her body away from him.

He let his hand fall and shook his head.

"I'm sorry," they said together.

"I wasn't going to hurt you," Cutter said. He walked to a chair and sat. He put his elbows on the table and cupped his face in his open palms.

"That's why I'm sorry," Lynne said. "It was a reflex."

He lifted his head and turned to face her. "That's why I'm sorry," Cutter said. "Do you think it's too late?"

"I hope not, Ely. This isn't what I expected. I thought that once we got past...that it would be past."

Cutter wondered if he'd caught up to Lynne, understood what she'd covered with the pause: Isaac's death, Eleanor, even his being caught on the floor with Grace.

Lynne sat across from him and laid her right hand on the table.

He could let it lie there, a petty way to get even with her that would come at great cost to him. No, to both of them. Her recoiling from his touch was terrible, but for him to choose to leave her hand there would be far worse. He took her hand in both of his. Her hand was soft and surprisingly cool.

He looked at her hand in his and remembered that he was wearing the ring he'd found in the garden. He'd have to say something before she noticed.

"I have something to show you," he said, and, disengaging his left hand, he held it out to her.

"A wedding band?"

"It sure looks like one," Cutter said. "Fact is, I don't know for certain."

"So, now you're wearing a ring and you don't know where it came from?"

"That's partly true. I know where I got it," he said, "It's the darnedest..."

"Let me see," she said, holding out her palm.

"You want to take a closer look? Not so simple," he said, embarrassed. "I got it on, but it won't come off."

"You tried?"

Cutter nodded. "I think it's on there for good unless I cut it off. They can do that, can't they?"

"Sure, but I'd bet you don't need to."

"I tried the soap thing already."

"Windex," Lynne said.

"You're kidding, right?"

"No. Come over to the sink."

Cutter held his hand out while Lynne sprayed it. "I'm sure this will do it," she said.

"I don't think so. It's really stuck."

"I heard this always works."

"Wait," he said. "Make sure the drain is covered. If you do get it off, I don't want it to go down the sink and disappear in the garbage disposal."

"Sounds like you're attached to it."

"More like it's attached to me."

"So, where did you get it?" Lynne asked, taking his wet hand."

"I found it," he said. "You'll never believe, in the garden by the pole beans. I was digging and there it was. Buried."

"Hold still," she said, tugging on the ring. "Don't bend your finger."

Cutter felt the ring catch on his knuckle. "See?"

"Patience," said Lynne. "Relax. This'll only take a minute," she paused, "I hope."

"Maybe I should try?"

"That sounds good."

"Give it another spritz," he said, holding his hand over the sink again.

"Let's try now," she said, after two more sprays.

Lynne seemed to be enjoying this. Maybe it was an adventure to her. Why had he been so worried?

He knew the answer. Off, the ring was no threat, on, with its inscription hidden, it could have come from anywhere. Or anyone. And that was it. After all the craziness with Grace! What if Lynne had thought that Grace gave him the ring—not intending or expecting that he wear it, but for sentiment—and he'd slipped it on, as he had, and it had gotten stuck.

He twisted the ring and pulled. "Success," he said, as the ring started over the first fold of flesh of his knuckle. "I think, anyway."

While he held his finger out straight, he pulled again, not wanting any more fuss. He grasped the ring, tugging, and he said, "I'll do it."

"Need help?"

"No," he said, uncertain that he didn't. And then it was over the knuckle and off.

He held it out to Lynne.

"No," she said.

"What no?" Cutter said, "why?"

"Just so," Lynne said. "Where are your glasses?"

"Next to the computer. But..."

"Wait here," she said. Cutter recognized the tone. She meant it. No sense fighting.

He squinted into the ring. He hadn't been mistaken. He saw writing. It was a wedding band, but whose? It had been in the ground for some time from the looks of it. This had been a new house when they'd bought it, so maybe it was a farmer's ring from back when this was a field. The ring would mean something to someone. Was the person whose ring it was still alive? Could they find him?

He was still peering at the ring when Lynne returned, bringing his glasses.

"Here," she said, holding them out with a strange showiness.

"It's a wedding band, for sure." He told her his theory about its belonging to a farmer.

"Does that mean you're not going to look? You're not curious, even about the date?"

"If you want to look, go ahead," he said.

"You found it. You look first."

"What's the big deal, Lynne?" Now that the ring was off, it didn't seem so important.

"You want me to do it, Ely? Fine."

She sounded snippy. Why was he pushing her? Not long ago he'd been afraid she was going to leave him, and now, he was falling into a fight over what? Bupkis, fly specks. A ring he found that meant nothing to him.

"I'm sorry, Lynne. I don't know why I got so stubborn," he said, sure that she was the stubborn one and half-expecting that when he proffered the apology, she'd offer one of her own.

"It's not important, Ely," she said.

What wasn't important, his apology? Or his offense?

And he did wonder how long the ring had been buried.

Strange, it almost fit him. Or maybe not so strange. He was average in his build. But weren't men smaller a long time ago? He could look it up when he got to the computer.

"So, what does it say?"

"OK." He put on his glasses and looked at the ring. 14K. No surprise. Fancy script initials and a date. EJC LMC June 3, 1974. How can this be?

"What is this, Lynne? They're our initials. Our wedding date."

"It's your ring, Ely."

"Mine? But I never got a wedding ring."

"That's almost right," Lynne said, "You never got it, but I bought it for you."

"You never gave me a ring you bought for me and had engraved?"

"Right."

"What was it doing near the pole beans?"

"It wasn't near the beans. That is, the pole beans weren't there. The ring was there before the beans. It's been there more than twenty-five years."

"I don't understand."

"It's simple. We got married I had a ring, you didn't. Years passed. We'd been married ten years. I used your class ring to get a size. I bought a wedding band for you, and had it engraved. It was going to be an anniversary present. We were happy, as happy as we could have been, considering. I was happy to be your wife, anyway, and I thought you were, too."

He knew what she meant, so he said, "Well, sure, Lynne."

He stopped himself from saying that he's always been

happy; he wanted to please her, to smooth things over, but she had to believe him. That he's always been happy, that just wasn't believable. Instead, he said, "I've never not wanted to be married to you." He wished that he'd said something closer to, "I've always wanted to be married to you."

Cutter shook his head. He couldn't imagine it: Lynne buried the ring and decades later he dug it up. Their tenth anniversary was after Isaac died. Their parents were still alive. They must have all been together, out somewhere, probably eating large slabs of beef.

"You never said a word about it, Lynne."

"No. I couldn't. You made a point about not wearing a wedding ring. You'd already stopped wearing your class ring."

"I don't remember making some principled stand against wedding bands."

Lynne laughed. "Of course you don't remember. But I asked you if you'd wear one, and you said no. You said you didn't want to wear one when you showed clients houses, and you didn't want to put one on and take it off like cufflinks—remember cufflinks?"

Cutter nodded. He remembered cufflinks. Tie tacks, too, for that matter. Not the conversation.

"I should have asked you about wearing the ring before I bought it and had it engraved. I had it wrong.

"I was going to give the ring to you when you said, of course you'd wear one. It was going to be a big surprise. Before we all went out for dinner."

Cutter didn't have to ask who.

"And then I would have given it to you, and you would have worn it to dinner. And so on."

"My father didn't wear a ring. Or yours either, for that matter."

"My grandfather did. I have his ring, you know."

"I never thought about it."

They were both quiet. Ely fingered the ring. "So, why didn't you let me wear his ring instead of going out and buying one?"

"I was saving it," Lynne said. "I thought things would be different, that we'd try again. And if we had a daughter, she could give it to her husband."

She had never talked about having a daughter, not even when they were trying to have a baby after Isaac had died. He couldn't imagine another child in the house, in the nursery.

"You can say one thing about me, Ely. I was a planner. I had it all figured out. And I got it all wrong."

"Not all wrong, Lynne. You didn't get us wrong."

"Enough wrong."

"Enough right," he said. "You're being too hard on yourself."

"I don't blame myself for what didn't happen."

Did she blame herself for what had happened, or did she expect him to shoulder the entire responsibility? Either way, he was sorry that he hadn't eaten some of that French Toast. And it was too late for that, not in the middle of this talk.

A wedding band! And he'd never known. "You aren't to blame," he said. He stopped short of saying, "It's my fault, all of it." Not everything was his fault, not losing Isaac, certainly not that, although he'd asked himself time and again what would have happened had he checked on him earlier. Would he have been able to save him? He still didn't know artificial respiration. This was old ground.

"Would you have worn it?"

Cutter bit the inside of his lip until it hurt. "I don't know," he said. "Would it be better if I said yes? Or would you feel worse?"

"It's sweet of you to care, Ely, but it's a real question. I don't want you to try to make me feel better, I asked because I want to know the truth. I don't want to be coddled. Not now."

"But you deserve to be coddled," Cutter blurted. He was dismayed. By saying so he'd achieved the opposite: doing just what Lynne had said she didn't want. It was a perfect paradox, a bind he'd bumbled into. "I'd like to think I would have worn it, not just as a fashion accessory, but full time."

"You said that you thought it would interfere with selling."

That sounded right to him. He would've said so. He thought so even now. The difference is that now he had a wedding band sitting on the table in front of him.

"I used a shovel, one with a sharp edge," she said, "and stood on it to make it go straight down."

Before he could make a gaffe from which he'd have no chance of recovery, Cutter understood that she'd switched the topic.

"And one of those asparagus cutter things to go down farther. And dropped in the ring. It was pretty easy to hide the cut. The grass covered it right up. After a few days I wouldn't have been able to find it myself. When you started to plant a garden there, I expected you'd find it for sure."

"And I did."

"I meant right away, the first time you put a shovel into the ground, I was sure you'd find it."

"I found it when I was supposed to find it," Cutter said. "When the time was right." He hated clichés and here he was, piling them one on top of the other—even though he was sincere.

"This has been quite a year for the garden, hasn't it, Ely?"

She wasn't talking about a bumper crop of tomatoes, though this year the garden had seemed to be more fruitful than other summers. It had been an extraordinary summer all around. And now it was coming to an end. He liked this time of year. Soon he'd be able to harvest fruit and vegetables, pick all the flowers he wanted and pretty much ignore the details and tasks of garden maintenance. Benign neglect. The bounty of the harvest in the fall seemed like a gift.

But if he hadn't been tending to the pole beans, he wouldn't have found the ring. Maybe he really was supposed to find it now. He'd said so himself, but though he'd been sincere, just a moment or two later he wasn't sure.

He picked up the ring, already cool in his palm.

"Do you want me to have it polished?" Lynne asked. "It must have scratches on it."

"Nothing unusual. Take a look."

She shook her head no and didn't hold out her hand.

"I trust you," she said.

He let the double meaning pass without a remark. "Then let's keep it as it is. For good luck."

"What are you going to do with it?" Lynne asked.

Not the good luck. No, she wanted to know what he was going to do with the ring. He wasn't about to do that Windex spray number every day. Once he put it on, it would have to stay on.

Or he could say that he'd put it in his top drawer in the box next to the cufflinks.

"I'd like to wear it," he said, pushing it onto his finger.

Looking at Lynne's face, her evident relief, he was confident that this time he'd made the right decision.

CHAPTER 19

And, on their way home from tennis Sam asked how Grace was getting along. Ely was grateful to Sam for not asking the direct question, letting him get off easy if that's what he wanted to do. "She's pretty interested in another property," Cutter answered, "and I think she's going to get this one."

"How long have you been trying to find a place for her? All summer?" he asked, pausing before adding, "I suppose you'll be glad to make the sale,"

"Glad enough, Sam," he said. "Everything's under control."

"She's given up on tennis?"

"I think it was a passing interest." He took a deep breath and continued, "Robbie called. He left a message on her answering machine— that call I said I had on mine? Same voice."

"No kidding!"

"We both have the same answering machine—neither one of us ever changed the message," Ely said, then murmured, "which, I guess, you already know."

When Sam didn't pick up that thread, Ely continued, "So Robbie assumed she'd gotten the first message."

"You told her?" Sam asked.

"Sure."

"How bad was she?"

Cutter looked at Sam. He was frowning, as though he knew just how drunk Grace had been when Cutter had arrived.

"Bad enough," he said.

"It wouldn't have been the first time," Sam said.

Then he hadn't been over-reacting to the open door and the music, to Grace's insisting that he show up—and fast. "I wasn't sure."

"Her ex-," Sam began, but stopped before explaining.

Ely didn't ask him to elaborate. He already knew enough about Robert to be sure that he didn't want to know more. Sam wouldn't push him, so he said, "The new property that she likes has an indoor fountain and pond with koi. Cathedral ceiling. Huge black granite fireplace."

"That's Grace," Sam said, with his first big smile of the day.

"You think she'll be all right?"

Sam shook his head, the smile vanished, "Don't know. Whatever happens, you can't fix everything."

Cutter nodded.

"Take care of yourself. Lynne, too. You're a mensch, Ely. I'm sure you were a *mensch* with Grace."

That was less praise than advice that Sam was giving him, and Cutter wondered what it would take for him to act on it.

"You think this will make a difference?" He held up his hand with the ring on it.

"A statement or a question?" Sam said.

"Both."

"Since when?"

"Lynne got it for me," Cutter said. "I've been wearing it," and he looked at his watch, "for about twenty-four hours and thirteen minutes." That was a part of the story.

"*Mazel tov*, I suppose."

"Definitely." Cutter injected as much cheer as he could into his response although Sam would see through his false heartiness. He hadn't thought about asking Lynne what she wanted him to say about the ring, about what she was planning on telling Ruth. That would have made this conversation easier on him. He wanted to level with Sam, and he wanted to protect Lynne.

The image of her in their back yard cutting into the earth was pathetic—poor Lynne probably standing on the shovel so her weight would provide what her strength lacked. Had she been furious with him then, thinking she'd never forgive him? After that had his bare hand been a poignant reminder to her of his unwitting rejection. He didn't want Sam to feel sorry for Lynne; it didn't seem fair to her. She had too much pride. If she hadn't had so much pride, she would've told him about the ring, or tucked it away somewhere for another more propitious time, a time when he wasn't so lacking in perception that he'd devalue her gift.

Dear Lynne. He couldn't imagine her tumult of emotions, what it must have been like for her to be out in the back yard after she'd buried the ring, not only at the beginning, but especially as their garden expanded, each year getting closer to where she'd buried the ring. So she had a secret, too. And maybe she'd even told Ruth about it at the time. She wouldn't have told her parents. It would have set them against him, which she wouldn't have wanted. But, he reminded himself, he had never wanted to wear a wedding ring. And a ring wouldn't have kept him out of trouble either—if his affair with Eleanor and his relationship with Grace could be called trouble.

"So?"

"For a long time, I wasn't interested in wearing a wedding band."

"And now you are?"

"Now I'm wearing one. Interested in wearing one? I'm not. But if it makes Lynne happy, that should be good enough reason." He chuckled, suddenly self-conscious, clarifying, "That is good enough reason."

"You'll get used to it," Sam said.

He might get used to wearing the wedding band, but as for doing something just because it makes Lynne happy—about that Cutter wasn't so sure.

Grace's house was filled with flowers: an arrangement on every surface. Her house smelled like a florist's shop. At a glance Cutter recognized roses, stock, carnations, baby's-breath, snapdragons. Most of these arrangements had the formal look of something designed by a professional.

"It doesn't look like a funeral parlor, does it?" she asked.

"Not to me," Cutter said, puzzled, until he remembered that flowers were de rigueur at Christian funerals; his immediate connection with Jewish funerals had spared him from associating flowers with death.

"Birthday?" Even as he asked, he was certain her answer would be no. He didn't remember her mentioning her birthday, and he felt sure that she would have pressed him into some sort of celebration.

"Anniversary!"

She sounded triumphant, but as far as he knew, she was divorcing, flamboyantly so.

"That's nice," he said. Maybe he'd tried a bit too hard to achieve a noncommittal tone. "That's nice" sounded cold, even to him. He'd try to make up for it, "They're pretty," he said, gesturing at the nearest bouquet of white roses.

"I love flowers," Grace said.

Cutter nodded. Though Grace had expressed an interest in having a garden in her new house, this house had a singular lack of flowers in the landscaping. If he'd been selling this place, he would have advised her to put in at least some impatiens along the front walk. The hostas were attractive and low maintenance, but a splash of color would have added to the curb appeal: A hanging basket of orange begonias, or on the front steps a pot of red geraniums, which Grace could have changed out before they looked scraggly, any of these would have helped. He'd say none of this.

He wondered who had sent all of these flowers and for what anniversary. Nothing to do with him he hoped.

"What's your favorite flower, Ely?"

"I don't know that I have one," Cutter said. He was feeling cornered, confused by his reluctance to say he had an inordinate fondness for iris, big old-fashioned iris that used to be called flags. He was expected to return the question.

Polite volley. No backhand slams just clearing the net.

"Aren't you going to ask me?"

Her tone was somewhere between petulant and flirtatious.

"Yes, of course." He struggled to keep irritation from his voice. "What's your favorite flower?"

"Not that question. Roses. Isn't that boring of me? The other."

"Roses aren't boring. They're beautiful," he said. Thinking about the thorns, he added, "and dangerous."

"Beautiful and dangerous." Grace chuckled. "Are you trying to tell me something?"

He'd stepped right up to that. "Nothing new."

"Do you think I'm dangerous?" She laid her hand on his arm. Today she wasn't wearing nail polish.

"I was talking about roses, Grace."

"I'll pretend to believe you," she said.

She looked and sounded like a petulant child. "Why shouldn't you?" he asked, not expecting her to come clean. That would have involved not only a clear look at him, but a steady gaze at herself,

"Let's not get into that," she said.

Grace was right. This wasn't a conversation he wanted to have with her. Were all the women in his life going to accuse him of being untrustworthy?

"So, Ely, you're not going to ask me, are you?"

"Oh, Grace! I'm not sure what you want me to ask," he said. The options were too many rather than too few.

"I can think of at least two good questions, but I'm only talking about the easy one," Grace said.

Cutter wished that he'd asked her straight off. That would have been better than getting into this. "Okay, then."

"Don't you want to try guessing?"

Cutter patted Grace on her shoulder, a gesture so paternal that it surprised him. "I've never been much for guessing games."

He'd tried with Grace. He'd wanted to figure out what was

expected of him, what would cause least damage—and yield the greatest advantage.

"Does that mean you won't give me a penny for my thoughts?" she said.

"That won't involve guessing, just a straight commercial transaction." He reached his hand into his pocket, searching for some loose change. Nothing.

"You're selling too cheap. Even so, I'm coming up empty handed." He held out his right hand, glad that had been the one he'd used to look for the change. He wasn't eager to show off his wedding band; she'd notice it soon enough, probably before he was ready.

"You always know the right thing to say, Ely."

That wasn't the impression he'd had. He'd been caught off guard by the flowers and Grace's announcement of an anniversary. "So do you," he said.

"See, that's just what I mean!"

Cutter was surprised by Grace's apparent sincerity. He managed to annoy, then delight her within moments. How did that happen? "I'm glad you're so easily pleased."

"Easily pleased by you. Not in general. You've been showing me houses, you know I'm picky."

She was picky. Most women were when they looked at houses, even more so when, like Grace, they were changing homes because they were divorcing. Sometimes he thought that the women who'd been left by their husbands were more difficult to please than those who had kicked their husbands out. It was all about control. They'd lost it, and now they wanted it back, especially at home. A woman's home is her castle, married or unmarried; he'd been told that when he'd started in the business. A lesson well-learned.

"No more than you should be. You have a right," he said. He tried to sound reassuring. It was easy for him now that she'd found a place she wanted to buy.

"I sent myself the flowers. You already figured that out, didn't you?"

Cutter nodded. He hadn't, but it was no shock.

"I knew I could count on you to understand! Meeting you has changed my life."

They were veering towards a dangerous subject, and Cutter tried to redirect the conversation by pretending he took it as an ordinary compliment. "That's very generous of you," he said.

"Generous? I'm not offering you a second cup of tea."

"Of course you're not," Cutter said, thinking it was an odd response. A second cup of tea wouldn't be called "generous." She was picking up on his tone, and he wished that she'd offered him a first cup, so he could fiddle with it. A sip of tea, an opportunity to stir in some sugar, both ways of filling awkward silence with a bit of stage business.

Grace clapped her hand over her mouth. "How could I? Oh, Ely, forgive me!"

This was the Grace who had burst into tears in the bookstore. He watched her face for a hint of reddening, an indication that she was about to cry. No, he was safe. He waited to see what offense she'd imagined.

"I haven't offered you even a glass of water. Let's sit in the garden and have a cool drink."

"All right, Grace, but don't you think we'd be better off getting that bid nailed down before somebody else gets the house?"

"If I don't get that one, I'll find another," Grace said, with such nonchalance that Cutter was dismayed. After all his work! And after all the trouble Grace had caused between him and Lynne! Though that hadn't been her intent, at least in the beginning.

"Joanne hasn't found anyone who wants this house, and if this doesn't sell. . ."

Of course, Grace had to sell before she could move. But losing momentum...

"I don't want to talk about that now," she said. "Iced coffee or tea?" She paused, then added, "Or something stronger?"

"Your coffee is plenty strong for me," Cutter tried for a light tone. It was early in the day for liquor, but he didn't want to say as much.

Cutter sat in the shadiest part of Grace's garden, wondering if it reflected her taste or her husband's. A few evergreens, stone lanterns, a water-flute fountain. A couple of well-placed, large rocks, a decorative bridge crossing a stream made of smooth river stones. It had the mark of a careful landscaper, schooled in Japanese gardens. Maybe he would feel tranquil if he sat here long enough, but if this garden was supposed to induce tranquility, Grace was no advertisement for its success.

No wonder Grace had gone for that house with the fountain. The sound of falling water was familiar. He was concentrating on the sound of the water, when Grace appeared, carrying a tray with two glasses and some plates and bowls.

"I thought a tiny snack might be in order. And no protests."

"Snack?"

"Cucumber with yogurt cheese," she said, "with garlic and fresh dill." She set another plate on the table. "Peanut butter on whole wheat toast—with asparagus and roasted pepper."

"Original," Cutter said, wondering how much he'd be expected to eat. Food like this doesn't just appear. She must have planned this snack and had it almost ready to go. When Grace leaned over to set the food on the table, she brushed against his arm.

"Iced tea for you," she said setting down a glass and a pitcher. "And a vodka gimlet for me."

Was that a tone of defiance that he caught in her voice?

She put the tray on an empty chair and sat down. "Don't look so disapproving, Ely. I'm a big girl."

"Sorry. I hadn't intended to..."

"Of course you didn't. But you are, aren't you?" she said, with her head cocked and a knowing smile.

"I'm not sure disapproving is the right word. It's so judgmental."

"And?"

"I have enough problems of my own—to be judgmental about, I mean. I don't need to focus on yours," he said. Judgmental brooding about one's flaws...not how he liked to spend his time. He'd observed that people who were insecure about themselves were often hypercritical of others, so much so that it had become a cliché, but he had a hunch that it could go the other way around, too. He was being candid about not wanting to focus on her problems: some of that was being self-protective.

"Is my drinking a problem?" she asked.

"For me? No." He felt like he should say more, but he didn't know what else to say.

"So it's not an obstacle."

"I can't think of what it's an obstacle to," he said. "Things are what they are, Grace."

"You're a good man, Ely. I'm a lucky woman to have you in my life."

That wasn't what he'd meant at all. Nor had he intended to tell her that there was nothing between them. And if he had, that would have been untrue.

"I suppose I'm going to have to ask you," she said. "I was hoping that you'd make it easy on me, but I see that's probably not going to happen."

What was she talking about now? He wondered why he found Grace so attractive when she kept him off-balance.

She took a deep breath. "Then why?"

Cutter was startled by her anguish in her voice. Although her "why" was too soft to be an actual wail or howl, it was an unmistakable expression of grief. He was at a loss until he remembered his ring.

She must have seen his wedding ring and said nothing about it until now. He reviewed the few minutes he'd spent with Grace to see if he could figure out at what point she'd spotted it. Is this why she wanted him to come out in the garden, so that he'd find it impossible to make a dignified undisguised retreat? He couldn't very well announce that he wanted to look at the fountain or walk up over the bridge that crossed the meandering river-stone stream. And even if he did, he will still be well within earshot.

He did the next best thing. He pretended that he didn't understand. He raised a quizzical eyebrow and said, "What's wrong?" Even as he asked, he knew he was being a heel.

"What's wrong? How can you ask that?" Grace said.

She'd gone from misery to puzzled anger. He preferred her anger. A moment later Ely felt self-satisfied, almost noble, because he preferred to be the target of her anger rather than the cause of her misery. Perhaps despite his weakness, he was a good man, after all.

"I'm sorry," he said, once more unsure of to which offense the apology should be applied. Had Grace asked him "what for?" he would be at a loss for a direct answer, and "for everything" would have been all wrong.

"Let me see it," she said, holding out her open palm.

"See it?"

"Your ring."

Cutter held out his hand for Grace to inspect. He was feeling uncomfortable, more so than he'd been when he'd shown Sam. He looked for words to describe his feeling: abashed, guilty, embarrassed.

She tapped her empty palm. "Here," she said.

The way she held out her hand was like the gesture Lynne had used. He set his fingers on Grace's palm. He'd forgotten how tiny her hands were. His hands weren't large, but, when his hand was with Grace's, it looked huge.

"Oh," she said.

Cutter had no idea that he could be so aroused by fingertips tracing lines on his palm, even by Grace's fingertips. Oblivious to his gaze, she stroked each of his fingers except his ring finger. He closed his eyes, abandoning the last of his resistance to her touch. The garden had high walls, was hidden from the neighbor's windows by trees. They must have as much privacy here as in the house.

Grace's head was bowed. Almost overcome, he reached to brush a tendril of damp hair from her neck, but before he could, she raised her face. Her eyes weren't red with tears, though her face was flushed. She had never looked so loving, so fragile, so accessible.

"Grace," he whispered.

He touched her lips with his fingers, and lips parted. He whispered her name again.

"No," she said.

"No? But why?" he said, surprised at her refusal. Had he been so mistaken?

Grace laughed, she put her index finger on the wedding band and made tiny circles, but she didn't say a word.

"The ring? That doesn't make any difference, does it? Nothing's changed."

"You never wore it before, so something's changed," she said.

"Nothing's changed between us, Grace," he said although he knew that wasn't true. He'd never felt for Grace what he'd felt a moment before, what he was still feeling.

"If you say things are the same with us as before, then they must've changed with Lynne, no?" she said.

"Look," he began, hoping that Grace would interrupt him

before he said something stupid that would have consequences he couldn't undo. But she didn't, and he continued, "This doesn't have to have anything to do with Lynne, does it?"

"The ring, Ely, the ring. You're not going to tell me it doesn't mean anything."

"Would you believe me?" he asked.

"Is there anything inside the ring?"

"My finger," he said, trying to lighten the mood. He knew as soon as he'd spoken that he'd made a mistake.

"Not funny."

"What difference does that make?" he said.

"I don't know why I asked." Then she shook her head. "Oh, yes, I do know." She laughed again. "I thought you might let me look."

"And so?"

"You'd have to take off your ring and give it to me. And I saw something in that. I wanted you to take it off your finger. For me."

"I can't do that," Ely said, his voice soft.

"You mean you won't," she said.

"It doesn't come off." As far as he knows, it really doesn't come off. Nonetheless, she's right. He doesn't want to remove the ring, certainly doesn't want her to hold it.

"I bet I could get it off if I tried."

"I'm sure you could, but I don't think that's a good idea. And, besides, it shouldn't make any difference." Shouldn't...by whose standards was that right, he asked himself.

"This is one hell of an anniversary, I'm having." She drank some of her gimlet. "So, let me understand. You never wore a ring until now, and now you want to..."

Even though her voice trailed off, Cutter had no doubt that she knew what he wanted, and how much he wanted it. "I can't expect you to understand," he said.

"So, all summer whenever you were with me you took off the ring? You weren't wearing it that night in the bookstore either. You had a date with that woman, that Evelyn, didn't you?"

He knew she meant Eleanor, but he didn't correct her. And he wouldn't tell her that she was right about the date.

"I didn't wear a wedding band then."

"I know you didn't. That's what I just said."

"I should have said, 'I really didn't wear it...'"

"I don't get it. This isn't new, right."

"Right." Cutter wished he could skip this part. "It's like this. We didn't have a double ring ceremony. Lynne gave this to me, got this for me, for our tenth anniversary."

"And you'd take it off whenever it was inconvenient to have a wedding band."

"I can see why you'd think that, Grace. But that's not quite it."

"You're being evasive."

Cutter smiled. "I suppose I am. I'll try to be direct. She bought it for me then, but I only started wearing it all the time a couple of days ago."

"And I'm supposed to believe that this makes no difference. Why now?"

"I put the ring on after a long time of not having worn it, and discovered that it goes on, but it doesn't come off."

"So, that's all."

"That's all." Cutter didn't want to tell her more, as much for his sake as for Lynne's.

"And you think we should be together in bed, and you'd be wearing your wedding band and that's all. Essentially all."

"I can understand why that would bother you. It's not what I had in mind."

"Isn't it?"

"I wasn't thinking about the ring," he said. "As for the rest, yes."

"It's not going to happen like that, Ely."

Grace drained her glass and stood, looking down at him. Cutter searched her face looking for a vestige of the desire that he'd seen earlier. Nothing.

An invisible jay called from a tree, thief-thief-thief! The garden might well have been a place he could have found some tranquility, but he'd lost the prospect. "You're sending me away?" he asked.

Grace sighed. "I am, Ely. I'm sending you away."

A flash of blue. The jay settled on the edge of the fountain basin, drank, cocked its head, and flew back to the tree where he vanished again in the foliage.

He had to say something. "I never intended...I told you I was married." What would those little cucumber things have tasted like?

"There's married, and there's married," Grace said. "I wasn't sure before which you were."

"I'll call you in a couple days. Or you can call me before that..." Cutter said. So much was at stake here.

Though the light behind her was so bright he couldn't see

her face, when Grace shifted her weight, Ely knew she was going to make him leave without seeing him to the door.

He waited for her to say something. This must be what she was feeling all those times, he thought. In possession of that understanding, he let himself out, careful not to slam the door as he left.

CHAPTER 20

Ely turned on his side, his left hand under the pillow. His wedding band cut into his finger. He shifted his arm, and when that was no more comfortable, he turned to lie on his back. No better. He bent his arm at the elbow and held it at right angles to the mattress. The ring was still too tight. He turned to lie on his right side and rested his left arm on his hip. His finger felt like a swollen sausage about to pop. He held his arm straight up in the air. If blood flowed out of his hand, maybe the ring wouldn't be so tight. All his flopping around has done no good, and he's kept Lynne awake.

"Are you all right?"

He wasn't all right. The ring was cutting off his circulation. "I'm fine," he lied. He sat on the edge of the bed, his finger throbbing. How could it get so bad so fast?

Salt, he told himself. He must've had too much salt at dinner. He'd go downstairs and find, what was it, Windex?

"Where are you going?" Lynne asked.

"To the kitchen."

"Snack?"

Cutter heard no disapproval in her voice. Good. He didn't want to tell her his ring finger hurt. She'd get all upset with no good reason. Tomorrow he'll take the ring to a jeweler and have it sized.

"I'm hungry," he said. A little white lie couldn't hurt. He padded downstairs barefoot.

Rummaging under the kitchen sink, he found the Windex. Just the ticket to stay away from emergency room.

He held his hand over the kitchen sink. No sense dripping on the floor, making one more mess he'd have to clean up. He sprayed his ring finger, working to get some of the liquid under the ring. And then he tugged. No luck. He repeated the process, his hand dripping blue liquid into the stainless-steel sink.

Cutter had forgotten something, but he couldn't figure out what. The ring pressed against his knuckle, scrunching up folds of flesh. He gave his hand another spritz. Now his right hand couldn't get a good grip.

Maybe he should have told Lynne and asked her for help, but he wanted do this by himself. He wiped his right hand on a paper towel, then gave it another go. This time the ring began to slide off. At least he got it to nearly the top of, but not quite over the knuckle. Just a bit more now.

He added a couple more spritzes of Windex, then gripped the ring as best he could with his fingers, which were slippery again, and twisted. The ring popped off his finger, slipped from his grasp, fell into the sink, and bounced. It caught the light and glowed, gold against the stainless steel. The ring rolled like a hoop in a big circle, and it kept rolling, spiraling into in smaller circles as it wobbled on its looping path towards the drain. The drain! That's what he'd forgotten— the strainer. Now frantic, he was reaching for the ring when Lynne, standing behind him, said, "Ely?"

Startled, he grabbed at the ring as it rolled past his uncoordinated grasp and into the drain opening, disappearing into the darkness of the garbage disposal.

Ely groaned and held up his bare hand to show Lynne

what had happened. "The ring," he said. "It got too tight, and I couldn't sleep."

He extended his hand to show her the marks the tight ring had left on his swollen finger. Nothing. No sign of the ring's constriction. Not even a reddened knuckle where he'd struggled to pull off the ring. His finger didn't seem the least bit swollen.

"I thought I'd try that trick you showed me," he said, sheepish. "It worked, but..."

"We can get the ring out tomorrow—or a plumber can," Lynne said.

Cutter turned on the cold water and rinsed his hands. "I'm sorry, Lynne."

"Don't apologize," she said.

"I'm not apologizing," he said. "I'm trying to express my unhappiness. I wish this hadn't happened. I wanted you to know how I felt."

"That's sweet," she said.

He listened for sarcasm but heard none.

"Let's get some sleep, but first let me see that hand again," Lynne said. She took his hand in hers and rubbed it. "All better?"

"Yes," he said. Maybe now all of it really was better. Or could be.

When Cutter woke, Lynne was gone from their bed. He'd better remember not to use the garbage disposal. He was irritated with himself for being careless, and he remained irritated all the way through his morning routine.

Even before he got to the kitchen, he smelled the freshly brewed coffee. Lynn sat at the kitchen table, an almost-full cup in front of her, the folded morning paper, next to her plate. She was frowning. Maybe she was, after all, angry about his accident with the wedding band.

He didn't have long to wait to find out. "It's Grace," she said.

Grace! What now? Grace had been pretty upset yesterday. He would have heard the phone unless Lynne had gotten it on the first ring. It was too early for a phone call, but Grace was never one for convention. She wouldn't have called to talk about the wedding band. Aloud, he said, "Grace? What about her?"

Maybe Lynne was worried. After Grace had summoned him to her house and he'd gone against Lynne's wishes, he wouldn't blame her for worrying. Now she had less to worry about, though of course he couldn't tell Lynne that the wedding band had kept him from going to bed with Grace. He was pleased with himself for having resisted Grace; it was as though Grace had never sent him away.

"It might not be Grace," Lynne said after a long pause, "But something tells me it is."

"For heaven's sake, Lynne. Spit it out already." He could have snapped at Lynne because he felt guilty or because he was cloaked in self-righteousness; however, probably he was just letting his irritation at himself for last night's clumsiness spill into his morning with Lynne. He sighed, not trying to disguise his discomfort, and apologized.

Lynne shook her head. "So, this is it," she said and launched into an explanation. The whole time she spoke, her hand lay over the newspaper.

Lynne told him about a bad car accident—the driver, a woman, didn't survive. No purse, nothing to identify her, except an answering machine that the police found in the car. "The answering machine made me think of Grace," Lynne said. "She might have been driving to her husband's—ex-husband's—to have him listen to the recording. She would have been upset, maybe driving too fast." She pushed the paper across the table. "It's not pretty."

He unfolded the paper to find a photograph of a white car, smashed into a tree, the whole front end crumpled. Cutter reminded himself to breathe. He'd seen dozens of photos like this one, and, until today, he'd always been unmoved. He'd never seen the point of the crumpled car image on the front page.

"Withholding name of the deceased until next of kin have been notified," he read aloud.

"Who are her relatives?" Lynne asked.

"Her son, Robbie. Do you count her ex as a relative?"

"I guess. They'd have trouble finding her son, wouldn't they?"

"I think the government can find anybody. Anywhere. There'd be passport records, I guess," Cutter said.

"Do you think you should do anything?"

"I ought to do something," Cutter said. He wanted to do something. The rending of garments came to mind, but that wouldn't do, even if he felt so inclined. If something G-d forbid happened to Lynne, he would be wild with grief.

"Is that her car?"

"She had a white car. It could be her car. I don't know. It could be."

The banner headline read: "Unidentified Woman Dies in Car Crash." Lynne had told him what he needed to know, but he read anyway:

"An unidentified woman died last night when her car hit a tree on Route 70. No passengers were in the car.

A witness told police that a cat ran across the road, and the car swerved to avoid hitting it. "I thought she was going to run over the poor thing, but she didn't. She must have lost control because the car swung back into the lane and then off again and hit the tree."

The witness said she phoned 911 and the local EMT group and police arrived "within minutes."

The name of the deceased is being withheld pending notification of next of kin. No pocketbook was found on the scene, but an answering machine was found in the back seat of the car."

"Do you think she was going home from Robert's, or was she on her way to see him?"

Cutter shook his head. He hadn't had time to ask himself the question, but now that Lynne had broached the topic, he thought the answer would explain a lot about what happened.

Or maybe it wasn't Grace after all?

"It must have been hard for her," Lynne continued. "After everything fell apart. To lose her son and her husband one after the other like that. Do you think she regretted…?"

"Sticking with her husband?" Cutter finished Lynne's

sentence. "Not from what she said. I got the feeling that she wanted things to work out with him. I think she would have gone back to him even at the end, after everything.

"She might have been drinking when she went to see Robert. I know she wanted him to hear the message and holding a phone up to the machine wouldn't do it. Not the way it should have been."

"It could have been an excuse to see him," Lynne said.

"She asked me," Cutter said.

"About?"

"Oh, maybe she was wondering aloud more than asking. Or maybe she knew what she should do and wanted to hear it from me. She needed to tell Robert."

"Not telling him would have been a good way of punishing him," Lynne said.

"I don't know, Lynne. If he cared so much about his son..."

"A good punishment. Well, not so much a punishment, but revenge. She could take satisfaction in his not knowing," Lynne said.

"Grace wasn't like that," Cutter said. Hadn't thought Lynne was either.

"And how do you know?" Maybe he'd overstepped some boundary, undefined, in defending Grace. He hadn't intended to say something that would upset Lynne. He hadn't wanted to compare the women, with Lynne being less kind and less honorable than Grace.

He took a deep breath and tried to start over. "Well, I suppose I don't know. How could I? Even if I'd said, 'Are you seeking revenge,' or some such thing, what sort of answer could I have expected?"

"Not revenge. I said that wrong," Lynne said. "Regaining control of her life. That's something she'd lost. Any control of her life at all."

Lynne was talking about herself, too. So, that's how she'd felt, helpless. And he'd done that to her, more than once. He hadn't realized until now how frightened Lynne had been, how she'd felt that her whole life was out of control. Lynne had never been what he would have considered a control freak, and even now, after a lifetime together, he could discover something about his wife if he paid attention. He should apologize, or, better yet, find a way to make it up to her.

"Was he living with somebody?" Lynne asked.

"Robbie?"

"Her ex."

"I don't know," Cutter said. "Or I don't remember, anyway."

"You'd remember that, wouldn't you?" Lynne said.

"You'd think so. But I don't."

"Because if he was, that would make it harder for her to go there. More awkward."

"I suppose." But Grace hadn't minded talking to Lynne. She'd done it on purpose that time on the phone—maybe she wouldn't have cared about meeting some shack-up honey. She might have bonded with her, or tried to, for all he knew. Or maybe arriving with the tape would trump the shack-up.

That's what Grace would have counted on. Show up with the answering machine after making sure Robert was there—she would have done her homework—and play the tape. Right. What she'd counted on was that maybe the babe answers the door, Grace smiles her way into the living room, and then, bam!

But if Robert had been cool to her, didn't much care about hearing the tape, or if he'd heard it, was moved, but then, instead of hugging Grace, hugged the honey—Grace wouldn't have done well.

Or maybe the accident happened on her way there. In which case maybe Robert still didn't know about the recording. Or at least he hadn't heard it. If he'd heard it, would Grace have had it with her in the car? "I should call Robert," he said, though that was neither a call he wanted to make or a conversation he could imagine having. So far there's been too much speculation: maybe, maybe if, if, maybe.

Cutter looked at the photo of the car again. If the photo showed the license plate, that would be the identification Robert would need. If he'd seen the photo. Not everybody took the paper these days. "I'm looking for the license plate," he said to Lynne, "It's not in the photo."

"I know. I looked before. I thought that would tell us. We could call Joanne. She has a key to the house."

"Or we could call Grace," Cutter said. "If she answers, all is well—that is, for her, not for the poor soul in the car. If she doesn't, and there's no answering machine that picks up, we have another indication." And, he said to himself, God willing, it isn't Grace.

Lynne handed him the phone. "You have the number," she said. It wasn't a question.

Cutter nodded. "It's on my cell-phone. Or I can look in the phone book."

"Really, Ely, this is no time to bullshit. Just call her."

She was right. This wasn't a time for pretense. The number

was on their phone, too, from the other night when she'd called. Unless Lynne had done one of her phone number purges. His hands trembled as he punched in Grace's phone number.

He closed his eyes: Grace at the table in her garden, holding her hand out for his ring. The ring that had gone down the drain. The least of his problems now. What would he say if Grace answered? Thank God, Grace, we were afraid you'd been killed. Would he tell her he loved her? He loves Lynne. But Grace... three... four... five...

And then a breathless woman answers the phone. "Grace?"

"Who?"

Cutter was afraid he was going to cry.

He repeated the number. No. He'd reversed two digits. Of all times to do that. But understandable. He explained to Lynne, punched the numbers in again, but with care. Again, he counted rings; he counted to ten, let it ring until it's obvious: there would be no answer.

Cutter stared at the phone. He could do it again. What's the use? He was kidding himself if he thought he could find Grace.

Lynne put her hand on his shoulder. "It's all right, Ely. You can feel awful. I'm not angry."

Cutter tried to manage a smile. It didn't feel right. "I'm going to call her husband. You know, in case, just in case..." His voice trailed off.

"That's a good idea. Do you want me to look up his number?"

"That's all right. I can do it," he said. She wants to do

something, Cutter thought. I can't leave her out of this mess if she wants to help. I've already cut her out of too much. "But I'd be grateful if you would."

And then, to his amazement, he realized that, in fact, he was grateful.

"No luck, Ely. Nothing in the phone book. Should I try online?"

He nodded. "Might as well." And then he added, "Thank you. You're being more help than you can imagine. It's not just that you're looking up a number." He put his face in his hands, his elbows on the table and stayed that way for a moment. Lynne was standing across from him, her face inscrutable.

He could attempt to dissemble, but at what cost? He'd already tried to hide too much from her, never thinking what she might have hidden from him. Enough! He admonished himself to stop wallowing. He had plenty to deal with now, no need to add more by self-pitying speculation.

"I don't want to think I'm being noble. If I do, I'll worry about what happened with you and Grace that makes this so damned altruistic.

"Besides, Grace is probably dead. I can afford to be generous," she said as she walked away.

I couldn't expect more than that, Cutter thought, and it would be better for both of us if I let it go. He wondered if there were a blessing to say over an averted argument, or for one that was concluded.

And then Lynne was back, shaking her head. "Nothing useful."

"Call the police?" Cutter said, hoping she would do it.

"They'll know who owns the car," Lynne said, "so I guess we can try that. But there's the notification of next-of-kin clause. We might be friends, but we're not next-of-kin."

He was grateful for the "we."

"I'll call," he said, "tell them what I know about the answering machine. Maybe they'll phone Robert and help him get in touch with their son.

"I hate going through this. I don't know how much I have to tell them. It's none of their business," he said.

"Not all of it. Leave out the unimportant details."

"Adultery is an unimportant detail?"

"To the police. In this case, yes. We're not talking murder here." She paused and added with what just a bit too much emphasis, "or suicide."

Cutter sighed. "I suppose I have to be the one to make this call."

Cutter blundered from sentence to sentence, disconcerted by his being aware that he was talking too much, making his relationship with Grace evident. But Lynne already knew, and the policeman wouldn't care. The police had already listened to the answering machine. Why wouldn't they? And they wouldn't tell him. But he could establish himself as someone who had a right to know if he told them what he knew about the message on the machine. What it said, not its background. That he wouldn't have to do. Or at least he hoped he wouldn't. He'd known they would ask questions. Methodical questions, and he was put off-balance when they asked fewer questions than he'd expected.

He'd had his back to Lynne while he talked. He hadn't wanted to check her face for clues, which would be distracting, as well as upsetting to both of them. He would have liked being alone for this part, but he couldn't leave the room to make the call or ask Lynne to leave. She had limits, and he would be bumping up against them either way. "Yes, I can do that," he said, "Of course. If you think...Yes."

He turned to Lynne, "They want me to come in."

"Aren't you going to hang up the phone?"

"Oh," he said, and stared at the receiver. He must be even more upset than he'd known.

"When are you going? Do you have an appointment?"

"Now. Soon. No appointment. Soon," said Ely.

"Eat some breakfast, Ely. You don't know how long you'll be there."

"I'm not hungry."

"You will be."

"Don't, Lynne," he said, as she set out a variety of cereals and milk and fruit. She'd taken eggs out of the icebox, and, from the cabinet, the bowl she usually uses when she scrambles eggs.

"You'll call Sam?"

Cutter knew it was an innocent question. She wouldn't know about Sam's history with Grace.

"I don't want to go there, Ely. And I don't think you should go alone."

"I'm a big boy," he said although he did want Sam to go with him. "But if you think it's a good idea, I'll phone him."

What would he say while Lynne was listening? If Sam

didn't know, it would be a shock. Nothing to do for it but call. He needn't have worried how to tell Sam what had happened. Sam's first words to him were, "I know. Grace is gone."

CHAPTER 21

Cutter had just clicked his seatbelt shut when Sam said, "I knew when I heard about the answering machine in the car. Too much of a coincidence for it to be anybody else."

"Lynne took a pass on coming along for this one," he said, wanting let Sam know that Lynne and he had talked over what Cutter was doing.

"Can't blame her," Sam said.

"Ruth knows?" Cutter asked.

"She knows it was Grace in that car. Pretty sure, anyway."

"How much did you have to tell her?"

"Minimal, Ely. No more than a need-to-know basis. What was there to say?" he paused. "She brought it up to me this morning. Lynne had told her about the phone message and the machine."

"I haven't said anything." Cutter said, though Sam hadn't asked. He hadn't told Lynne about Sam and Grace. It wasn't his to tell. He hated keeping secrets from Lynne, but he had kept his own, he could keep Sam's, too.

"I didn't think you would. I knew you wouldn't."

"This isn't what I'd expected. Not how I thought it would end up. Not that I thought much," Ely said. Maybe he had thought about a lot of things—but not Grace's death.

"So, now what?"

"I go in, they ask questions. I suggest they find Robert, and that's it."

"I'll go in with you. Who knows how long you'll have to wait."

"Give me ten minutes, say, maybe fifteen. No sense in your getting involved with this end of it."

"But if?"

"Right," Cutter said, knowing that Sam was looking ahead. "Then... well...then I'd be grateful."

Later Cutter would remember little about his interview with the police. Cutter explained, this time in more detail than he'd given on the phone, that he sold real estate and had been showing Grace places. The Lieutenant had seen right through him, asking questions about how well he'd known Grace, for how long, and some details about her habits, questions to reveal the extent and nature of his relationship with Grace. He was afraid to lie, afraid to tell the truth. He wished he had his wedding ring back, not that it would have offered him any real protection from the questioning.

Despite his having imagined scenarios of Grace telling Robert about Robbie's calls, he'd missed the obvious. She couldn't have told Robert. If she had, he would have phoned the police by now. He might have been unfaithful, but he wouldn't have left Grace unidentified.

She might have gone to the house and found only the girlfriend, been upset and crashed. Doubtful.

"They tried phoning him, and there was no answer. Just a machine like the one he'd left with Grace," Cutter told Sam. "So they want to know if I would try to identify the body. Her."

"And then?"

"Then they find Robbie, wherever he is. Passport. Visa. State Department information. I don't know how, exactly. But

I suppose it's not that hard. They probably can get Robert's cell phone number, too."

"Sounds like it wasn't too rough."

"The Lieutenant asked whether Grace was suicidal. And if someone would have wanted her dead.

"I told them I couldn't imagine that anyone would have wanted her dead, and, as far as I knew, Grace wasn't going to kill herself."

"Did he ask how you knew?"

"Oh, yes. I told him that she'd been high-strung when I met her, that over the past months while she's been house hunting, she's calmed down. The phone call from Robbie threw her off-stride, I said, but it was good news, not bad."

"You had to give examples?"

Cutter shrugged. "I gave examples. She used to cry a lot. She doesn't anymore—didn't, that is. Not inappropriately."

"This I didn't say: she threw me out the last time I was with her. Before she would have bawled. Very together. Self-contained. She knew what she wanted, but she was much cooler."

Then Cutter paused.

"On the other hand, she had some sort of anniversary thing going on. And they'll find flowers everywhere when they check her place. I think it was the anniversary of Robert's leaving. But she wasn't about to kill herself, not when I was there."

"And when you left?"

"Not then either, not that I could tell. It was the wedding band, Sam. She wanted me to take it off. And I wasn't going to."

"But you're not wearing it now."

"An accident. It's down the drain. I'll get it back. Have it sized. *Kleinekeiten.* Little stuff can be fixed.

"She's at the hospital where they took her after the accident. They'll have to send the body somewhere. Morgue. Mortuary. I hope Robert sets things up," Ely said.

"You think he'll wait to hold the funeral until the son comes home? If he does."

"For sure. He'll come. I heard those tapes."

"But you're supposed to go to the hospital?"

"Since they can't reach Robert. Maybe he's on vacation. Summer's almost over. Who knows?

"It was a bad accident, Sam," he said, shaking his head.

"I don't think she intended to drive into the tree. She wouldn't do it like that—if she would have at all," Sam said.

"She was too religious, Sam." Cutter paused. "He asked me about that. When I said she was religious, he asked me if she went to church a lot."

"What did you say?"

"The truth. I didn't know for sure. Church wasn't something she talked about much. I told him that she'd suggested I light a candle. And, of course, he wanted to know why. I said I'd taken a spill, didn't go into details.

"She wouldn't have killed herself. Not like this," And then Cutter said, "They showed me photographs. From the accident."

"The photo in the paper looked bad."

"Right, but the photo in the paper was of the car. These were pictures of Grace herself. After."

Sure, she'd been drinking before the accident. He couldn't have prevented that. She'd been in a state when he'd arrived. If he'd dropped his ring into her hand, everything would have been different now. Maybe he'd still be going to identify her body, but he'd be wondering when or if the police would be showing up at his house, looking to match up his DNA with what had been left behind after lovemaking. Sex. It would be the insurance company behind it, trying to show that Grace had killed herself so they wouldn't have to pay whatever policy she'd had.

But the witness said Grace had swerved to avoid hitting a cat. Where had the cat come from? And where had it gone?

"You could tell it was Grace?" Sam asked.

"Pretty much, I could. But they asked if I could be sure. I said I couldn't without seeing her, so I suppose that's why we're going.

"Then what?"

"I go back, make a signed statement. And they take it from there."

"We're supposed to use the Emergency Room entrance," Cutter said.

"I guess that makes sense."

"He said he was phoning to let them know we'd be coming. Or that I would."

"Protocols. What would Grace have wanted?"

"Not this," Cutter said, certain of this answer. "She always looked, well, spiffy.

"A vodka gimlet," he added.

"What?"

"She was drinking a vodka gimlet when I last saw her. And she put out some yogurt cheese on cucumbers. For a snack, she said. She told me I was being judgmental."

"Were you?"

Cutter nodded. "I suppose I was. If she hadn't been drinking, maybe she wouldn't have had the accident."

"But you don't know for sure that she'd had much to drink at all. And it was later, wasn't it, that she had the accident?"

"Hours. Of course, she had hours to get smashed." He winced at his choice of words.

He wanted to change the subject, searched for something neutral. "Do you remember if she had on those bangles of hers the day she wanted to learn to play tennis?"

"No," Sam said. "I didn't notice. I wanted to be somewhere else."

"Of the three of us, she was the only one who didn't mind. She had, I don't know, a sense of being in the right place, no matter what," Cutter said. "Even when she cried."

He paused, then said, "Sam, I want to be somewhere else now."

"Understandable. You'd gotten to know Grace. You were, how would you put it, fond of her? I know I was. You saw that for yourself. Nothing surprising about it."

"Fond. A good word, Sam. Sanitary," Cutter said. Does anyone still use that word?

"I wasn't trying to..."

"I know. This isn't easy on you either. How are you going to manage with Ruth?"

"Ruth's okay with my going along with you today. She knows it was over. And, besides, Grace is gone. Nothing left to be jealous of."

"Could be easier to be jealous of somebody who's gone. No imperfections."

"That's the way you feel?"

"All the little irritations disappear. You don't speak ill of the dead. And I feel guilty even thinking ill. You know how it is."

Cutter drifted into silence. He tried to remember Grace's face in the garden, but could call up only the fountain, the bright sunlight, her gimlet glass beaded with water, the plate of cucumber slices.

"It is what it is, Ely."

"I don't want to see her, not the way she is."

"It's not going to get any better," Sam said, "except for make-up of course. If that's what you mean."

"No, make-up won't bring her back."

"You had a choice. You didn't have to be on your way to the hospital morgue right now.

"At every step you had a choice. You called the police. You agreed to come in. And then, then when they showed you the photo you said you couldn't tell for sure."

"I wasn't..." Sam was pushing him, but why? What did it matter to Sam?

"You weren't sure it was Grace? With all the evidence that pointed to Grace being the driver? And yet you said you weren't sure. You knew what that would mean."

"I suppose so."

"So, you wanted to see her again. Without a room full of people. Without Lynne. Without Robert. Even without Joanne."

"I'd forgotten Joanne." Sam was keeping him honest.

"Sure. But there's not much she's forgotten. And you didn't want her staring at you and whispering about her having found you two on the floor. And you know she's capable of doing just that."

"There's still the viewing and the funeral."

"But this is different, Ely. It's a private way to say goodbye."

"There's bound to be someone in the room with ..."

"Us? You were going to say 'us,' weren't you."

"You know me, Sam," Cutter said. "But there's the rest of it, too. I'm bound to remember her like this. I don't want to think of her lying dead on a gurney or in a big drawer."

"Then why?"

"Why did I agree? What you said. But with reservations,' he said, shaking his head. "Sometimes I try to remember Isaac, and instead of his grabbing my fingers and waving his little arms, I see him dead in the crib, and in his small coffin."

"Do you ever talk with Lynne about that?"

"No. I'm ashamed about forgetting. What's the point? It'll hurt her," he said. "And she'll think less of me. It'll be the opposite of a bond that we have."

"Does she ever look at albums?"

"Oh, yes. She's a great one for looking at pictures. The yearbook. Our honeymoon. The baby-album. Everything. But we stopped taking pictures."

"You don't anymore, do you?"

"No. I hadn't thought much about it. It just seemed natural not to."

"And it was natural to take them before?"

"Before he died. I guess that was when we stopped. Except for every now and then. A vacation. Or when you took them at birthdays and anniversaries."

"You don't think there's anything to remember?"

Cutter shrugged. "I thought I'd remember what I'd remember. The photos were for the future."

"Meaning Isaac. But you took them before he was born."

"I think we took them thinking he'd have them. Even before Lynne was pregnant. We counted on having children." He shook his head.

"We take a lot for granted," Sam said. "All of us. Not just you."

"I suppose you're right. And, in a few minutes, I'll have the ultimate lesson of why I shouldn't."

The police had, indeed, phoned ahead, so when Cutter and Sam presented themselves at a desk in the Emergency Room, it took only a few minutes for the clerk to check a clipboard and a computer before Cutter was sent down a long hall, past an elevator where he was to turn right. They stopped at another small office and were joined by an aggressively pleasant young woman. Sam had walked with him, but when it was time to see Grace, he sent Cutter in without him. Cutter looked over his shoulder: Sam was sitting on a black vinyl bench, head bowed, looking at the floor.

Cutter found himself in a small room, not much larger than a good-sized elevator with no place to sit. The woman instructed him to wait, and she disappeared through double doors. He knew she'd be returning with Grace, with Grace's body, and he stood, shifting his weight from foot to foot, then leaned against the wall. The wall was almost the color of the gimlet Grace had been drinking. Over the slight metallic rattle of the air vents, in the distance the public address system announced a series of calls for doctors and nurses. None of this had anything to do with him, none of these routine requests or emergencies were for him, and because he was freed of all responsibility to respond, he found the voices soothing.

He had nothing to do but wait.

He closed his eyes for a moment as he leaned back. He and Grace are standing together looking at their reflections in the mirror of her dining room. They're like teenagers exulting in how happy they look, the two of them. The swinging door opened, bringing a whiff of antiseptic air: pine oil disinfectant and something Cutter didn't want to put a name to.

He stood almost at attention as the nurse pushed a gurney into the room. On it lay a figure covered by a light sheet, and Cutter waited to find out what would happen next. He didn't have long to wait. The nurse looked at him, and he understood that he had only to nod for her to lower the sheet, revealing's Grace's face. She was accustomed to this first viewing of the dead by a mourner. One who had a right to be here. He felt like an imposter.

Yes, undoubtedly Grace. Her face was in repose. He felt a

surge of relief. Years ago, he'd been called into a hospital room to see a dead uncle, and the nurse had placed a sheet over the lower half of the face; unaware of why she'd done that, ignorant of her kindness, he lowered the covering to reveal his uncle's face distorted with a rictus, the mouth in a horrid grin. The nurse had scolded him, but what he'd seen had been punishment enough.

Today he'd been afraid that Grace would be grotesque, disfigured by death. He hadn't wanted to see her beautiful mouth contorted. He was ashamed of his relief. After all, Grace was dead. A large bruise covered half her forehead. She was wearing her hot pink tank top with her orange shirt. She'd changed her clothes to go see Robert. What besides telling him about the phone message had she wanted to happen?

A lock of her hair lay across her forehead, over her eyebrow. He fought the urge to brush it back off her face, as he'd started to brush back the tendril of her hair in the garden. He had no right to touch her; it was a type of violence even to see her like this. The moments for tender gestures were forever lost.

The nurse stood guard by the gurney. "Do you want some time alone with her?" she asked. She'd probably noticed his hand twitch with a suppressed gesture.

"No," he said, "Thank you."

He didn't know if he'd actually seen or only imagined that she raised an eyebrow before she replaced the make-shift shroud.

The nurse was waiting for him to leave before she'd roll the body back into the other room, to slide it into its refrigerated drawer, the paperwork on its way to completion. She made no move to push the gurney away, so he said, again, "Thank you," and backed out of the room, not wanting to turn his face from the lightly shrouded form of what was left of Grace.

"Anything I can say is a cliché," Cutter said to Sam. "I have to go sign a form, and then we can go home."

"I hope they find Robert," Cutter said. "She can't stay here. They'll probably move her to a morgue somewhere, and then, I don't know…"

"It's not time to worry about that," Sam said.

Sam was right, but it was easier to worry about the details than to confront the central fact: Grace is dead.

When they got to the police station, the forms took a matter of minutes to fill out. "Can you give him a message?" Cutter asked. "I'd like to know when the funeral…"

"Sure," the Lieutenant said. "But don't count on anything."

That figures, Cutter thought and managed a smile for his answering thanks.

At home, Cutter called out, hoping to find Lynne. Instead, he found a note on the kitchen table—characteristic for her to leave a note before she went out. It was folded up into an A-frame shape and set near a white saucer in which he found his wedding ring. The note said, "Back in early afternoon. Thought you might want this." He did want it, and it fit. If it got tight, he could take it off again, this time being careful. Next week he'd take it in and get it resized.

He hadn't eaten all day. He rummaged in the fridge and pulled out some vegetables and sliced chicken for a salad. He poured some orange juice. He took his plate and glass out to the garden. He murmured the blessings and ate, grateful for the food and for being home, grateful, even, for meaningless routine.

He has to figure out something to tell Lynne that wouldn't be hurtful. If he could find something that wouldn't be hurtful.

He'd turned his cell off just after he left Grace's house. He hadn't wanted a barrage of calls. When he turned it on, he found one message from Grace, "Ely. I'm sorry, really, I am. I've phoned Lynne. I left a message and told her that she's a lucky woman. Forgive me."

Her voice was blurry. He'd never know what she'd done that required forgiveness. Lynne hadn't said a word about a message from Grace.

Lynne was in the doorway of the kitchen. "It's hot out here. Do you want to come in, or should I bring out some iced tea?"

"Your choice," he said, hoping she'd come out. She was right about it being hot, but the weather would turn soon, and it would be too cold to be outside.

Lynne set down two glasses of iced tea, garnished with mint. "How are you?" she asked. It wasn't small talk.

He shrugged and drew a line in the droplets of water on the outside of his glass. The water ran down the glass and through the wrought iron top of the table, onto his leg, startling him. "I'm okay," he said, trying to sound better than he felt. "Okay."

"It was a dumb question," Lynne said. "I don't know what to say. I don't know."

Cutter waited to see what she would say next.

"Everything's always so...complicated," she said.

"I'm sorry," he said.

"You never meant to, Ely. I know that."

He wished she would look at him. She seemed to be studying a cloud.

"Something interesting?" he asked.

"I don't know," she said. "I keep looking at the sky, hoping—maybe it's hoping, maybe I'm just afraid—that I'll see a face, too."

"If you see His face, I hope it looks more official than when I saw it. It was so tacky, if you can say that about Him."

"It was difficult for you when I didn't believe you, wasn't it?"

"I think that in some ways you did believe me. You wouldn't have told people if you hadn't."

"I guess I did," she said after too long a pause for the answer to carry weight.

He wanted to say something about Grace's last phone call to him and tell Lynne he knew about Grace's call to her. There was nothing on the answering machine, and he wondered if Grace had called the right number. He'd never have imagined such an error except for the mix up with Robbie's phone calls. Maybe some random woman had received a message from someone who was a stranger to her, telling her that she was "a lucky woman." And maybe nothing that happened was really random.

"Her face was bruised up all on one side," he said.

"I thought seat belts..."

"Me too. The answering machine might have flown into the air and hit her when the car crashed into the tree," he said. It wouldn't have been fastened into a seat belt.

"Could be. She must have left the house fast if she didn't take her purse. How would she have gotten back in without her keys?"

"She could have hidden a spare set, or left a set with the neighbors, or maybe left the door unlocked," Lynne suggested.

"I was thinking how different it is ..." he stopped himself. Different being alive or dead?

"What?"

He shook his head and changed the subject. "Everything's different, isn't it, from what we imagined it would be?"

He was thinking about Isaac, how they'd be anticipating being grandparents, that they would have cartons of his stuff in their basement, and diplomas and pictures on their walls. Decades of artifacts. Memories of decades of love. A son, coming and going. Decades ahead. Cutter's eyes filled with tears, but he said none of this to Lynne.

"No," she said. She sounded almost angry. "Not everything." Her voice was softer now. She touched his arm and leaned towards him and brushed his cheek with her lips.

"Not everything."

He looked at her, astounded, understanding: it wasn't all wrong. When she bent to kiss him, a stray lock of hair had fallen onto her face. He reached up and, with a gesture that might have been a caress, he brushed her curling tendril of hair back into place.

CHAPTER 22

In the morning, Cutter turned to harvesting the trellised pole beans hidden in the leaves' luxuriant growth. His searching fingers discovered the beans his vision missed. He set careful handfuls of beans in the trug next to a few small ripe tomatoes. Soon he'd have to harvest them all, green as the tomatoes might be, the greenest perfect for pickling with dill and garlic, the rest to be wrapped separately in newspaper and stored to ripen in the cool basement.

Long ago he'd all but given up on tender perennials, though every few years they'd dahlia—Lynne had turned "dahlia" into a verb when he was digging up tubers after first frost. To prepare them for winter storage had always seemed a lot of trouble, even for the promise of blooms with the intense brilliance of mid-century Technicolor. No matter what Cutter did, he lost some to rot; he found small consolation in knowing that as for the dahlias, if he'd done nothing, he would have lost everything.

Soon enough, too soon, he'd have to take down the garden, or else, through the winter, face the consequence: rows of dead plants like ranks of an inexorable advancing army momentarily halted in place, insistent reminders of mortality.

Cutter didn't understand viewings, and this one was both painful and awkward. He'd have to move along in line with Lynne, allowing only an apparently reverent pause at the casket. He regretted not having accepted the nurse's offer of time alone with Grace. If he'd heard Grace's phone message, he might have accepted, might even have moved the lock of hair from her forehead.

Now makeup concealed the bruise on her face, but the lock of hair still lay across Grace's forehead. She'd didn't choose this navy dress, Cutter thought, before dismissing her wedding band as another decision she hadn't made. On the navy dress lay the small gold cross he'd fumbled fastening. Her nails shimmered with the same pink Lynne had worn all summer. Had Lynne noticed?

He and Lynne made their way to the front row to Grace's ex-husband and son, Robbie, who wore a wedding band, probably Grace's, on his pinkie. Cutter flinched at their effusive gratitude, hoping Lynne's kindness covered his discomfort as she murmured teary condolences to Robbie. Why was she crying about Grace?

Going home, Lynne dabbed at her eyes with a tissue, "I'm glad Grace knew he loved her."

So, that was it. Cutter didn't believe that a drowning man's life flashes before his eyes, but he'd experienced times—and this was one of them—that he saw Isaac's short life like a home movie run at triple speed.

"Even so, I'm a lucky man," he thought, having in mind Grace's message to Lynne. And he said aloud, "I'm a lucky man."

Lynne laughed. "Maybe you are," she said. "And maybe I'm a lucky woman, after all. Maybe we make our own luck."

Cutter wished she hadn't added "after all" when she considered her own felicity. Even if Lynne were right about making our own luck, idle wishes aren't enough to bring good luck. Maybe luck wasn't what happened but how we saw it. But a cat in the path of Grace's car, the tree she hit—he couldn't see those as good.

"Maybe we do make our own luck, Lynne. I'd like to think we're both lucky. That we can make ourselves happy."

"I'm sure you would," Lynne said. "It would be easier like that, wouldn't it? No one to blame but ourselves?"

If so, he'd be able to escape blame, maybe even escape responsibility. After all, the thinnest of lines lies between responsibility and blame. He didn't remember blaming Lynne when he went off with Eleanor, and he couldn't forget the miasma of guilt when he'd returned from his dates with Eleanor. He'd felt guilty tonight walking away from Grace.

Later he was sure that Lynne hadn't been in his mind when he'd been with Grace. He'd been looking at Grace, seeing only Grace. That's how he remembered it—and no one would ever know enough to set him straight.

"That must have been the woman he was with," Lynne said.

Cutter tried to hide his confusion in silence.

"You don't know who I'm talking about, do you?" Lynne asked, suppressing laughter.

He attempted a self-deprecating smile and said that he didn't.

"The flashy blonde," Lynne said. "Sitting right behind him. She put her hand on his shoulder. He patted her hand, but he didn't turn around.

"I didn't think she'd look like that. She looked so...small."

If he'd trusted his voice, he would have said, "Of course

she looks different. She's dead." And no matter his tone, he would have sounded hostile, antagonistic, at best, defensive.

"Was she?" Lynne asked.

"Petite," he said. "But feisty." And silently added, "a real firecracker.'

After the funeral, Cutter circled to drive Joanne to her office. She produced a stream of chatter directed at Lynne, exempting him from conversation, but not without the risk that Joanne might bring up the accident, embellishing the story with ungenerous observations about Grace lying on top of him. Joanne wasn't cruel, but she was insensitive. In a rare moment of good taste, or, perhaps, because she had a greater interest in the housing market and divorces. she spared Cutter that humiliation.

He was about to congratulate himself on having escaped, when, as he pulled up in front of her office Joanne asked, "So, what did Grace say about your vision, Ely?"

"I don't remember," Cutter replied, sorry his answer sounded like an obvious fib, chosen when a more inventive lie was likely to result in even greater disruption.

"You always were a man of discretion," Joanne said, a remark Cutter thought catty rather than congratulatory, and without a pause Joanne thanked them both for "letting her tag along" and that "it was a comfort being with friends at a sad time."

"She didn't sound sad," Lynne said when the car door had closed behind Joanne. And after a beat added, "I don't blame you for not wanting to tell her what Grace thought."

"I really didn't remember."

"And now?"

"I don't remember. If it's important to you…"

"It was something, wasn't it, your vision."

"You were embarrassed by it, Lynne." He heard the accusation in his voice and retreated, "So was I."

"Will you miss Grace?"

"I suppose," he said, calculating that his more-forthcoming truth wouldn't upset Lynne as much as obvious prevarication. "But I hadn't expected we'd be seeing one another forever. After settlement, people don't stay in touch. You know that."

"I didn't think Grace was 'people.'"

"Whatever Grace was, she was. And now, she's not." Lynne was jealous, and he didn't know how to reassure her. He'd thought they were on a better footing than this.

"Did you mean it when you said you were lucky?" she asked.

"Of course I did."

"Grace told me I was lucky," she said.

"Oh?" Should he tell her about the message he'd found on his cell phone?

"Why do you think she said that?" Lynne asked before he had to make that decision.

"I couldn't presume to speak for her." He hated sounding so stilted and self-righteous—so scared. "What matters isn't why Grace would think that—or anything, what matters is if you think you're lucky. That's what matters to me."

Lynne's deep breath was almost a sigh. "What's going to happen, Ely?"

"What's going to happen? When we get home, I'll make some lunch. I'll call the office and check for messages. If I don't have to go in, I'll work in the garden. If you think you'd like me to, I'll grill some chicken for dinner."

"That's not what I meant."

"Did you mean what you said the other day?" He waited for an answer, and when she shook her head no, he went on.

"I hope you mean that you don't understand, not that you didn't mean what you said."

"I don't understand."

"When I said that everything was different from what we'd imagined, you said that not everything was different. You meant that?"

"Yes."

Cutter smiled. "Then you know what's going to happen as well as I do."

He put his arms around Lynne, relieved and gratified when she put her head on his chest and, instead of her just tolerating his hug, she put her arms around his waist. He wanted to tell her that she'd been a good sport, but that seemed to make light of what she'd been through. She'd been wonderful. No, too vague. He couldn't have asked for more. No, that sounded phony or weaselly. Everything sounded wrong to him. Maybe he didn't need words, not for this.

When Lynne stepped back, he studied her face for some sign of what she expected of him. "Lynnie?" he said to her frown. He surprised himself by calling her "Lynnie." He couldn't remember the last time he called her that.

"I'm sorry, Ely," she said, her eyes filling with tears.

Nothing new had happened to upset her, nothing he'd seen. "What is it, Lynnie?" He wanted to make her feel better, so she'd be happy again. They'd gone through a bad patch, but it was going to be fine. He ran his left thumb over the smooth curve of his wedding band. Sam was right—he got used to the ring. It didn't bother him now; it was a comfort. The jeweler had done a fine job of resizing and polishing, and, in time, the ring would look like it had always been on his finger.

"I'm afraid," Lynne said.

"It'll be all right," he said, though he couldn't have said what the "it" was.

"I don't think it will, Ely. I'm afraid it's broken and can't be fixed after all."

"What, Lynne?" Cutter said, apprehensive.

He reached out to stroke her hair, and, though she didn't pull away, she shook her head and her face contorted.

He'd seen this expression on Grace's face. In the past, Lynne had teared up, but she hadn't been flamboyant in her crying. Grace had been flamboyant. Cutter clenched his teeth. He hadn't meant to think about Grace, not now.

"Do you want to talk about it?" Of course she does, he chided himself, that's why she brought it up.

She shook her head no.

"That's not fair, Lynne," Cutter said, surprising himself with his spontaneity.

"What does 'fair' have to do with anything? When has 'fair' meant anything?" Lynne said.

"We should sit down, Lynne. Whatever's wrong—broken—

as you say, isn't going to be fixed while we're standing in the kitchen."

Lynne laughed, and kept laughing until her laughter became wrenching sobs.

Cutter wanted to touch her, but his arms hung as if weighted, and he looked past her to the garden. If he could get her to the garden, he was sure he could set things right. "Let's sit down outside."

He watched, helpless, as she continued to sob, and then quieted. "We can sit here if sitting is so important to you. What's the difference—chairs outside or chairs here?" she said.

It's better out there, he thought, but that was the wrong answer. "Or the den? We can sit on the sofa there. Together."

"I don't see what's wrong with the kitchen. We've talked here before, haven't we?" she said. "But we can go to the den."

Lynne sat in the wing back chair, thwarting his plan, and Grace shimmied into his mind. He couldn't sit on the arm of Lynne's chair, so he sat on the sofa, as close to her as he could, and leaned forward, his forearms on his thighs, turning his head to face her. He hated not being able to see her properly, and he was too uncomfortable to stay in this position. This was too important to be squirming around.

"And how is this better than the kitchen? Really, Ely."

At least she wasn't sobbing now. How dark it was in the den! He reached over, turned on a lamp, leaned back and waited.

"It's your cheap trick, and I don't like it. You're manipulating me, and I know it. So do you," she said.

Caught. But even when she recognized what he was doing—if he could keep his mouth shut— she'd tell him what was bothering her.

Later he'd say that nothing had prepared him for this, and later still, he'd realize that he had chosen not to see.

"I suppose you're wondering what's gotten into me," she said.

Cutter nodded but stayed silent.

"Grace," she said. "I took a good long look at Grace at the viewing. And then I knew. You saw me crying?"

He nodded again.

"And you didn't ask..."

He had to speak now. "You told me it had to do with children, what you said about Robbie." This was difficult, but he had to continue. Sorrowful, he shook his head. "What did I miss?"

"When I was in bed with the lights out, I kept seeing Grace in her coffin."

Cutter said he understood but stopped before telling Lynne that he'd had the same experience. For once he had enough sense not to say something stupid and hurtful. Maybe, at last, he was learning. It had taken him long enough.

"I realized that I was going to die, too," she said.

Instead of watching Ely to see how he was responding, she looked down at her hands in her lap. He didn't say anything, not to manipulate Lynne, but because he was wondering if she'd noticed that Grace was wearing the same radioactive pink nail polish that Lynne wore ever since the day he saw the Face in the sky. Nail polish? This couldn't be about nail polish.

"I know," Lynne continued, misconstruing his silence, "We're all going to die. I know that—but, I mean, it's one thing to know it intellectually, another to feel it, really feel it."

"So, that's it?" He tried to sound empathetic. After all, he was mortal, too, but he had trouble understanding: he didn't believe that she was crying because everybody is going to die.

"That's it. I realized I don't have forever."

"I wish we did have forever," he said. And he meant it.

"Not 'we,' Ely. 'I,'" Lynne said, emphasizing the pronouns. "I don't have forever."

So, she wasn't talking just about mortality, she was talking about them. "But I thought you said you were lucky. That you were happy."

"I said 'maybe' and that we make our own luck. That's what I'm talking about now. Why I asked you what was going to happen."

Cutter groaned. He was as startled by the sound he'd made as if it had come from behind him in the dark. "I only partly understood. Maybe not at all."

"I guess so," she said.

Cutter heard misery in her voice, but he no longer trusted his understanding of Lynne. "I thought you said you were happy," he repeated, as though saying it again might make it happen.

She shook her head. "I said maybe we make our own luck. You said something different. You'd like to think that we make our own happiness."

So, he'd been right at the time, she had been unhappy. Or still is. "How long?" he asked.

"Too long, Ely. Don't tell me that's a big surprise. You haven't been happy either. If you had, you wouldn't have..."

"I've always wanted to be married to you," he said. This time he said it right, but it wouldn't matter.

"You said it yourself, we're responsible for our own happiness. I'm taking responsibility for my happiness now," Lynne said. "I'm not blaming you."

But you are blaming me, Cutter thought.

She continued, "But if I stay now, I'll blame myself." She was breathing as though she'd been running uphill.

"Please, Lynne..."

"How much longer do you expect me to try, Ely? I thought about it. Say, we went to therapy. Ten years? Of course not. Five? I asked myself...I don't want to stay another five years the way we've been. And then I said to myself, well, suppose another year." She started to cry again and wiped her eyes with the back of her hands. "Even just a year, that was too long, too."

"But why now?" Cutter said, anguished.

"Say it was Grace. Or say better late than never. Suit yourself," Lynne said, unexpectedly determined and collected. Then she stood and added. "We can talk about the details later."

Cutter, still sitting, watched her go.

Ely waited for the shadows of the pole beans to creep over the tomatoes. Would Lynne or he, maybe both of them, be moving, poking into somebody else's closets, testing the glide of kitchen drawers, peering at grout and bathroom tiles—

considering the potential? If so, the garden and the house were among the "details" that Lynne had said they'd be talking about. Negotiating.

He stared at the sky where he'd seen the Face. Maybe the Face was behind the sun, or next to it. The sun had become as pale as the moon, but when he looked away, in place of the sun, a luminous darkness hung in the center of his vision. He saw the Face superimposed on the blank disk that blotted out whatever he turned to see.

For years Ely had imagined going alone to the desert or to the ocean's edge for the long fast and prayers on the Day of Atonement. He murmured the only words from the service that he remembered, "But Penitence, Prayer, and Deeds of Charity annul the severity of the judgment."

His fate hung on Lynne's forgiveness, too.

Ely had wanted to pray and repent in an immense terrifying wilderness. The ocean would have done as well as the desert: the stillness of the desert or the crashing of the waves. In wilderness he would be—and feel— small, helpless, at His mercy. He no longer needed desert or sea: he had become his own wilderness.

Miriam N. Kotzin writes fiction, poetry, and creative nonfiction. Her novel, *Right This Way*, joins *The Real Deal* (Brick House Press 2012), her collection of short fiction, *Country Music* (Spuyten Duyvil Press 2017), and a collection of flash fiction, *Just Desserts* (Star Cloud Press 2010). She is the author of five collections of poetry, most recently, *Debris Field* (David Robert Books 2017). Her fiction, creative nonfiction and poetry have been published in numerous anthologies and periodicals such as *Shenandoah*, *Boulevard*, *SmokeLong Quarterly*, *Eclectica*, *Blink-Ink*, *Mezzo Cammin*, *Offcourse*, and *Valparaiso Poetry Review*. She teaches creative writing and literature at Drexel University.